D0847032

I play the drums in a band called *okay*

I play the drums in a band called *okay*

A Novel in Short Stories

TOBY LITT

HAMISH HAMILTON
an imprint of
PENGUIN BOOKS

HAMISH HAMILTON

Published by the Penguin Group
Penguin Books Ltd, 80 Strand, London WC2R ORL, England
Penguin Group (USA) Inc., 375 Hudson Street, New York, New York 10014, USA
Penguin Group (Canada), 90 Eglinton Avenue East, Suite 700, Toronto, Ontario, Canada M4P 2Y3
(a division of Pearson Penguin Canada Inc.)
Penguin Ireland, 25 St Stephen's Green, Dublin 2, Ireland
(a division of Penguin Books Ltd)
Penguin Group (Australia), 250 Camberwell Road, Camberwell, Victoria 3124, Australia
(a division of Pearson Australia Group Pty Ltd)
Penguin Books India Pvt Ltd, 11 Community Centre, Panchsheel Park, New Delhi – 110 017, India
Penguin Group (NZ), 67 Apollo Drive, Rosedale, North Shore 0632, New Zealand
(a division of Pearson New Zealand Ltd)
Penguin Books (South Africa) (Pty) Ltd, 24 Sturdee Avenue, Rosebank, Johannesburg 2196, South Africa

Penguin Books Ltd, Registered Offices: 80 Strand, London WC2R ORL, England

www.penguin.com

First published 2008
1

Copyright © Toby Litt, 2008

'The Return of the Grevious Angel' by Gram Parsons © 1972
Wait and See Music, assigned to TRO Essex Music Ltd,
of Suite 2.07, Plaza 535 Kings Road, London SW10 0SZ.
International Copyright Secured. All Rights Reserved.
Used by Permission

The moral right of the author has been asserted

All rights reserved
Without limiting the rights under copyright
reserved above, no part of this publication may be
reproduced, stored in or introduced into a retrieval system,
or transmitted, in any form or by any means (electronic, mechanical,
photocopying, recording or otherwise), without the prior
written permission of both the copyright owner and
the above publisher of this book

Set in 12/14.75 pt Monotype Janson
Typeset by Rowland Phototypesetting Ltd, Bury St Edmunds, Suffolk
Printed in Great Britain by Clays Ltd, St Ives plc

A CIP catalogue record for this book is available from the British Library

UK edition ISBN: 978-0-241-14282-0

www.greenpenguin.co.uk

Penguin Books is committed to a sustainable future
for our business, our readers and our planet.
The book in your hands is made from paper
certified by the Forest Stewardship Council.

For Henry and George

Acknowledgements

The author would like to thank Adam Warner, real-life Canadian drummer and God-hating Buddhist; Tony O'Neill, expert on the virgin of Guadeloupe; Richard Thomas, where vox meets roll; Matt Thorne, for the new sounds; Julian Grenier, for the old sounds.

All the band members of Senator, Eratnos 5, The Rotanes, Space Band, Platinum Demon, The Psychic Arabs, Squadron is Pill, Mujaki, Benzoin Silica, The Unhip, Click, Innocent People, Heat the Feet, Obviously Five Believers, The John Wesley Harding Band.

Also, Levon & John, Keith & Ringo, Mo & Karen, Charlie & Clem, Linn & Roland, Philly Joe & Bill, DJ & Elvin. Boom-tssk!

Versions of these episodes have appeared in the following places: 'Dog $^{\#}$1' (as 'tourbusting1') and 'Lindsay' (as 'tourbusting2') in *Exhibitionism*, Hamish Hamilton, 2002; 'Roots' (as 'tourbusting3') in *Talk of the Town, Independent*; 'LA' (as 'tourbusting4') in *The Stinging Fly*; 'Yoyo' (as 'tourbusting5') in *Ambit* and *Inculte* (French); 'Lydia' (as 'tourbusting6') in *Stand*; '333' (as Girl333') in *3:AM – London, New York, Paris*, Social Disease, 2007, and *VLNA* (Slovak); 'Forest' (as 'Tree/Forest') in *Hype Magazine* (Czech). Thanks to all the editors.

And I remembered something you once told me
And I'll be damned if it did not come true
Twenty thousand roads I went down, down, down
And they all led me straight back home to you.

Gram Parsons,
'The Return of the Grievous Angel'

DOG #1

'Wouldn't the coolest thing now be to be Japanese, eh?'

We are in Rotterdam Europe lost in thick fog together.

'A bridge over a river next to a church. Haven't we walked past this once before?'

That's me, name of Clap, dissecting the bridge-river-church interface. With me, Nippo-theorizing, is Syph.

We are from Canada. We are in a band called *okay*, lower case, italics. We are on our second European tour.

'I mean, think about it. We can't match those copycats for hipness. No way. You see, Clap, we've completely forgotten how to be ourselves. But *they* know how. They know that it's about *choosing* who you want to be, not being destined to be anyone in particular. And they are better at choosing than we ever were.'

'Can we sit down for a minute?' I say. 'I'm not feeling too great.'

'When the Japanese are punks, they are the greatest punks ever; when they are rockabillies, not even Elvis can touch them.'

Twenty days in.

This is it – we have reached the point of self-annihilation. So much of what comprises who one is has been left behind. Jackson Browne found a phrase for it, Running On Empty. In this non-state you can go for two days without having a single real thought. *How did I get here?* – that is the thought that most intrudes. The non-thought is always – *next, next, next.* Next gig. Next girl. Next goodbye. Aspects of it I do sincerely appreciate – I love the sense of left-behindness. You never use a bar of hotel soap more than once – if at all. (And if you're really sensible, you carry your own with you: so that's not a very good example.) But if you don't like something – a magazine containing a bad review, a tape that's gone fucked in your Walkman – you just drop it. Within seconds, it is miles away. Another country. (As the lyrics to my favourite of our songs go: 'I've reached out in the dark to touch/Things a thousand miles away.') Similarly, if you freak out some girl and she has hysterics at you, she's two towns behind before her slap even hits your face. You become impervious to pain – of a non-serious sort. Self-harm becomes a bit of a game. (Not that *okay* are great ones for stage-diving. It's not part of our image.) You eat nothing but shit. You look like a piece of shit. And you talk shit a hundred per cent of the time.

Twenty days to go.

'You see them,' Syph continues to talk shit, 'walking around downtown – children dressed like souvenir teddy-bears – groups of girls with their heads close together and their hands over their mouths – couples holding hands, each so cool you can't decide between them – serious young men buying huge stacks of CDs – salarymen, who break into a sweat as they move from the pavement to the road – senior citizens in beige and fawn golfing clothing.'

I am the drummer. Syph is the lead vocalist. We have a bassist, Mono. We have a rhythm guitarist, Crab.

Our mothers did not call us by these names – though Syph's is starting to. None of us knows if she knows what it means.

'Do you remember when we were on tour in Tokyo?'

'I feel bad. I'm sitting down. You can keep walking.'

I sit down on a low concrete wall with black railings stuck in it looking out across a street of cobblestones and grey-green walls.

'Like, no-one gives blow-jobs like the Japanese. It's the kind of thing they probably have instruction manuals about that are a thousand years old. Like the Karma Sutra.'

'The *Kama Sutra* is Indian.'

I stand up, lean over the railings and puke into the hedge.

4

'They do ancient things with their tongues and with the roofs of their mouths.'

I hear a whining sound.

'Did you fart?' I ask.

Syph looks shocked. He can't remember.

'I don't think so,' he says. 'Was it in tune?'

I lean back over the railings and look beyond the hedge. I see a paw, an ear – black and white.

I turn back to Syph. I say: 'I think I just puked on someone's dog.'

'Are they Japanese?' he says, and does ancient things with his tongue.

'What are we going to do?' I ask.

'We need to score.'

Syph is right – we smoked the last of the grass before the border. Syph is superstitious about carrying grass over international divides. He says it has to do with Paul McCartney. But he is quite happy about having speed in his pocket while making passport control. Which means that, until we score some dope in each new city, he is unbearable. And because he is likely to speed his way into getting arrested, I always go with him to try and track something down. If we are lucky, there's someone from the local fan club to help us connect. But *okay* aren't very big in Rotterdam, as we are finding out.

'I'm going to have a look at it.'

'Whatever,' says Syph, and plucks his Marlboros from his suit pocket.

Members of *okay* wear suits at all times. We play gigs in suits and we play hockey in suits. It's part of our image.

Our music is slow and formal with lyrics about love and guilt. We also sing about the sea.

We sound like the Velvet Underground on quarter-speed.

Climbing over the railings feels surprisingly easy. I haven't eaten anything in two days. Maybe I am getting the better of gravity.

I fall into the hedge, branches digging into my legs through my suit.

With a flip of my arms I roll off onto a patch of grass.

'Are you okay?' says Syph.

'Dollar,' I reply, keeping very still.

Whenever one of us uses the name of our band in a context not relating specifically to our band, that person is required to put a dollar in the stash-pot. It is a band rule.

'You didn't break your back?'

'I'm fine,' I say. I haven't opened my eyes yet. I don't feel any pain in my body.

Then a warm wetness crosses my nose and I smell a bad smell. I open my eyes into the face of the dog.

'Hi,' I say.

It continues licking.

I'm not sure if the bad smell is the smell of the dog's breath or the smell of my puke, which runs all down the dog's back.

I roll away.

The dog tries to follow me, to carry on licking, but it is tied to the railings by its lead.

'You've gone all quiet,' says Syph, then laughs. 'Is the dog Japanese?'

'Throw me your smokes and your lighter,' I say.

He throws them. I light up. I throw them back.

'Shit,' he says. 'That almost went down the drain.'

'Sorry,' I say.

I lie on my side on the lawn in Rotterdam Europe looking at the dog.

It is a mongrel, black and white. It doesn't look like anything much. Except thin. It looks kind of bony and shaky. Like Syph.

To this day, he's never been able to find a pair of pants that stay up. His mother used to make him wear suspenders or dungarees. For a while his nickname was Huck.

The girls always loved him. Still do.

Some nights I get seconds and some nights thirds and

maybe once a tour I'll settle for fourths. But Syph always gets firsts.

We drummers have our own distinct kind of girls. They are enthusiastic long before you are successful and loyal long after you're shit.

Drummer-girls tend to have long hair and large breasts and bring their own contraceptives and leave when asked.

Lead-singer-girls, from what I've seen and heard of them, are model-like and neurotic and bring drugs and want to do really weird sex-things on you so that you never forget them.

Some nights Syph doesn't even get laid, because none of the girls in that town comes up to his high standards. But that is rare. Syph's standards vary from town to town. Sometimes he ends up with Little Miss Rancid-and-a-half. (And I end up with her mutant grandmother.)

'It's a nice dog,' I say.

I look down at myself. There are a couple of muddy paw prints on my shirt. There is a bit of puke on my lapel.

'I think it's homeless.'

'Hey!' I hear Syph shout. 'Hey! Yeah!'

'Yeah?' I say.

'Come over here, I wanna talk to you. Yeah, come on. Yeah. Hi, I'm Steve.'

It was a girl. It wasn't hard to tell.

'What's your name?'

There is a giggle.

'I'm Inge.'

'Would you like a cigarette, Inge?'

'I have to go.'

'Hey, Syph!' I shout. 'Ask her if she knows whose dog this is?'

'Who is there?' Inge asks.

She was *so* beautiful. I just knew it was going to break my heart all over again to watch Syph closing his hotel door behind them as they walked in, smiling.

'That's my drummer,' said Syph. 'He's found a dog.'

7

Inge says, 'A dog?'

'Yeah,' says Syph. 'Woof-woof.'

Usually the beautiful ones laugh at Syph's less funny jokes. And the more beautiful they are, the more they laugh. And the sooner that door closes behind them.

I decide to stand up.

'Do you happen to know where we might chance upon some blow?' Syph is now doing his comic Englishman.

When I get to my feet I find myself standing face to face with an angel called Inge, with only a vomit-covered hedge separating us. Inge is very slim with short-cropped white-blonde hair. Her eyes are dream-blue. And oh her skin . . .

'I'm Inge,' she says.

Syph rises to stand slim-hipped beside her.

'I'm Brian,' I say, hating my name totally.

'Where is the dog?' she asks.

'It's down here.' I point. 'Is this a garden or something?'

'I think it is a park,' Inge says. 'I will come round.'

Without turning towards Syph she starts off.

When she gets a few paces away Syph looks at me and mouths: *mine.*

I shake my head.

'Musical differences,' I say. This is the threat anyone in the band always makes when they take something so seriously that they are prepared to break up the band over it.

'I saw her first,' says Syph. 'You wouldn't even have said hi.'

'If it hadn't've been for the dog, she'd've walked off.'

'I tell you, if she goes for me I'm having her.'

Inge has found a way into the park.

'Hello,' she says, and holds out her hand to be shaken. 'Brian.'

She has an angel's ankles.

'Hi,' I say.

We shake.

Then she turns her attention seriously to the dog, address-

8

ing it in Dutch or whatever language they speak in Rotterdam. She can't fail to notice the puke, but she doesn't seem to associate it with me. I reach in my pocket and take out some gum to chew, to get rid of the smell.

Syph climbs up on the railings, jumps the hedge and joins us.

'What does he say?' I ask. 'Does he belong to anyone? Are they coming back?'

Inge says, 'I think he was left because they want him not.'

'Sometimes they have addresses on their collar,' says Syph.

Inge says, 'There is no address.'

Inge stands up.

'What were you going to do?' she asks.

I look at Syph. Inge's eyes follow mine.

'Well,' he says, 'we are actually going to score some blow. Do you know where we could find some?'

Inge turns back to me – a little shrug, eyes rolling to the heavens-where-she-belongs.

'I was going to wait here to see if his owner came back. Then I was going to try and find a police station.'

And please can I kiss you?

'Give me your handkerchiefs,' she says.

Members of *okay* have handkerchiefs in the breast pockets of our suits at all time. It's part of our image.

'We must clean the dog.'

I hand over part of my image quite happily. Syph is flirting with the idea of refusing and of using his refusing as a way of flirting.

'Give it her,' I say.

Inge cleans most of my puke off the black and white dog with our handkerchiefs.

'You want them again?' she asks.

Syph says, 'Nope.'

I say, 'Yep.'

Inge hands them back, and I wrap them in the handkerchief I always keep in my side pocket for real use.

'I will take you to the police station,' Inge says.

Syph looks at me with *no way* in his eyes.

'But we have to be somewhere else,' he says. 'Don't we?'

'I'll come with you,' I say.

Inge kneels down and unties the dog's lead from the branch of the hedge.

'But we need to score,' says Syph.

'See you back at the hotel,' I say.

Inge looks inquiringly at both of us.

'Come on, boy,' I say to the dog.

Inge speaks to it in the Rotterdam language.

We walk off, leaving Syph behind.

Outside the park gates we turn left into the fog.

'You are drummer in a group?' Inge asks.

I am stunned. She's been paying more attention to Syph than she's let on. She really doesn't like him.

'Yeah. We're on tour. We're playing tonight at some club.' As I am halfway through the line, I go on with it anyway. 'Would you like to come?'

'Maybe,' she says. 'The police station is very close here.'

I hear footsteps running behind us in the fog. I don't need to look. Things have been going too well. It is Syph.

'I thought I'd lost you guys,' he says.

Inge leads us up to a doorway and into the police station.

Inge tells the policeman the story in the Rotterdam language. He then asks us to confirm a few details in English. It seems like Inge's left out any mention of the puke. I am glad of that.

We give them the name and address of our hotel.

Inge gives them her address and telephone number.

Inge and I say goodbye to the dog and watch the policeman take it off down a long white corridor.

On the foggy street outside the police station, Inge says, 'What is the name of your band?'

'It's *okay*,' I say. 'Spelt o-k-a-y.' And just so she knows, I tell her the name of the club we're playing at.

'Do you know where we can score?' whispers Syph.

Inge looks at him pitifully.

'Come on,' she says, and leads us off round the corner.

Unexpectedly, she stops, reaches into her rucksack and brings out a clingfilm-wrapped chunk of dope. She breaks off a corner and hands it to Syph.

'God,' he says. 'The woman of my dreams.'

Inge turns to me.

'You are a kind person,' she says, and kisses me on the cheek. 'Good-bye.'

I watch as she walks off into the fog.

Syph doesn't even look. He is sniffing the dope.

'This is really good shit,' he says. 'Let's get back to the hotel.'

That evening the lighting set-up means that I am unable to see anything of the audience – it is just a sheet of white light which applauds whenever we finish a song.

Our set-list goes: 'Thousand', 'Blissfully', 'Jane-Jane', 'Motherhood', 'Sea-Song $^{\#}4$', 'Hush-hate-hum', 'Walls', 'Queen Victoria', 'Long Cold Lines', 'With Strings', 'Gustav Klimt' and 'Work'. We encore with 'Sea-Song $^{\#}1$' and our cover of 'Marquee Moon'.

Syph dedicates one song to a girl we met today. Thanks. For services rendered.

At the end of the encores, I walk straight up to the mic and say, 'Inge, if you're here, I'll see you in the bar.'

Two Inges show up, neither of which is the right one.

Back in the dressing-room there is a drummer-girl but I brush her off.

'I'm going for a walk,' I say.

'What?' says Mono.

'A walk?' says Crab.

'See you back at the hotel,' I say.

'Maybe,' says Syph, who has one girl sitting in his lap and one opening him a beer.

For an hour or so, I wander about trying to find my way back to the park. But the fog has gotten even thicker and everywhere looks even more the same.

I stop a cab and tell the guy to take me back to the hotel.

Inge is sitting in the lobby with the black and white dog at her feet. As I walk up the dog I puked on recognizes me and starts to strain on its lead.

'You didn't come to the gig,' I say.

'I was there,' she says. 'I left.'

'I asked you to meet me in the bar. Didn't you hear?'

'I thought you would get another girl. I wanted to see. I came to wait here.'

'What, you were testing me?'

'I don't know,' she says, smiling. 'Maybe.'

'Hi,' I say to the dog.

Someone has obviously given it a bath. And love. He licks the salty spaces between my fingers, looking up at me with wet eyes.

'Brian meet Brian,' says Inge.

'They let you keep it?' I ask.

'I went back and told them that the story we said before was a lie. I told them that I lived with you and that you didn't want the dog, so that you made me give it to them. I told them that we had split up and that I wanted my dog back. They didn't want the problem of a dog. They gave it to me without question.'

'Do you have a boyfriend?' I ask.

'No,' she says. 'I have a dog called Brian.'

I am very close to saying woof-woof.

Just then, Syph and his two girls, both Japanese, plus Mono, Crab and their girls, plus several other girls and a couple of boys come through the hotel doors.

'Great dope,' Syph says to Inge as he walks up.

His girls are already getting jealous. They touch him even more.

'Musical differences,' I say to the whole band. 'I'm afraid to say.'

'Nice doggie,' says Mono.

'Irreconcilable musical differences.'

'Really?' asks Crab.

'You have dope?' asks one of Mono's girls.

'Yes,' I say. 'I think so.'

Syph says, 'No way.'

'Yoko,' says Crab.

I smile at Inge and she smiles back.

'Let's go,' Inge says.

And I say, 'Okay.'

That last bit didn't really happen. It's just how I daydreamed it the following afternoon on the tourbus. Cologne was next. Then Munich. Then Berlin. Nineteen days to go. What really happened was that I went back to the hotel, alone, only to find Inge not there. No sign of that dog, either. Then I went for a walk, to try and find the park or the police station. But I couldn't. I got lost again in the fog. Then I stopped a cab and told the guy to take me back to the hotel. That detail was true. Syph and the others were there in the bar with a group of girls. None of them was Japanese. But one of them I saw straight off was a drummer-girl. I think she had long hair and large breasts and brought her own contraceptives and left when asked. It's just, you meet so many and remember so few.

LINDSAY

I'd like to tell you about Lindsay, now, if you'd like to hear.

(I think I mentioned her yesterday or the day before, when we were in that bar, in, you know – that one with the . . . yeah, right. Wild, huh?)

I knew Lindsay all the way through high school, but we never really dated. I have my suspicions that we kissed, once, maybe – I can't remember where or when. And I can't think why. I didn't even like her then, and she was in love with – well, I'll tell you that later.

(This isn't for the profile, you understand. This is just, like, between you and me. Because I *like* you.)

Anyway, I can't remember the first time we met, either. Though it was probably in a corridor somewhere. You always meet the most important people in your life in corridors or on stairs. Never in rooms. Don't you think that's weird? And we would've not even – whoa, let's try that again. We didn't shake hands. We just, I guess, shrugged and said *hi*.

Just saying that to you now makes me think I can see it all over again: Lindsay pulling the hair out of her eyes with a half-curled finger. But that's way too convenient to be a real memory, isn't it?

(Can I borrow another cigarette? I always fucking forget to buy them when we pit-stop.)

Anyway, we were just starting to form the band that later went on to make history as *okay*.

(Thanks.)

Only later did we get our famous nicknames. I wasn't yet Clap: I was just plain Brian. And Lindsay was just plain Lindsay – and Lindsay, really, was always just *plain*. She looked unfortunately like Carole King or Laura Nyro. One of those great women songwriters who you just love, and really try hard to find attractive, but just can't. Nina Simone, even. Where you love them with your eyes closed and them singing, but you can't even bear to have their poster on your wall.

We used to rehearse over in this shack that used to be attached to a church. But the church was gone. Someone bought it – the whole thing – and moved it to another town. It was made of corrugated iron.

And I heard, where they moved it to, they put it inside *another* church. And they called it something like 'the heart of the Lord'. Because the new church didn't feel like it had any o' dat ol'-time religion in it: so they drove down the road, stopped off and bought some. Seriously.

One of the walls of this shack was wood, the rest were iron. Sometimes, if you got the feedback going just right and loud enough, you could make the whole thing shake like it was going to fall down on top of you.

Lindsay was our first fan. Also, I suppose, our first groupie – though I think only two of us actually slept with her.

(I'll let you figure out who.)

When we were just banging away, sounding really trashy, she would sit there behind one of the amps – nodding her head like we were the Velvets or something. In the beginning, Lindsay was really important to us – really encouraging. When we were down, she'd say, 'Hey, you were really getting somewhere today.' In fact, she could hear things in us that we couldn't hear ourselves. She heard *through* us. I think, back then, she heard everything we've ever done since – right up to the break-ups and beyond.

I know a lot of people have come along claiming to have discovered us. But it's Lindsay really that was the first. If you asked the others, if you asked Syph, he probably wouldn't even remember her. She's exactly the kind of thing he was always trying to forget.

What makes me feel really guilty is that we kind of dumped her early on. Like a girlfriend who's becoming an embarrassment. We had to. There was a reason. Banging away at our practice sessions in that iron shack, we were actually getting to be quite good. But no-one knew it, and when we told people, they wouldn't believe it. In school we were actually known as 'the band that Lindsay hangs out with'. You see, association with Lindsay was making us out to look like losers. The logic went something like this: the girls thought, *They must be really sad and unsexy if Lindsay's the only girl who hangs out with them*; the boys thought, *Why go and see them play, there's no-one there but Lindsay to pick up?* And so Syph dumped her for us, on our behalf. He found some lame excuse, like she'd been stealing patch cables or something, and he balled her out and threw her out and that was that.

Almost immediately, a better class of girl started to come around. In other words, getting rid of Lindsay *worked*. It helped give us a start. When we played, the girls came. And when the girls came, the boys came. They all liked the music.

I remember the first time we played to over fifty people, and that was like a big deal for us back then – Lindsay was there, standing at the back, crying: all through the gig, crying. She tried to speak to Syph afterwards, but he just blew past her – blew her off. I stopped and talked for a while.

'You're doing really well,' she said. 'You sound really tight. You're going to make it.'

And we did, in a sort of a way. We weren't the Beatles or anything. But we started to get the opening slots. We could headline locally. Play anywhere we liked, locally.

Next thing we knew, we had the deal, cut the record and started to go off on tours. We went to Great Britain first of all. Support slot. Before we'd even toured properly at home. I've always liked Great Britain. My mother came from there. My grandmother still lives there. This music paper, the *NME*, gave us a really good review for one of our singles. 'Sea-Song $^\#$1' I think it was. And lots of people turned up for this gig at the Marquee Club. Like that Television song, 'Marquee Moon'.

But you know all that shit already. I'm going to try to stay focused on Lindsay from now on.

We were away for about two months. Did Holland, gateway to Europe, and then Belgium, Germany and Spain – or maybe not Spain. Italy. When we got back, we went into the studio to record. That was the second album. The shack had long ago been knocked down, and the 'good old days' were knocked down with it. We started to get really serious about things like The Snare Sound – which is when you know it's starting to go a little wrong. Honestly, no-one cares about The Snare Sound. Or like, one per cent of people do – the ones that listen on hi-fis that cost more than they get paid in a year.

So, Lindsay wasn't around to hook up with. I only saw her again by accident. She was working in the library – behind the counter, checking out books. I went in there to get something by August Strindberg, who this English music journalist told me I'd, you know, *empathize* with.

(That was how come we wrote the song 'August'. It wasn't the month, it was the gloomiest fucking playwright that ever stuck a pair of cripples on-stage and made them hate each other. But I guess you know that already. Done your research all the way, haven't you?)

I didn't recognize her at first. She was wearing these bottle-thick glasses. Her hair was done up in bobbie pins. Not fancy ones with butterflies on or anything. Just plain brown slides. And her hair was the same old Carole King Jewfro – you know, thick, really thick. And the slides just couldn't cope. They kept pinging out onto the books.

I stood looking at her from behind one of those turnaround things they stack paperbacks on. The sight of her made me want to cry, really. I mean, she had never looked anything like good. But it was as if she were trying *really* hard to look shitty. And nature was giving her more than all the help she'd need.

Here we come to the second thing that makes me feel

guilty: I didn't speak to her that time. I found a back way out, so I didn't have to walk past the counter again.

I was feeling bad the whole way home. I couldn't stop thinking about it. What if she'd seen me? What if she knew I'd decided not to go up and talk to her? She'd think I was playing the big star.

(But then, what the fuck – I was going into a library! We hadn't made any money then. None at all. Top Ten album, and *no money*. Believe it.)

All the band met up that night in a pizza place, and we were surrounded by really good-looking women. Syph was playing the local hero. Really, he was such a *knob*. Dropping names of people he'd seen, like, for five seconds crashing the Executive Lounge at some airport. Like he'd jammed with them all night in the studio. And I couldn't stop thinking about Lindsay.

So, anyway, the next day I go round to the library. And on the way I even buy her a bunch of flowers. I don't know why. I wanted to say sorry for not talking to her the day before. But I also didn't want her to know that I hadn't talked to her the day before. So I realized I couldn't give her the flowers. So I hid them behind a fence before I got there.

(Went back to pick them up later, and they'd gone. Some fucker had seen them and stolen them. To give to his poor disabled mother, I hope. (Isn't it weird the things you remember?))

I'm rambling, I know. It's the JD talking. What was I saying?

(The library – right. The library.)

It was a big yellow building. Made out of concrete. But somehow yellow. '70s yellow – like California sunshine going down on the hood of a gold Chevrolet. She was in the exact same place, and I pretended just to notice her when I went up to get the Strindberg book out. It was black and had about four plays in. One of them was *Ghost Sonata*, the play the journalist had namechecked. Lindsay was so delighted to see me, it made me feel even worse about the day before. We agreed to go for coffee, after she got off.

(I can remember *so* many girls working behind counters who, before the band made it, I'd wanted to ask when they got off. But it never worked out – if I did ask, they never said *around six thirty*. And now, when it didn't matter at all, when it meant something completely different, it was the easiest thing in the world.)

I turned up back at the library. I told her I'd gone home, but I'd just gone and sat in the park and read that weird fucking play. I was so nervous I could hardly read. I don't know why. I have no idea. I mean, this was Lindsay – Lindsay who looked like Carole King: I didn't find her at all attractive. I couldn't remember having talked to her that much, even when we were rehearsing in the shack.

She came down the concrete stairs in the sunlight. My hands were shaking, like a half-hour after a great show – adrenalin. I was glad to see she hadn't done anything with her hair or her appearance generally. That would have suggested she had *hope* – which would have broken my heart. I didn't want her to have any hope as far as me and loving her was concerned.

(Does that sound cruel? I meant it to sound kind. I felt really . . . compassionate towards her. God, that sounds even worse, doesn't it?)

She noticed the shaking in my hands.

'Caffeine,' I said.

'Yeah,' she said. 'I know. It's terrible. Shall we go get some more?'

We went and sat there, in one of the booths in the coffee shop. It was an old high-school hang. A few of the students knew who I was, and looked at me, but this was before anyone started coming up for autographs.

Lindsay said, 'I was surprised to see you getting that out.' She meant the Strindberg.

I explained about the journalist.

'That's very studious of you,' she said. 'It's not exactly rockstar behaviour.'

I flashed back to Syph, bumping past and cutting her at that first big gig.

'Well,' I said, 'I'm not exactly a star. I'm a drummer. Drummers are never stars.'

'Except Ringo,' Lindsay said.

As I laughed, even though it was a bit lame, I realized how much I *liked* Lindsay.

Liking isn't meant to be a particularly strong emotion: the whole liking vibe is meant to be pretty mild. But sometimes, you know, you can just be overwhelmed with how much you like someone. And at that moment I *liked* Lindsay more than I've ever liked anyone. I wanted everything to go well for her. Her job. Her life. Love.

We talked about Strindberg for a while. She'd read him, and knew a lot more about him than I'd managed to pick up in the previous four hours. Then she started to ask about what life in the band was like. I told her. I told her the old stories, but I tried to put some truth back into them. I didn't exaggerate as much as usual. I really wanted to give her some idea of what it was like, although I wasn't sure if that would make her feel bad about not being there with us. She wanted to hear, I think. I wasn't just torturing her. Thinking back, I should probably have insisted on asking her more questions. Because this coffee date – which wasn't a date – set up our relationship for what was going to be the rest of it. She would ask; I would answer.

My liking-buzz started to wear off. Lindsay's breath smelt a little, and she had a slightly annoying way of dropping her jaw and going *Wow* whenever I said anything even remotely starry. I tried to keep liking her as hard and as much as I had when she told the joke, but it just didn't work. It was easier to concentrate on telling her the stories that she wanted to hear. We talked till late. I kissed her on the cheek when we said good-bye. Even half-hugged her.

I'd like to say something like *As she turned away from me, smiling, I thought, Maybe there's just a chance –*

That would be a lie. I had a girlfriend. I *thought* I loved her.

I saw Lindsay a couple more times, before we went off on tour again.

And that was how we fell into the rhythm. I'd be gone like five, six months. When I came back round, older, tireder, more famous, richer – having had huge amounts more sex (I decided pretty soon I didn't really love that old girlfriend of mine) – I would go to the library. Lindsay would be there. It seemed like from one tour to the next, she didn't move from the Books Out counter. Her hair never got longer or changed.

In all the madness that goes on, she was the thing I clung to. I would be getting loaded in some Tokyo strip bar, and I'd be thinking about Lindsay stamping books. She was my *O Canada*.

Whenever I heard Joni or Carole or Laura, and I had tapes of theirs for the bus, I thought of Lindsay. I often wished she were more beautiful, so I could make her into my poster-girl – put her up on the wall in my head.

Sometimes, when I made it home, I'd even go to the library intending to start something with her: her goodness was so much more important than all the sluts on the road who just want to say they've banged someone in the band.

But when I saw her, standing like she always did, where she always did, I knew it wasn't meant to be.

We became like old people in our habits. We'd go out for coffee, and try and sit in the usual booth. We'd order the same thing. At some point, I'd get that same *whoosh* of power-liking. (Power-liking, I like that.) Then it would fade away. She'd ask me questions; I'd tell her what she wanted to hear. Sometimes, I sounded to myself like Syph – Thurston Moore this, Michael Stipe that. Lindsay was my hometown reality check. She was the valve on the decompression chamber.

So, one time, when I got back from a whole six-month deal

– touring the fifth album (the live one) – it destroyed me to find she wasn't there.

I mean, I was half-destroyed just by her not being at the Books Out counter. I'd always believed there were worn places in the lino where she used to stand. Another librarian was in her place. A boy. He knew who I was. When I tried to ask him where Lindsay was, he was like, 'You know *Lindsay?*'

'Yeah,' I said. 'Where is she?'

I knew he was going to ask me for my autograph. He just had the *look.*

'You don't know about Lindsay.'

'What about her?' I said.

'She left.'

'Left where?'

'Left town, I guess.'

'Left to go where?'

'I'm not sure. I can ask.'

'Ask,' I said.

He hesitated.

'*Then* you can have my autograph,' I said.

He went off. I heard him say *asshole.* Perhaps he *hadn't* wanted the autograph.

When he came back he said, 'They don't know.'

'Let me talk to them,' I said. 'It's very important that I find out where she is.'

Because, you see, in all those times we'd gone for coffee, I'd never got her number or found out where she lived. She was always at the library. I didn't need her address.

The librarian-boy goes and gets the head librarian, Miss Watts, who was like this figure of myth from my childhood. She used to be as tall as New York City. (Crab had nicknamed one of his amps Miss Watts.)

'How are you, Brian?' she asks.

We chat for long enough for it to seem polite, then I ask about Lindsay.

Pretty soon it becomes clear that Miss Watts really *doesn't* know where Lindsay went. Reading between the lines, it sounds like Lindsay especially didn't want Miss Watts to know where she was going.

I was able to get Lindsay's home address out of her.

Miss Watts asked for my autograph, for her daughter.

When I dropped by Lindsay's old place, it was an apartment block. After pressing all the buzzers, someone let me in. The elevator had piss in one corner. Her number was 44. No-one was in.

I left a note with my number.

No-one rang.

All that time I was away on tour, Lindsay wasn't behind the counter in the library. She was living in an apartment block where people pissed in the elevator.

And that's Lindsay for you. That's all I know.

I hope she's happy, wherever she is. Whatever she's doing.

When I think of her these days, though, she isn't in the library. She's back behind the amps, reading some philosophy book. She looks younger, and better than she ever really did – like your memory of Carole King when you're trying to be kind in your mind about what she looks like.

Hey, on second thoughts, maybe you could put something about her in the profile.

Just a line at the end.

'Lindsay, if you're out there, call.'

Something like that.

Or maybe not.

(Hey, forget it. You know. Forget. It.)

Friends make jokes about you being famous, to let you know that's what you've become, and that it's starting to worry them – as it should.

I never thought we were *that* big a deal, until we paid our third visit to England.

First time over had just been us supporting a band called John Craven, who split shortly afterwards. Their fans hated us, and we only had about five of our own – and those were too poor or shy to travel from gig to gig.

Second time was better. We headlined, and sold out half the midsize venues we were booked to play. There was a TV on the bus. At least a hundred of the fans I met claimed they'd seen us on the first tour.

But the third time (just promotion, no gigs), we had girls waiting for us at the airport. It wasn't Beatlemania, but it was a little freaky. Our last single had gone Top Twenty there – on the back of that video with the ghosts in it. After which, most of our interviews seemed to be with British magazines – not all of them music ones. Style entered our lives, along with, for a brief while, stylists.

After this, we rapidly became blasé. Fame gets old fast. England was our first taste, though.

We were driven from the airport to our hotel in downtown London, which our efficient British PA informed us was where all the best bands stayed. We asked who, and when she named them they all sucked but were huge. It wasn't a great omen.

Some of the same girls from the airport had rushed here, too. They wanted Syph and Syph, of course, wanted them right back. He stood in the lobby for about half an hour, chatting them up – as if *You, follow me, now* wouldn't have done the business.

In the meantime, I went up to my room (alone), had a shower (alone), ignored the complete lack of timid knocks on the door and came back down –

– just in time to see Syph put something in the hands of one of the girls. She was the most beautiful – long glossy-black hair and big eyes done in kohl that a year from now, six months even, she'd be sneering at. She was young, too – too young: sixteen or seventeen.

As I walked up to Syph, she started off towards the elevator. She turned and waved, shyly but knowingly, when she got in. I was surprised Syph didn't just follow her. I knew where she was going; I thought I knew what would happen when she got there.

'No!' said Crab, to something else.

'I'm sorry,' said the PA, who was small, Asian, tough and dressed in tight black.

'What's up?' asked Syph.

'We have to get on a fucking train . . .' said Crab.

'There's a TV show,' said the PA. 'It shoots tomorrow morning in Manchester. They've just confirmed.'

'*Morning*,' said Mono, like he'd say *death*.

'So we'll go tomorrow,' Syph said.

'It starts at seven,' said the PA. 'I know you wouldn't want to miss it. It is broadcast nationwide. Five chart places, at least.'

'Shit,' said Mono.

'We'll do it,' said Crab, who later in the junket, thanks to much more of this puppyishness, was granted the privilege of one night in the PA's room. (He never said what happened. Nothing, we think – either that, or some very heavy SM.)

'But –' said Syph. 'But I –' He made a gesture that included the whole of the lobby and, by implication, the whole of London.

'There's a very nice hotel we've booked you into there,' the PA said. 'And I'm sure there will be girls.'

'Well, honey,' said Syph, despicably rock'n'roll, 'if you put it like that.'

Two minutes later – this is the way things were starting to happen for us – we were in a limo on the way to the station.

I didn't want to mention the beautiful black-haired girl in front of everyone. Not because I didn't want to embarrass Syph but because I didn't want to give him the chance to embarrass me back – by being not at all embarrassed, by treating it as if it was nothing.

I waited until we were in the lobby of the Manchester hotel – which, as the PA had promised, and Crab was confirming back to her, was very nice.

'Can I have a word?' I asked.

Syph, thinking I meant drugs, came across. 'That girl you left behind,' I said. 'You will call her, won't you?'

'Yeah, yeah,' Syph said. 'Sure.'

'As soon as you get up to your room.'

'Definitely.' But his eyes were around the lobby and over by the elevators and anywhere else that girls might be.

I knew *he* wouldn't call, so I did. I went upstairs to my room and, after taking my London room-key out of my pocket, dialled the number on the dangling metal triangle. (It had been an old-fashioned hotel.)

The desk clerk I'd seen through the revolving doors two hours earlier answered, still on shift. I explained who I was – he said he knew.

'Can you put me through to –' And I gave Syph's check-in alias: Thomas Jerome Newton. (Long story.)

The phone rang about ten times before the young woman picked up.

'Hello,' she said. Her voice was very English, pure and doorbell-like.

Again, I explained who I was. My accent convinced her, I think.

'Where's Syph?' she asked.

'We're in Manchester,' I said, expecting upset. 'We're doing a show. So Syph won't be back today.'

'Oh,' she said.

'I think,' I said, carefully, 'well, that you should go home. You can meet him again when he's back in London.'

'But he'll be back in the next few days, won't he?'

I tried to reason with her. As she spoke, I listened to the sound of the London hotel room. She didn't seem to have the TV on, the acoustic wasn't that of the bathroom.

'Go home,' I said, then hung up, went to bed.

We did the show in Manchester – and were told immediately after that we'd been booked for another in Scotland. 'Really important market,' said the PA. 'They buy lots of records up there.' We left without even changing.

It was only in the Glasgow dressing-room, afterwards, that I spoke to Syph. 'Did you call the girl?'

'What girl?'

'The one in London – in the hotel.'

'Oh, yeah. I called her.'

'No, you didn't. I did. When I called, she was still waiting for you.'

'I did – I called her.'

'When?' I asked.

'After you, obviously.'

'And she was still there?'

'Well, she answered.'

'I told her to go home – she was still in your room.'

'Have we still got rooms in London?' asked Crab.

'Cool,' said Mono.

'We couldn't cancel them,' said the PA. 'The hotel wouldn't allow us. Don't worry. The record company's paying.'

'We should call her now,' I said.

'Why?' said Syph. 'She won't still be there.'

I asked the PA if she could call the London hotel for us on her cellphone. She did, then handed it to me. Again, I asked to be put through to Syph's room, memorably number 333.

'Hello,' said the girl.

I handed the phone over to Syph, thumb on the holes where the sound goes in.

'Tell her to leave,' I said.

Syph took the phone and immediately started to chat the girl up again. He walked over to the corner of the room and I thought to myself, *Try trusting him, for once. Let him gently persuade her home with promises of future sex.*

'We're going to Paris now,' announced the PA. 'This is really building well.'

'Not back to London?' Mono asked.

'Maybe tomorrow,' the PA said.

'Anything you want,' said Crab.

When Syph handed the cellphone back to me, it was off.

'You did tell her to leave, right?'

'She's gone,' he said. 'History.'

I pulled up the last-dialled number and pressed Connect. The desk clerk put me through to 333.

'Hello,' said the girl.

I hung up.

Syph knew from my face what I was about to say. 'She didn't *want* to leave,' he said. 'She wanted to wait for me.'

'Didn't you tell her there wasn't any point?'

'What can I say, dude, she seems to think there is.'

He pulled the cellphone away from me and handed it back to the PA.

'Car outside for *okay*,' said a production assistant, head round the dressing-room door.

'Everybody out!' shouted the PA, who had already learnt that direct orders were the only way to move us.

We shuffled off.

In the limo, I borrowed the PA's cell again, called the hotel again, got 333.

'Hello,' said the girl.

'Go home,' I said.

'Oh,' she said, 'I thought it was him. He just called.'

It was time to be cruel. 'He called because I *made* him call.'

'No, he called because he wanted to speak to me.'

'Did he ask you to leave the room?'

'. . .'

'Did he?'

'He said he might not be back for a few days.'

'But did he ask you to leave?'

'Not exactly,' she said.

'He's not going to be back until at least the day after tomorrow. Surely you have better things to be doing with your time than sitting in an empty hotel room.'

'I don't.'

'You must.'

'I want to be here. It's his room.'

'It's not his room. He's never even been in it.'

'It *is* his room. They booked it for him therefore it's his room.' She wasn't stupid, this one.

'He may never come back,' I said.

'I'll take the chance,' she said and – really, she did – hung up.

Over the next few days, we went from Paris back to Scotland, Scotland to Liverpool, Leeds, somewhere even more industrial-looking, then back to Manchester. We even passed through London, doing three radio interviews back-to-back. But we didn't return to the first hotel. A plane to Brussels. A train to the Hague. Occasionally, I would call – by now I'd got hold of a functioning cellphone for myself ('Hello,' the girl said), but as soon as she heard it was me and not Syph, she would hang up. I tried to get him to speak to her again but he was totally stubborn. 'If she wants to stay, she wants to stay.' He had other girls, he had other concerns. In the end, I gave up. I'd thought about speaking to the desk clerk and asking him to have the girl thrown out, but I knew there was a big chance she'd just end up waiting for Syph on the sidewalk outside the hotel. However neglected she was, at least in room 333 she was safe. I thought about all the meals she must have ordered – all the TV she must have watched. Just like us. The whole thing was so immensely sad that we could probably have written a pretty good song about it.

The girl in room 333 – She's waiting for me – Patiently – Eternally. Or maybe not that good.

We went back to Paris. Then to Barcelona and I don't know where else. I gave up keeping track. And then and then and then. Our original schedule was forgotten as more and more important markets demanded our physical presence. We did the single a hundred times – playing live when we could, otherwise miming. Finally, we returned to London and to the hotel.

Syph wanted to go up alone but I made it absolutely clear that I was coming with him. I needed to see this girl – to try and talk to her.

Syph had no key. That was what I'd seen him put in her hand, back in the hotel lobby, ten days and twenty thousand miles ago. So we just went up to the room, unannounced, and knocked.

She answered the door – her face all delight – not a flinch of resentment, not until she caught sight of me over Syph's shoulder. 'You,' she said. 'Why don't you fuck off and leave us alone?'

For a second, I couldn't be bothered, then I changed my mind (maybe my heart) and *could.*

Pushing past them, I entered the room. The curtains were drawn. The bed was made. The TV was off. It looked like hotel rooms do when you first walk into them. There was no bad smell.

I could hear the girl saying to Syph, 'I waited for you.' And him replying, 'I'm glad you did.'

I went and opened the mini-bar. It was full. Perhaps it had been restocked. Perhaps the bed had been remade.

'I didn't drink anything,' the girl said to me, bitterly. 'Only tap water. I didn't eat anything, either.'

'You didn't?' said Syph – even he was shocked.

'Well,' she said, 'I had a couple of chocolate bars in my bag. But I didn't eat anything of yours.'

On the desk, beside the lamp, was a bowl containing complimentary packs of peanuts, potato chips.

The girl looked beyond-ghost: inch-thin arms and panda eyes.

I walked out – all the way out of the hotel. I walked until I found a wall I could retch and weep against. After that I just walked.

By then, they were probably fucking.

YOYO

Yoyo from the fanclub website (hi Yoyo!) has been nagging me very nicely for over a year to put something on paper (hotel stationery – the best & most romantic) about the very, very, very beginnings of *okay*.

I think she wants to hear about when we were young, innocent, idealistic – stuff like that.

And after all the bad shit that's gone down, especially recently with Syph (although I'm glad to say he's getting better – with relapses – thanks for all the cards & emails), I thought it might not be a bad time to remember when we started out – remember it, I mean, whiles I still can.

I wish I could describe it better. Success of the sort we've endured isn't too good for clear recollection. Here's what I have.

Young, innocent, idealistic – one, two and three – I wish I could be sure we ever were. Rather than the four ego-monsters we've become.

But it's very hard to remember what it felt like to unload my second drumkit (the first was a kiddie Christmas set I knocked to hell by age twelve) from my cousin's van and carry it, piece by piece, up the stairs and into Crab's room.

Of course, *then* he wasn't called Crab. He probably would have known what crabs were, in theory. But he was yet to have his first visit to the white-walled clinic above the doll and puppetry store. *Young*, we were definitely that: fifteen years old when we started rehearsing seriously.

I think, now, that you probably play the drums differently if you've had to carry them to wherever yourself. It's such a fucking huge labour to move the things that, when you set them down, you want to make them speak in a particularly special way. Maybe that's hippie-thought, I don't know. Perhaps it's just that, having to bear the burden of them, you really want to punish them for being such a painful instrument – painful to transport, not to play – playing them was never less than a joy. Particularly when we got to somewhere (not my parents' house) where I could bash the shit out of them.

And that's what our first rehearsal room was, Crab's sock-and-crotch-smelling attic. But *okay* truly started in another room – a room about ten feet by twelve that Mono had found, somehow. It was just out back of a store selling spare parts for motorcycles. The owner, T-Bone, could care about the noise. He was so deaf from tuning engines that I don't think he even heard us.

Musicians will yammer on for ever and ever about chemistry – almost as much as they'll bitch about not getting paid enough. But the truth of it is, or was, from the first occasion the four of us played together, we sounded like a true band.

We'd all done stuff before – played with other kids in other styles: prog, pop, punk.

okay, which didn't have the name yet – which wasn't to be *okay* for over a year – *okay* really and truly started (have I already said this?) the moment Syph opened his mouth to sing over the slow-roaring noise Crab, Mono and I were making.

Innocent? – innocent I don't know about.

Right from rehearsal one, along with the pleasure in knowing we *worked*, there was a kind of resentment. (I'm sorry, Yoyo – sure you were hoping for band-of-brothers, but this is the dirty truth.) We knew that we were tied together. Anything about another band member that annoyed you now was, because we sounded so damn good, going to be paining you for years to come.

We didn't doubt our success. That, too, makes us sound uninnocent. We were aware of the standard of bands our age, and we knew that we were far better than all of them. Syph had somehow managed to find a way of performing without being embarrassing. A true front-man. And though I wouldn't want to sit down and read the lyrics to our first few songs as poetry, they too were far from laughable. Quite unlike the guy who wrote them, who was an absolute knob from the get-go. Really, Yoyo – he was, is, and please God will be for a long time yet. If he weren't, he'd just be some guy. And Syph was never some guy.

To backtrack even further:

Our first meeting. I've told this too often in interviews. I know when I say about Syph dropping out of a tree in front of us, it's probably a story I made up years ago and now believe is true. But I do believe it's true.

Me, Crab and Mono were out walking around the neighbourhood. I think we were discussing how much Rush sucked or whether Leonard Cohen really banged Janis Joplin in the Chelsea Hotel (*innocent?*) – perpetual topics. And Syph, who had just moved in round the block, fell all the way down from quite a tall branch.

He landed on his ass, and made a huge wailing screech of a cry as his ankle twisted.

You can check with the others, but the first word I remember hearing him say was *motherfucker*.

We ran over to him and picked him up. All of us hoped he'd broken his leg – in those days, a trip to hospital counted as excitement. But he felt it up and down and said it wasn't too bad, it didn't feel broken. We asked where he lived and then helped him hop home.

The way Syph tells it, I know, is slightly different. He says he'd been sneaking around the new neighbourhood for several days and had caught us practising. He liked what he heard, wanted to meet us. (Mono was singing back then – and anyone could have told you we needed someone better, or more confident.)

When Syph asked his mom, she just said (like moms do,

35

seeing no difficulties), 'Why don't you go over and introduce yourself?' But this wasn't enough for Syph. He wanted to impress by making a big entrance.

I don't know how long he'd been waiting up that tree for us to come past.

So, according to Syph, he didn't fall, he jumped. Also, according to Syph's revised version, his ankle wasn't twisted at all. But I was there – I saw him land awkwardly, I saw the ankle swell up, and I saw the look on his mom's face when she answered the door.

We were invited in, rewarded with milk and cookies. A bigger reward was Syph's mom, who immediately went in at number one of our collective crush chart. She only seemed about ten years older than us – slim, quick, flirty and hip. And *divorced.*

To begin with, at least two of us were much more concerned with getting to talk to her than with Syph's injury.

He was charismatic, I suppose – that immediately made us want to ignore him. To punish him for having something we knew we'd never have. Skinniness helped. But he had cute eyes and, from the way we lusted after his mom, we could be certain girls lusted after him.

He took his sneaker off, and his foot ballooned (I swear it did). But his mom checked for breaks, too, and found none – so we were able to go up to his room. He was under orders to put his foot on a pillow on the bed. We helped set him up, whilst looking around, impressed, definitely. He had cool stuff. Rare posters of the right bands. Plus there was a guitar, acoustic: a Guild – a serious guitar.

'Can you play anything?' asked Crab.

Syph showed he definitely could, even lying on his back.

'And I write songs.'

Without being asked, he started in – no embarrassment, instead, that thing which has always been his greatest gift: shamelessness.

The song . . . put it this way, it didn't make the first album. But it did make the first gig. It was called 'Celibacy', and was about moving away from where he'd grown up. (For the first year I knew him, *all* his songs seemed to be about that. He missed the north, the snow.) We tried our hardest not to be impressed, but started smiling at the strange changes in the bridge. There was strong implied harmony, too.

'We're a band,' said Mono.

'Would you like to join?' asked Crab, without even calling us into a pow-wow. There was no point – whether he'd plotted it or not, Syph had just sung his way into our lives.

What was the last of the one, two and three? *Idealistic*, yes. This is hard. There is an idealism of whores, I'd say. They're all sentimentalists, if only in their weepy love for cash. Our motives were always mixed, and we tried to be honest about that – with one another and also in our songs. Money was quite important. Fame was very important. Music was some-times more important than fame and sometimes less impor-tant than money. We liked the way we sounded and we wanted other people to like it, too – as many people as possible. Stadiums.

Of course, in our heads, we competed with the biggest, with The Beatles. That's the thing of being in a band, especially a bass, drums, lead, rhythm combo. We thought we could do something similar, although the great breakthroughs (even then we sensed) had already been made.

There was another thing, too, a fascination. I'd known Crab for five years and Mono for eight. A large part of the thing about wanting success was wanting it for yourself, but there was also the fascination of doing it with your friends, seeing it happen to them and, through them, feeling it happen to yourself.

That's where Syph was a difficulty. He came in as an outsider and stayed as a permanent latecomer. *okay* needed him but it didn't always want him. We played together but, after the tree-climbing-falling, we only played music – with Mono and Crab, I'd played *played* played. We had sandpit history.

Syph brought the excitement. Without him, we'd be – I don't even want to think what we'd be. Certainly, we wouldn't be being asked by charming Japanese fans (hi Yoyo!) to reminisce about fifteen–twenty years ago.

What else do I remember? One thing, above all, from after that first rehearsal. It's not really to do with music – at least not directly.

We arranged to meet again the next weekend and start practising for real. Everyone swapped phone numbers, and we were very band-y – no hugs but lots of smiles and yeahs and hummings of riffs as we packed up.

Middle of that week, I'm walking down the street in the centre of town. Coming towards me I see just the most beautiful girl in our school, Katie Proudhon (Catty Proudhorn, as she inevitably got called), and with her? alongside her? – to my young, innocent, idealistic astonishment: Syph.

Years of experience have now taught me that, to him, this kind of company is nitrogen. He breathes it in without noticing, without metabolizing it. To me, it's oxygen. Most of the time, I'm gasping.

So they come towards me, and I put on a scared smile and I think how great it will be to speak to such a lovely girl. Even if, and I accept this completely (almost completely) (alright, I work really hard to accept it) – even if she walks away with Syph and is his girlfriend and wife for ever.

And Syph sees me. I see him see me. (He denies this now. Ask. He *denies*.) Syph sees my smile, and he steers Katie Proudhon round me.

He *steers* her.

As if I'm *dog mess* on the *sidewalk*.

'Hi,' I say, to their together-backs.

I'm astonished, *mortified*. But like the jerk I am, I say, 'Hi.'

And, still steering her, Syph says – and he doesn't look round and he certainly doesn't *stop* – Syph says, 'Hi.'

Motherfucker.

After recording, releasing and touring the live album, we – the four band members – sat down in a skanky diner and decided what *okay* needed was change, radical change.

Enough of hotel rooms, enough of road-food, enough of contempt-fucking – what all of us required was a zone of long hibernation.

And so, we did what we hadn't done since the very beginning: loaded our own equipment into the Big Van, and drove –

(Alright, we took two roadies, Shed and Monkey Boy, but they were almost band members anyhow. Don't tell them that, though.)

– drove East.

One reason we could do this was, for once, we were all single. Syph never kept a girlfriend for more than a week, and that was only if we were doing a six-night residency – in NYC, say. Crab split up with Kerrie three weeks into the live-album tour, after they'd been seeing each other for a year. (The band record at that point, a year of solid faithfulness.) Mono had been divorced two years, and was still living out his depraved version of *la vida*. And me, Clap, you probably know a little too much about me already: homeless: hopeless: helpless.

It was *okay*'s intention to reconnect with 'the country' (meaning Canada). Not an original idea, but –

– basically, no band can do anything that hasn't already been done by the four great archetypal bands: The Beatles, The Band, The Velvets, The Stooges. These bands did every variation upon every move a band can make.

We drove our van cross-country to Northern Ontario,

looking for our own homegrown version of Dylan and the Band's Big Pink. We took our time, secret-gigging on the way.

I think when we first got there – and one of us is still there – we thought we'd found it. (I won't say where *there* is – don't want to spoil it for the old chap.) On the very edge of a flat stretch of the most beautiful water you have ever seen, a three-storey house with an alpine-sloped roof and a huge basement.

The owners had two of our CDs, and were Dylan aficionados – they didn't take much persuading to move out. Money, also, was involved.

Town was about two miles back along the track. It had a population of 350 – shaped like a T, with a long main drag and a couple of churches off to left and right built on less expensive land. The stores were old-fashioned, and not chains. Junk food was available, however. We wouldn't have stopped there otherwise.

Town was the colour of asphalt and blackish wood – what gave it colour was the sky and the trees against the sky. Its yearly cycle was a round of dulling to gray and brightening to green. We caught it at the start of the end of spring, if that makes sense.

For the first few days, life in the house was perfect. Monkey Boy had found a supplier of decent weed. We relaxed and I – I'm not sure about the others – started to hanker after some good ol' unplugged music-making.

Syph posed around – *getting inspired*, he said it was. This meant having female photographers come and take his picture up against trees in forest groves. He spoke to some music journalists, too. Probably telling them about the great new material we were hard at work on.

Mono went fishing. He is terrible at it, and whenever any of the rest of us went along with him, we always caught more, but he loved it.

Crab installed himself at the far end of the roughest local

bar, put on his *eat shit* face and prepared himself for greaser homage.

The roadies were down in the basement, setting up the equipment – a modest sixteen-track mixing desk, etc., etc.

In the afternoons, we could hear them banging around: they weren't a bad rhythm section, and Monkey Boy could sing in his own sweet way. He had often soundchecked when our lead singer was otherwise engaged.

After he ran out of photographers, Syph set himself up on the barstool next to Crab – who hadn't received any homage, greasy or not. Syph was different, though. Within about a half-hour, the crush (female) was such he had to move the party back into a booth. Crab followed him, and together they began to make artistic arrangements out of their empty bottles – much to the amusement of the five or six local girls who fit round the table, too. One whiff of Syph, that's all they needed. I don't know what it is he sends out – weasel, skunk, buck or coon; it works.

I joined Mono by the lakeside.

You can see where the split was starting to develop.

Two weeks in, and we hadn't spent a single hour down the basement. The roadies had it all ready to roll – drumheads tuned, strings shiny-new. We still heard them, trying the equipment out in a variety of styles: gospel, country, blue-grass, funk. Whenever we were ready, they were ready. Syph had been generous: both Monkey Boy and Shed would get to engineer whatever we laid down – credited, with royalties.

This was roundabout when Syph fell in love. A strange phenomenon, never before been known to have occurred. Mainly we knew this was serious because to the woman in question (definitely a woman, not a girl) Syph made no protestations. *I love you* with a wink and a grin, was one of his best lines. He could conduct an entire seduction, saying nothing else. Apart, maybe, from *Hey, what's your name?*

The woman was called Major. Half Native Canadian, Sitka tribe, born in Alaska, brought here by her mother (after the divorce and the attempted murder), working the cosmetics counter in the town's only pharmacy – Syph saw her come into the bar the third Saturday night.

I was there too, and I would like to say I saw in her what Syph saw. The rest of the band, plus roadies, were also there.

Up until this point, this epoch, our table had been doing its pale cowardly impression of Led Zep's dominion over the Whisky-a-Go-Go, *circa* 1972. There were empty bottles of JD on the table, of which we were all secretly keeping a count. Apart from Crab.

Mono had been monologuing about fishing techniques, and I was distressed to find myself fascinated – hooked.

'Look at her,' said Syph. He had his arms round two local girls, but they could tell straightaway they'd lost him. He was a lunar module, they were just booster rockets.

The band must've heard something in Syph's voice, because we all looked over.

Major had entered the bar on her own, so she wasn't hard to spot.

'Mmm,' yummy-yummed Crab. '*Beefcake*, eh?'

Syph slapped him. 'Don't ever speak like that about the woman I love.'

We thought he was joking. We mocked him, pretending he meant it, and in this way found out he did.

I'll never know how it happened. The moment she walked through the door, Syph turned from hound dog to lap dog. (He was never not going to be canine, but he had in a second gone from a leg-rutter into a heel-worshipper.) I've never known a thing like it: she *transfigured* him.

'Well, go and speak to her, then,' said Crab, assuming this was the role Syph wanted him to play.

'I can't,' said Syph – he seemed paralysed by the idea, and delighted by his paralysis. It was years – put it another way, I don't think he'd *ever* felt at a disadvantage, sexually, when faced with another human being. Major scared him, as well she should. She was taller than him, broader than him, and probably stronger than him. She looked like an Olympic swimmer, a specialist at the butterfly. Syph had never gone for the Amazonian type before, not that I'd seen. The rapid destruction of the most delicate beauty, that had always been his speciality. But with Major, he must surely have felt himself to be the potentially delicate one.

'*Talk* to her,' I said to him, about an hour later. He had become boring with out-loud longing.

'I *can't*,' he whined.

Mono got frustrated with not knowing, and went and asked the barman who she was – the barman gave him the basics: the pharmacy, the cosmetics counter.

Next time Major went up to get drinks, the barman told her about Mono asking who she was. I saw him nod in our table's direction. Major followed his eyebeam, picked out Mono, thought she caught his eye, smiled. But he was staring right through her, describing to me the joys of nightfishing.

After she came in, Major sat down as part of a large group of women, many of them familiar from the stores in town. Most of them were ten years older than us, sturdy of leg, and none of them gave any sign of knowing who we were – although we knew word had gotten round within about a day of our arrival.

Major took another trip to the john, passing right by our table. Syph's eyes followed her, like puppies chasing a butterfly.

'Talk to her,' Mono said.

'I can't,' Syph said.

This time he seemed genuinely tortured by his paralysis.

Early the next morning, we left the bar – Syph not even taking one of the local girls back with him to his room.

Mono, Crab and I traded glances – they were humorous but also anxious. What if it were true? Would we have lost the old Syph? – the one upon whom we could blame all our own lapses? the one who made the worst of our behaviour seem mild?

Another consideration was whether Syph would start maybe writing songs.

As we went to bed, I got the answer – an acoustic guitar starting to plang-plang down in the kitchen.

Next day, we found Syph in the studio with Monkey Boy. They had been up all night, and had laid down rough mixes of four tracks.

After breakfast, Syph played them back to us. The first was called '*Coup de Fou*'. It was clear almost from note one that this was 'a solo project'. Drums, bass, guitar – it was all there already. We weren't needed.

That afternoon Syph took a ghetto blaster down to the cosmetics counter.

From what we later heard, Syph walked up to Major's counter, slammed the monster boombox down and pressed Play. His first heartbreaker kicked in. 'You make me feel like a baby, baby.'

A female customer almost immediately came up and shouted a question about combination skin. Major tried to answer, couldn't be heard, so pressed the eject button on the boombox. She then spent ten minutes in close discussion of the virtues of various foundations.

Syph, defeated, took up his tape-recorded declaration of love and walked. He'd had refusals before, of course – girls who seriously *did* love their boyfriends, girls who loved God. But it was at least a decade since he'd been ignored.

He hiked the long way back to the house, went down in the basement and immediately set to work on another two tracks.

'You didn't talk to her?' asked Crab.

'Couldn't,' said Syph. 'Just couldn't.'

*

Mono and I went fishing, though I was getting bored. I tried to talk to him about the Major-situation, but he replied by questioning whether he was using the correct ground bait.

A little later, Mono said the sight of that flat expanse in front of him, rippling under the wind, made him feel true calm. It had the opposite effect on me: I wanted to throw stones into it.

The fact there would never be real waves on such a stretch began to make me weirdly fearful. I wanted the sea; I wanted to surf. (I've never surfed before, but now I got a mad craving.)

I handed back the rod Mono had lent me. 'I'm going for a walk,' I said.

'Yes, you are,' he replied, Buddha-like.

Frustrated, I went for a long hike along the forest trails on my own – and found it far more satisfying than fishing: the birds, the insects, the whole natural vibe, man.

From then on, Mono went fishing on his own. This he did at increasingly unrock'n'roll hours of the day – early morning, after sleeping eight full hours.

Syph didn't dare risk another failure. He spent the week hard at work in the studio, writing and recording an album's worth of devotional material. Monkey Boy and Shed split shifts to keep up with him – the other band members were still surplus to requirements. I bought some decent backpacking boots and went for more long hikes. Mono got to bed early, so that he could be down by the lakeside well before dawn.

About this time, Friday of the fourth week, it came clear that *another* album had already been recorded in the basement. During the first couple of weeks, the roadies had put together their own set of fourteen tracks. Now, it seemed, Syph had made late-night promises to start up a record label in order to release it. Mono wasn't concerned but Crab and I thought this could be the end of the band. We confronted Syph. He told us, no, it was just something he needed to do. The label would be called Major Record Label.

Saturday morning, Syph had a plan. He drove over to the bar we'd been frequenting, spoke to the manager. The roadies spent the rest of the day shuttling equipment and sound-checking. Without even asking, Syph had set up a gig for us. Crab and I refused to play, so Monkey Boy, Shed and Mono took the stage. They were pretty good, not as good as *okay* but okay.

Syph spent the whole evening looking out for Major. The gig was entirely for her benefit. He was going to do a solo acoustic set of all the songs he'd written her. But she never showed.

Mono turned in early, wanting like most days to get up before the dawn and fish.

Syph, distraught, by the end of the set was getting drunk. I enjoy plinky-plinky on-the-edge burnout music – Neil Young's *Needle*, Big Star's third. Syph was going for something like the same effect. I felt sorry for him.

The bar cleared, as a result.

Syph had a long maudlin talk with the barman, then went off to make a fool of himself for the third time.

We later heard he'd persuaded the barman to give him Major's address, and had gone round to serenade her.

Turns out, she wasn't at home – was somewhere else entirely. In fact, I may as well tell you now, she was camping out by the lake, wanting to get up before dawn and fish. (I *know*.)

Come morning, she and Mono picked roughly the same pitch, and when it became clear nothing was biting, they said hello and had breakfast together. Then she went into work.

Mono kept quiet about it that afternoon, whilst playing bass on some new Syph tracks. He had ditched the gentle acoustic style, and was off into the angry clatter. As drummer, I was now his main man – and I was glad to be.

We laid down three pretty good tracks, keeping going till 2 a.m. Mono again went off early, the better to fish in the morning.

Whilst we slept, Mono's luck changed – he and Major had a dream morning of bites, hookings, tugs, nettings.

Thinking little of it, they came in their joy to show us their catch. The house was very quiet. None of us was up, except Syph, who still hadn't gone to bed.

Mono and Major walked in, a line of fish hung between them, and Syph *knew*.

Before Mono knew, before Major knew, Syph *knew* that they were one another's final destination.

He also knew, I think, that it meant the band was over – in the original form. No-one was ever going to persuade Mono away from this place again. The wide stillness of the lake, the careful speech, the values, the fish – he was at home. We wouldn't be a living-in-eachother's-pockets gang any more.

Mono introduced Syph to Major, and Syph started crying.

Major excused herself and, when she had gone, Syph tried to punch Mono – he missed, and Mono calmly retaliated. With a single jab to the gut, he laid him down gently, like a baby into a cot, leaving his beautiful face undamaged.

'Now why did you want to do that?' Mono asked.

'Go away,' said Syph, deathbed-scene style.

Mono went after Major – and they realized what was going on about halfway to town. They didn't come back to the house, carried on going to hers.

When we got up later, Syph was bent over at the kitchen table. He explained the situation.

Bless Syph, bless what he was before he was in the band, and bless what he's now returning to.

He took the whole thing as 'educational'. The anger was gone. He'd already written two gorgeous songs of leaving.

We rehearsed them, recorded them, one take each, no Mono, and he left before Major came off shift at the cosmetics counter. He took with him the tapes of his own album and the roadies'. Both were released.

You've probably heard theirs, *Mountain Men*, big hit, Grammies and all; Syph's – *Hook, Line and Sinker* – is a little harder to find, but worth finding.

LYDIA

Just like the song says, I fall in love too easily.

I wish I could stop myself, but I can't, it's a function of me being alive, of me being me.

There was that girl in Rotterdam, Amsterdam? Rotterdam, Inge her name, who is still there or thereabouts – in my heart.

I've fallen in love three times today already, and I haven't even gone for lunch yet. There'll be another *then*, guaranteed: all waitresses, I fall in love with.

I really shouldn't be allowed out the house: it hurts too much. There are so many alternate lives I could be leading, in the parallel universes of these women's arms.

I want to live with one of the English ones, a rich girl if not an actual princess, in a castle her family has owned for five hundred or a thousand years. (I wonder, does it make any difference, five hundred or a thousand? To the plumbing, probably. Not to the girl.) I'd like there to be at least one warm room, for wintering in. I think of these details.

But sometimes, girls fall in love with me, too.

Yes, there are groupies, but that's not exactly what I mean. What I mean is, they fall in love with me in a way that's disturbingly like the way I fall in love with them. Hopelessly, in other words – immediately, stupidly and in a way designed to ensure maximum loss of dignity. And this is what I'd like to tell you about, because it's different.

I was in England, perhaps following my yen for an aristo-cratic beauty but more likely because *okay* had finished a month's promotion in Europe (*Underlings*, the B-sides and rarities collection) and I couldn't face getting on another airplane. It's amazing how some deeply scary turbulence over Portugal impacted on the life of Lydia I-Won't-Include-Her-Real-Surname. Chaos theory in reverse: a thunderstorm above Lisbon brushes dust off the butterfly's wing that Lydia definitely was.

We met cute, in the bar of the hotel *okay*'s new management had booked me into.

I was sitting there on my own – such a beautiful thing, that; unhassled and away from the other guys in the band. No publicist. No questions to answer. Nothing I had to do *that* minute, that evening, *that* week. Time without a schedule was a different thing, chewier.

So, I was sitting there in a big velvet booth with a neat double vodka in front of me, nicely iced, trying to decide whether or not any of my friends in London were really my friends – and if they were, whether that made me want to contact them more or less. There are occasions on which what you most want to see are vague and largely facetious acquaintances. Cocaine-friends – or 'mates', as they call them in the UK, with the implication that some form of mating has gone on, among all the matiness. And then again, some-times what you need is a friend so old and true that you can be ugly and selfish and generally a 'twit' – all the while knowing you'll be forgiven, eventually.

I was leaning towards wanting a genuine Canadian grown-up-with-them person when I saw Lydia and Lydia saw me.

And I *knew*, just as I've known (of myself) in the past. Oh, I knew so many things – I knew about her months of cool, drizzling endurance, about the sunbursts of searing, flame-yellow hope – I too had lived beneath that emotional sky. I knew of transient and hopefully-permanent relationships. And I knew that this was one that could go a certain distance but which would never make it to the end, or anywhere close. I also knew, above all, that she knew who I was. Her glance showed sweet recognition.

She was there with a female 'mate' – later, they told me they had been to a 'naff' rom-com and didn't want the night to end in disappointment. Her friend came with hope, too – a hump of hope. They were fellow hunchbacks – carrying round that great useless lump of optimistic stuff on their backs: deformed by it – aching in every bone to be relieved of it – hating and growing it like an angry zit rather than a romantic burden.

She whispered to her friend and her friend whispered back. I had seen these head movements before, seen them on all five continents – the dip, twist, jerk and shake. Like defunct dance-crazes. There is a rhythm to it. Finally it comes down to shake and nod, shake and not. Reluctance and encouragement. No and *yes*.

Yes usually wins. The smaller the town, the more exciting yes seems. But even in capital cities, yes has an edge.

Do it, yes.

I was expecting both of them to come over, but Lydia was braver and more foolhardy than I'd given her credit for.

The walk across, as I felt it for her, was very wearying. I tried to help by not staring at her approach.

'Excuse me,' she said, the traditional opening. 'I'm sorry to bother you, but...' I hated it that this was an unoriginal experience for me – in fact, a screamingly tedious one. 'But are you ...'

'Hello,' I said. 'Yes, I'm –'

'Aren't you that gardener from television?'

She had heard my accent, and realized her mistake. 'I'm sorry – I didn't –'

But I was the more horribly shocked. Not that I'd been so wrong – that my knowing had been disproved. Not *that*, and not that she didn't know who I was: drummer with a mid-rank Canadian indie band. No, what shocked me was that I'd felt the whole of this encounter from her side. There was a very wounding quality about Lydia, right from the start.

'No, it's okay. Why don't you –' I said.

I was in her embarrassment with her, beneath her sky as it blushed into excuse and anecdote. Go into reverse, she thought. Reverse gear. Get back to the bar. Drink up and leave. Or leave the drinks and go. Laugh about it in the taxi home – or the bus. They looked like maybe they used buses.

'It's just, you look like him. A bit.'

'A gardener?'

'He's famous.'

'Well, that's something at least. Would he be here?'

She looked back at her friend. And this time I wasn't so sure what her face would be saying: *Join me, Rescue me* or *Don't you dare leave me.*

The friend, good friend, got down off her barstool and walked across the room. She walked very carefully, so as not to upstage Lydia – her skirt was shorter than Lydia's, and her legs longer. But she was walking towards me as a famous gardener, not as a semi-famous-in-some-circles-and-countries musician.

'It isn't him,' Lydia said, when her friend got close.

'No, I'm only me,' I said. What surprised me most about this situation was that, despite these two young women being neither my friends nor my acquaintances, I was quite enjoying it – being misrecognized for someone else public. It took some of the pressure.

'Oh,' said the friend, 'we thought you were –'

'You must like him a lot,' I said. 'What kind of gardens does he make?'

They looked at one another, each hoping the other would answer. I liked that they weren't too drunk, hardly at all. I liked, also, that they seemed to be trying to answer seriously, informatively.

'Very "architectural",' said the friend. 'He uses metal quite a lot.'

I decided to flirt. 'You think I look like a famous gardener of metal?'

'From over there you did,' said the friend. I was worried she would take over. I could feel Lydia mentally exiting from the evening.

Reader, I pitied her. (That's an allusion to Charlotte Brontë's *Jane Eyre*, Miss Ullshawn – see, I didn't forget *every-*

thing from fifth grade. I think my English is pretty good, for a fail student.)

I introduced myself – looking all the while at Lydia – and, to end the confusion stage of things, explained who I was and what I did and why I was there. Then, unthreateningly as I could, asked, 'Why don't you sit down?'

'Sure,' she said, suddenly confident. Again, I was pained – this was the flood-of-liking moment. For me, it goes both ways at the same time: I like her; she likes me! Two waves crashing into one another and whoosh.

The friend was a little more hesitant. I think I had disrupted their girls-together evening. But as the friend was aware of Lydia's singleness and her hope and the fact I might, despite not being off the 'telly', be someone worth having met – as the friend was a kind sort, she sat down too.

I had shifted round the booth so they weren't flanking me pimp-style; Lydia was closest, the friend opposite.

There was a moment, a definite moment.

Then the friend introduced herself, taking over again, briefly. And then Lydia, quietly, brought her name out. She was far shyer about it than, later on, about stepping out of her dress. This, I empathized with: by that point you are committed – it's in the tentativeness that torture lurks.

We talked – for over an hour, while the lovely waitress brought us drinks which I insisted went on my room bill and which they tried to give me money for. When I promised that my management, and not me, would really foot the bill, they quit. Both understood the joy of drinking on someone else's tab: alcohol tastes lighter – like the air above vodka.

I felt I knew what was going to happen, and switched to singles – so as to be ready for it. Not for sex but for explanations, more talk and deeper. Tonight was neither for London friends nor acquaintances; tonight was for a complete stranger who, fittingly strangely, felt as known as myself.

I looked at Lydia and, by slow steps, worked it out. So many of *okay*'s songs are about wrong romances. But in all pop and most rock there's a basic belief in the true love, the soul-mate, the long-awaited other. And I'd done so much waiting. And Lydia had, too. And now we'd found one another. But not in the way we should have done. She was attractive. I could say, *she had a beautiful figure* but that would be senti-mental: she had a very sympathetic face and beautiful breasts – truly gorgeous and loveable. But the bits in between, the supporting bits, weren't model-like. They were sketchy and touching. Her legs, when I saw all of them, were comic in some way – not advertisement legs; friend legs, sister legs. Her legs made me want to cry almost as much as her breasts made me want to cuddle, nuzzle, semi-suffocate. But I knew it would feel wrong – wrong for both of us, eventually, though with her lessness of experience it might take her a year to realize. I'm sure she knew a lot about heartbreak, for want of a non-country'n'western word, but she certainly didn't know as much as me about strangers in hotel bars, strangers in hotel bathrooms. (Very few people do.)

We talked about their lives. Lydia worked in arts adminis-tration, her friend in telecommunications. They felt mildly glamorous to be in my company – though the fact I'd arranged it so they weren't sitting either side of me made it feel both less glamorous and less sleazy.

'Okay,' said the friend, just after twelve. 'It's now or never for the bus.'

Well, I'd been right about that, at least.

I didn't avoid the moment's eye-contact that was the necessary next. Lydia understood: 'I think I might stay a little longer.'

I said nothing. I didn't need to. I felt weak with Lydia's brave achievement – her liking hurt me. Mmm, and her love. It was important to be deeply kind to this young woman. I wanted to treat her like I wanted women to treat me, women I loved. What I wanted was not to be politely put off – I wanted them to let me have the pleasure and catharsis of a fuck.

Yes, we would talk for another hour – more soulfully, even sobering up a little. Yes, I would invite her up to my room – just so she could see what the suites looked like in a 'posh' place like this. Yes, I would maintain the guided-tour pretence for a couple of minutes after we got upstairs: I wouldn't jump and hump her. Yes, I would seduce her by using her name just as I would want a woman I loved to use mine – to speak it as if it were a name to be spoken many times more, in together-future.

I found the making love difficult, having seen Lydia's legs. Once the idea of sisterliness entered the room, it was very hard to dissipate. I tried for a while to get off on it, but eventually decided to focus on her face and her breasts. It sounds horrible and sexist. (I'm not ripping her body to bits.) But they were exquisite – and they were exquisite because they were truly *hers*, not just voluptuous add-ons that didn't fit with her personality.

(This isn't going the way I meant it to.)

Making love, note, not having sex: my lump-o'-hope wanted me to try – I knew it wouldn't work, and it didn't. This wasn't a woman I'd ever love as I'd loved the ones who didn't care for me or let me near them.

Afterwards, she went to sleep very soundly.

As I lifted my arm from behind her head, she woke up a little but I kissed and whispered her back to sleep.

Then I got dressed.

I wasn't able to pack everything, but I took my passport, a few clothes and a book for the flight. If she wanted to steal something of mine, I didn't mind: as I looked round the dim room for the last time (it was still only three thirty in the morning), I wondered what it was she might take. Everything? Might she rip my clothes up in anger at being abandoned? Not Lydia. Nothing – would she want nothing? I hoped not. I tried to inventory what I saw.

When I left, I left no note. I kissed the air silently above her head, said *I don't love you. I'm sorry* and walked out of the room.

I was lucky with the taxi and made it to London Heathrow in under an hour. Lucky, too, with the airline – ticket on the first flight out. I could have flown business class, but didn't: I felt a little emotionally tough and wanted my travel to reflect that.

I was sure I'd done the right thing. I only hoped that, next time I met her and it didn't work, my so-long-awaited would leave me as absolutely.

MODEL

One night, in my hotel room, in Paris, in the middle of everything, I had a long conversation with a model who was, incidentally, very attractive and, inevitably (or else she wouldn't have been there), very stoned.

She told me all about it: being beautiful. I don't think she meant to. Her nature didn't include lectures – nothing conventionally didactic, though educational. Truancy was written all over her, misspelt. But recently written. She was a good girl trying not to be.

I was thirty-five then, and the naked body of an eighteen-year-old model made me think first of all of death – my own and death in the abstract. After that, I could usually bring it round again to desire. Some nights, though, and those were becoming more frequent, sadness won. Sadness, from time to time, was all there was.

I should probably accentuate the positive. At least, given my position (middle of a modest drum-stack – out-of-shot and out-of-focus for 90–95 per cent of the videos – one quote per all-band interview – millionaire) – given my ignominious and by-proxy glamour, I still occasionally got access to the bodies of eighteen-year-old models.

It would be dishonest not to note there was a downside to this, too. Along with access to their bodies came an open invitation to enter their minds – and that, as I hope you can imagine, was a corner of Hell that Virgil somehow neglected to show Dante. Probably thought he couldn't take it.

Her name, that night, was Barbra, spelt like and in tribute to Streisand.

She was best known for a lingerie campaign in Europe – which had picked her up the tabloid nickname of Bra-Bra and, more cruelly but less frequently, Baps.

Like I said, and probably don't need to say again but will, Barbra was beautiful. But, in the flesh, there was something not exactly off-putting but quite *taming* about her.

Which was why she ended up, at 2 a.m. Central European Time, with me and not with Syph.

I've heard one reason Marilyn Monroe looked so radiant on-screen was that her face was covered – cheeks, nose, everything – with a very fine pelt of white hairs. This is why she remained peachy, right up through *The Misfits* and *Something's Got to Give.*

It was also why quite a few men, confronted with the real Norma Jean, and not the celluloid goddess, found her more than a little grotesque.

Of course, this didn't *stop* them from doing what they were going to do: sexually punish her for being sexual. In fact, it probably added to the viciousness of their attacks.

Poor Norma.

Poor Barbra.

I'm not saying Barbra was at all fuzzy-like-a-peach. But there was a definite teddy-bear quality to her, close up. She would prefer a cuddle, and she looked like she needed it. Anything else brought thoughts of soft-toy violation – and if that's your thing ... It isn't mine.

Barbra called out to be treated with kindness. And so, without sounding too knight-on-steed, I rescued her from the end of the evening.

I should, perhaps, mention the evening. Just to give you some context: after-show party in Parisian warehouse (yes, they do have such things in such places). Our French fans are some of our most loyal (read crazed) and attentive (read obsessive). There's a noticeable difference between gigs there and, say, Belgium. The Belgians come to rock, the French to think about the existential nature of what it would be to rock – or some shit like that. So, we were on a mild high, a slightly frustrated we-didn't-break-on-through buzz.

'I can't even *look* at people,' said Barbra. 'I can't look at *men*.

If I look at them, they look back and they see me and then it's like the whole eye-contact *catastrophe*. They think I'm interested in them and come over and try and chat me up – when I wasn't looking at them for *that* at all. I don't even *dare* to look at men I find really attractive. I just go and stand as far away from them as I can, sometimes in another fucking *building*, and I think about what it would be like if they *did* come to find me. It's lonely. I'm shy – no-one understands. And I *want* to look at people. I'm *interested*, you know. I want to see what they're *like* – what they look like, what they are doing. I think I'd like to be some kind of *artist*, or maybe a photographer. Then I could hide behind the camera and no-one would fucking see *me*.'

Fucking – the word *fucking* – really didn't suit her, but she'd picked it up as a habit, probably around the same time as those other habits, puking and cocaine. Fourteen, maybe fifteen, maybe younger – I was getting out-of-date. Anticipating forty.

And I'm going to cut out some of the Valley Girl *like*s and *you know*s and *really*s – she used lots but, *you know*, you don't *like really* need them. Barbra was from Washington State, upstate, but sounded like she was from everywhere. Secretly, she was Canadian, she just didn't know it – had a wide-open and snowy soul.

'It's lonely,' she said.

I won't interrupt much more, but she used the word *lonely* almost as much as *like, you know* and *really*.

'It's so fucking lonely. I mean, like I said, I'm interested in people. How am I going to learn anything about the world if I get *attacked* every time I look at it? Someone said to me this morning, at the shoot – they wanted me to be more, what was the word? *Aristoscrat* – he wanted me to be more aristocrat. It was the photographer. *Really*, he just wanted me to lift my chin a little higher. Like that. Anyway, I'm getting lost, this is good shit, *aristoscrat*, hah! This famous fucking photographer said to me, "Beauty is distance." He said it like he was a phisollopher – I mean, a phillo-soffa, a pheelosofr, philosofpher. "Beauty is distance." And he let that hang for a few moments, while everyone listened to him and I stood there freezing in the Summer Line. And then he said, looking at me with a strange look, "That's why we all want to get close to it." And everyone clapped, stylists, everyone, like he'd said something really intelligent and *true*. And what I really hate is that I think probably he *did* – but I'm sure he stole it off of someone *genuine*, a real deep thinker from the past.'

Line of coke.

'I'm beautiful. I wouldn't be here if I wasn't. And people are always trying to get closer and closer until they're all over you and up *inside* you. Did I tell you that people touch me up *all* the time? Not just men. *Women* will stand so I can feel their *nipples* against my *arm*. It's fucking *true*! What's *that* about? These aren't *lesbians* – not all of them. I'm not charismatic, I know that. It's not *real* talent. Not like you guys. That's why it's lonely. Because I know I *have* it and I know it will *go* and so I better *enjoy* it while it lasts, like *everyone* is always *telling* me, usually because they want to *bang* me, but having it makes you sort of *not* able to enjoy it. Do you understand? It's easier for them to think they would enjoy it if they had it than for me to enjoy it being me and having it. You're cute. No, you *are*. Believe me – you may not think so, but I see your inner cuteness. I have x-ray vision and superkinetic powers, and you are a cutie.'

Line of coke.

'I want to touch you,' I say, guiltily. 'I'm not that different.'

'At least you fucking ask,' Barbra says. 'To some of them, I'm just a piece of *meat*. People talk about me all the time as if I wasn't there. "Her hair's looking a bit *frizzy* today." "Can we do something about the *bags* under her eyes?" "I really don't think she has the right *look* for this *campaign*." "God, is that *cellulite*?" And they're always moving me around, putting me in this position or *that* stupid fucking position, not asking, and sticking fucking pins in me. I really should be a doll. In

62

French they call us *mannequins*. I learnt that today. See, I'm interested. Anyway, this photographer who said about beauty – after we're done, he invites me to his apartment. His *Paris* apartment, I should say, he has one in New York and one in *Miami*, too. I thought he was gay enough for me to be *safe* with him. Some of the others came, too – his assistant. And when we got there, he got out *another* camera, a little *digital* one this time, and he told me *to take my clothes off* like we were still working. I said, "Why?" and he said he did this with all the girls he used. He said he liked a *record* of them. And I thought about saying why didn't he just use some of the shots from the shoot. Shots from the shoot – hah! Pretty funny. But I didn't say that because I was a bit scared of him. And he says, "Come on, you're *wasting* my *time*." So I ask who else has done it, and he takes me into his bedroom – big view of the Eiffel Tower – and pulls out this drawer and there's a book inside it, like a photograph album, and when I open it I see *everyone* – all the models going back, like, ten–fifteen years. But they're not just *standing* posing, like for the record, like he says. He's got them all on their hands and knees looking back over their right shoulder, like *this*.'

And she shows me. And I'm dismayed not to be more dismayed.

'And not just that, but they have their fingers in their – you know – in a really porny way. Spreading it apart so you can see all of it. And this is the record, because when he turns the page I can see he's blown up this part of the photograph for all of them. And underneath, in tiny tiny neat writing, he's written their *name* and a *date*. He turns the page – more models – he turns the page – more clitorises. "You see," he says, "it's an *art project*. And I want *you* to be part of it." So, anyway . . . Do you have some *Coke*, please?'

At first, confusingly, I think she doesn't mean soda, but it turns out she does.

I open the mini-bar and then offer her a choice of five different kinds. She goes, as I knew she would, for fat *Coke*.

'So what happened?' I ask, as I pop it and hand it over.

'I *did* it,' she says. 'He's an important photographer – and it's not the *worst* thing I've ever done. But I don't want to fucking talk about that fucked-up ... Let's talk about you. What's it like being in a band? You guys really *rock*, you know.'

And I give her the speech – one of the speeches (I think I have about five by now), which I playlist randomly and occasionally remix, cutting from one to the other. I give Barbra the gentle version, the I-don't-want-to-ruin-your-illusions vamp. She doesn't seem to have many illusions left, except about herself.

When we return to *that* subject, she talks for ten minutes or so about clothes. She has theories – what the designers are doing wrong, what women really want. I nod and ask her to explain more. Then she says, 'When I was ten, I used to be a real tomboy. I was climbing trees and fighting with my brother – some of the time even beating up on him. We lived in the country and I didn't know a *thing* about anything. I'd never even *seen* a fashion magazine. My mother didn't buy them. The first model I saw was on a poster when my daddy took me into town to get the truck fixed. It was up in the office of the mechanic, behind his desk. She was a blonde and was covered in something that looked like a fishing net, orange string in diamonds. Of course, it didn't cover her very well. She had brown nipples and they were stiff. You couldn't see anything else, which was lucky or I'd have screamed. I didn't scream, I just said, "Look, Daddy, she's got no clothes on." And he said "Who?" and I said "Her" and he said, "No, I don't think you'd call that clothes" and the mechanic, I remember he laughed at that. I was a little brat, so I kept on asking. "Is she cold?" I said. Which made the mechanic laugh again, but Daddy didn't. He was more serious. "It looks like she's on a beach," he said, "so she's probably quite warm." And the mechanic said, "She's *hot*." And my father laughed, but not really. I didn't understand what was going on – they

64

were laughing about something I didn't know. It annoyed me. I turned to the mechanic and straight out asked, "Is she your sister?" And he laughs fit to burst. He laughs so he can't speak. "It's not his sister," says my father. Oh, I was so obnoxious. I say, "Then why does he have a picture of her there?" And the mechanic says, "She's not my sister. Boy, I wish she was. Sure would have made bathtime a whole lot more fun." And my daddy says, "We'll be back in two hours. You'll have it fixed by then?" And the mechanic looks at me and says, "You're a very pretty little girl." I can't remember any more than that. I think we went to a diner and had burgers. Or to the movies. The next thing I do remember, we were in the truck driving home. "Why did he laugh?" I say. And my daddy knows who I mean. He doesn't answer. "Did I say something funny?" I want to know. "No, honey," he says, "the man was just laughing at something else." "So was she really his sister?" I ask, and he says, "Did she look like his sister?" "No," I say, "he was ugly and she was pretty." "He's a mechanic," says my father, "and she's a model." I thought about this for a couple of minutes as we drove. And I can't remember this, but my father swears it's true – after a couple of minutes I said, "Daddy, I don't want to be a mechanic." That's the family joke, that I said, "I don't want to be a mechanic."'

'I'm sure you'd make a very good mechanic,' I say, mechanically.

'Perhaps I should've,' she says. 'I never wanted to be a model, either. It just happened. But, after I finish, I want to do something useful. I want to have a *skill* that people want. I can be *original*. If I took photographs, people would see how *I* see things – they wouldn't be looking *at* me. I could show them how they look through my eyes. *All* of them. The *mechanics* and everyone.'

She starts to cry. And it is such a sad moment. And the saddest thing is, I've heard it all before. A hundred times, at least. Heard it all.

Every.
Single.
Like.
Fucking.
Word.

ELVIS

I have never been any good at endings. In relationships, I always hang on long past the points of viability, dignity, sanity, forcing my girlfriends – eventually – into full-on dump mode. That way I end up getting custody of a few delicately bejewelled regrets whilst they have to accommodate the buffalo guilt.

Here, though, for once, I am going to tell a story that is all endings. A true story, though not a good one.

The first ending was of the band. Some fool at a record company thought Syph capable of a solo career – I mean, a *successful* solo career. Not the long day's journey into nightmares on wax that is Syph's speciality when disconnected from his life-support system (a.k.a. us).

There was money involved. Too much of it, Syph insisted, at the this-is-something-I've-just-got-to-do meeting – far too much to turn down.

I knew from the looks they gave me that Crab and Mono knew how this would end. (Those guys are much better at endings than me.) They could script the humiliation, the apologies, the grovelling, the reunion. All it meant, in practice, was a year's holiday – at least, if we didn't plan on doing anything else.

I hadn't even started thinking about what I might want to do with myself when the second ending came along: my father died.

There was a message on my machine to phone home – from Betty, a friend of my mother. So I assumed whatever had happened had happened to my mother. I called, and Betty told me.

My house is only a couple of blocks from my parents'. I don't know why – I have a perfectly decent car, or two, or three – but I got on my bike and ripped round. It was probably the fastest way. I could cut across lawns and through back alleys. Head down. Sprinting.

Didn't matter how fast I rode to the rescue, I was still too late to save my father –

– save him from his heart.

He was an active man. He lived a healthy life and, if you believe the cereal boxes, it should have been a long one.

When I got home, he was still on the toilet. That's where he died. He was half resting back on the cistern, half sideways on the wall.

My mother was too calm. At first I thought it was because she didn't really care. I became angry with her. I wanted some hysteria – if she wasn't going to provide it, I was. Only later did I understand she was in shock. That's why she had her friend, who was round for coffee when it happened – had Betty call me and not call the paramedics.

Dad hadn't locked the door. It was the en-suite of my parents' bedroom, so there was no danger of Betty coming in. A sports magazine lay in the bathtub, wet. The toilet roll had unspooled until it was touching the floor. Perhaps one of his arms hit it, when he flailed around, made it spin. These are the details.

Together, all three of us, we lifted him off the toilet and into the bedroom. I was wearing tracksuit bottoms, T-shirt, sneakers, no socks. He was going stiff. We didn't have to wipe him – the piece of crap which killed him was still inside, and would be for all eternity.

My mother pulled his pants up while we held him above the bed. Betty closed his eyes, like it was something she'd done before – though later she confessed it was a TV-learnt skill. I stood uselessly, thinking about Elvis.

That was what I'd have to tell the band – that my daddy went like the King: on the john, straining.

It's not very rock'n'roll, that's what I thought. *Even if Elvis did it, it's still not very rock'n'roll.*

My father, I'd like to say, having stripped off all his dignity just now, was a wonderful and dignified and unrock'n'roll man. But although he wanted me to be educated and have a career like his (law), he didn't kvetch about it. He understood me and he understood what I was trying to do – even when that was telling him to go fuck himself.

I never used those exact words. I'm glad about that.

He said he liked our music. And, truly, I think he did. Some of it – the quieter songs.

When I checked the browser on his computer, the last few sites he'd looked at were all to do with us. He had also been ordering bulbs for the garden. Since he took retirement, that was where he'd spent most of his time.

The funeral was arranged very quickly. Betty had another friend, Clara, whose husband had died three months before, and Clara gave me and my mother a list of telephone numbers, some handy hints about where to buy a coffin and totally unexpected amounts of love.

My father was buried after a service in the church he had regularly attended since boyhood. Crab and Mono were there – Syph turned up, ten minutes late.

There's something drastically sad about middle-aged rock stars in mourning. The jewellery picked up on tour, the bangles and beads and earrings – it's all wrong, unnecessary. Wearing black was nothing new for us. We should have worn white, like John and Yoko in the 'Imagine' film.

With a lot of persuading, the band didn't re-form to play one of our melancholy songs. How could I drum grief? Grief isn't played in 4/4 time. I spoke, slowly and audibly, even for the partially deaf. I kept the in-church music to Bach, Schubert and Mozart.

There were a few fans waiting, when we got outside, and I was proud of them for not asking for autographs.

Afterwards, everyone came back to our house. They stayed for a while, we talked, we ate, then they left.

That was the worst moment. It was me and my mother

and my father's death and the rest of our lives without him, hers more than mine – I'd expected to have to mourn them; for her, it had been a fifty-fifty chance. Theirs had been a great marriage. She was sixty-one years old. He had been her third boyfriend. Fifty-fifty, and she had been the one to lose.

Although I wanted to junk them, the words *This isn't very rock'n'roll* kept sounding in my head.

I moved back in, just to be there – back into my old basement room. I played records, tapes. I played comfort music. Something was missing – not just my father. Something in me.

It is hard to be involved with and dependent upon youth, after a certain age. The young have yet to learn mercy – well, most of them. I got some really sweet cards and emails. They, too, made me think about what I might be missing. I remembered that girl Barbra, the model. I remembered what she had said about wanting a *skill*. I wanted a skill, too. She'd thought I had one – Barbra thought that bashing skins and watching Syph's skinny ass every night counted as a skill. I knew it didn't. Grief needs a tune. Grief quite likes a lot of voices raised in pitch-perfect lamentation. But grief isn't thump-thump-thump-thump, boom-tssk boom-tssk boom-tssk boom-tssk.

That's what I was thinking, during those first few weeks.

My mother lost weight, and she was never big. I worried that she might become frail and so tried to trick her into eating. But she was thinner in every way. Without her husband, who I suddenly saw quite clearly as that, there was less reason for her to take up space.

I kept very quiet. Didn't touch my sticks. Didn't drink, smoke, hardly spoke.

Then my thoughts went flip-flop. Grief, now I had spent some time there, was in fact very like thump-thump-thump-thump. There was a real eloquence to the repetitious stupidity of it.

I got on a train of thought, and I rode and I rode and I rode.

To Africa.

It was my mother asked me to leave. I would have stayed as long as she wanted. Longer. A month in, she said she appreciated what I had done but it would be better if we both got on with our lives. 'Stop wallowing,' she said, 'we're very privileged to be able to wallow. Most people can't afford it.'

I told her I didn't want to go – I didn't have anything to do. She told me I should find something. She told me in the same way she'd told me, on rainy pre-teen days, that I had no inner resources.

It was true. I had no plural, only a singular: drumming.

The train of thought took me through some fairly desolate ghost towns.

One night, I went to see Skullfukk, a local deathmetal band, and thought I'd found the answer. The Answer. They were *so* loud. Their drummer was a total monster. Skullfukk's noise left no space in the universe for anything but itself. And the noise was either all grief or all not-grief – I couldn't tell which.

In the bar afterwards, I found the drummer and tried to explain how profound what they were doing was – how moving I found it that he could drum that way, so defiant of death, so brave. He was coming from a very different place – and where he was going to, accompanied by a little drummer-girl, was even more different.

Then the train stopped off at a gay club. I don't even know how I wound up inside. I think I was just walking past and heard the siren thump-thump sounding. Paid my entrance, got looked up and down, down, then stood in a basement full of men who'd put a lot more effort into themselves than I ever had. I wanted to persuade myself I didn't feel as uncomfortable as I did. I bought a drink and, when I was offered, a couple of pills, too.

I wasn't offered anything else. They all knew I was hopelessly straight.

One really kind man listened to my whole tale of woe. He couldn't hear very well, over the thump-thump. I didn't want him to.

I explained about my mother, telling me to leave home. 'Mine did, too,' he said. We had a moment of connection, and I thought of sleeping with him just out of gratitude.

Our music, *okay*'s, has never had much of a gay following. That night, I could understand why. It, our sound, is full where it should be empty and empty where it should be full. Our melancholic euphoria just doesn't suit these lives of euphoric melancholy.

I told everybody I could grab that I loved them and they either thought it was the drugs, which wasn't untrue, or were wiser still – this sweaty, out-of-shape man with the tight grip would never, in any sense of the word, be gay.

I *so* wanted to be.

I looked at the men kissing and grabbing ass and felt truly proud of them. It made me cry. They were the national anthem for a country I had only just discovered. We were noble compatriots in the Democratic Republic of Thump-Thump.

The kind man put me in a taxi-cab and blew a kiss through the open window. 'Take good care of yourself,' he said, and meant it.

My last thought-train experience happened to me when I was completely on my own. I call it the Music Room, but it only amounts to a couple of drumkits, a stereo and a guitar I can't get much out of.

It was a week, maybe, after the night of the gay.

I'd just gotten off the phone with my mother and gone downstairs, nothing in my mind.

When I picked up the sticks, they felt comfortable – and the snare was crisp when I tightened the skin.

I played.

I played everything.

I played like a drum machine. I played like a monster deathmetal drummer. I played half of our set. I played 4/4. I kept on and on playing it – boom-tssk boom-tssk – for about an hour. I sweated, gasped, spat and near pissed myself. I tranced out.

And then it happened.

I stopped playing, went upstairs, phoned our management, got them to book me on the next flight to Africa.

'Where?' they asked.

'Africa,' I said.

'Which country, exactly?'

'Anywhere,' I said. 'I don't care.'

'What are you going to do there?'

I refused to say. It would sound corny – drummer finds World Music. Stewart Copeland. Mickey Hart. That wasn't what it was about.

'South Africa,' I said.

With relief, they hung up.

Three hours later and I was on my way to the airport. They had someone from the record company meet me at the other end. To her, finally, sworn to silence, I confessed what I was after.

Her name was Dorothy. I thought about the gays back in the club. I was a friend of Dorothy, too.

She was the blackest person I'd ever met. And she had the whitest teeth. It sounds a racist stereotype, but it was true.

I wondered if the record company had her in this job deliberately – so visitors got what they expected, or hoped for: an African-looking African.

'Can you take me somewhere?' I asked.

'If that's what you want,' she said.

okay are even less popular with South Africans than with gays. I'd been surprised even to discover we had a record company there. A few sad souls in gated compounds, American exiles – our market.

We took a taxi down dusty airport-environs highways to smaller roads and then to tracks. I saw black people walking with burdens. I tried to smell the Africa-smell everyone mentions.

Dorothy called her funky aunt. Her aunt knew some musicians. The musicians would be glad of an excuse for a party. Simple as that.

I could tell Dorothy was humouring me – it was her job but, also, I genuinely annoyed and amused her. Should I tell her about my father? I decided not to. Perhaps the management had already informed her I was Handle With Care.

When we got to the house, it disappointed me. I think I'd wanted something made out of corrugated iron, no drains. The garden was a neat square of greenish lawn.

Dorothy's aunt sat me down in the shade of a tree and gave me a beer. She was wearing jungle print.

I am so profoundly embarrassed about what happened over the next few hours that I don't really want to put it on record. (Shouldn't have started then, should you?) This was just the latest of the endings – there have been many more since, but none so awkward. Almost with my first sip of beer, I realized I'd made a mistake. It wasn't that I shouldn't be there – being there was fine, despite Dorothy's pained and painful smile. Fine, fine, fine. There was a lot that was colonial and horrible about my motives for coming. What the fuck did I expect? *Roots?* To reconnect with the spirit of the drum? To jam into the night with master musicians? Still fine. No, my being there wouldn't have been a problem – if only I could truly have *been there*. That's the thing Africa requires of you: *presence*. Although I'd come at the right time, after my father died, I was still too early: my body was there but my whatever, my thump-thump, wasn't. It was a terrible mistake. I thought I'd been following an instinct, and it turned out to have been the most cerebral, calculating, contrived of motives. I was such a fucking honky.

The musicians came, one by one. They set up and played,

beautifully. Effortless slithering rhythms that are a lifetime's achievement, transcendently twangling melodies – all I'd wanted and expected. Everyone apart from me was present. Not in a soulful way. They were just at an impromptu party.

Dorothy explained who I was, and the musicians insisted I join in. They gave me a drum.

Which was when I started crying.

I didn't stop until I was back on the plane – it was the same plane, I checked with the air-hostess, the same air-hostess.

I felt so *ashamed*. I'd tried to *use* Africa. Like deodorant. Or disinfectant.

Halfway through the flight, the world began to look better. The ocean was blue beneath us. I'd seen it from a thousand planes. I was reassured. It, Africa, had worked – worked by failing to work. The embarrassment of it was good for me. I had needed *exactly* that: to go somewhere completely wrong and then to run away, to be welcomed and to feel excluded, to try to do what I really do and to find that it isn't what I do at all – that it's never been what I do. My truth is my absence from myself, my isn't-ism.

For the next nine months, until the call came through from Syph, I did *nothing* but watch TV.

'I want – man, this is so difficult – I've been such a hosehead – I wanna get the band back together.'

For nine months, I watched TV seriously, passionately, with absolute devotion.

As an ending, from the outside, it doesn't look very happy – but, strangely, it was.

FOREST

If the *Tree* album had been a big hit, I'm sure we wouldn't have split.

It's a shame – going into the studio, we had some good songs.

I'll admit, there was also obvious filler, which wouldn't have happened earlier in our career. E, A and Bm, chunka, chunka, twelve bars of the stuff. Don't leave me, baby-ooooh.

But we were trying to get out of that studio before there was a murder – i.e., before one of us killed Syph.

That was the second set of sessions, the second studio.

The first studio had been in Geneva Switzerland. Brutalist concrete exterior. State-of-the-art mixing desk. Floor-to-ceiling window overlooking the lake. Nice nibbles always around. Very bad choice.

There were no distractions, so we made our own, resurrecting old feuds, animating new ones.

Once upon a back in the day, we might have appreciated the magnificent view – might even have looked at it, now and again. But we recorded (like we always record) mostly late at night, so what we saw was not an expanse of subtle water but our dysfunctional life-size selves in a huge black mirror.

There was a strip of lake-edge lights, around head height, which meant that none of the others could make eye-contact except directly. Sitting where I was, low down on the drum stool, I caught all the flicking searches they made for one another. We played towards the unseen, behind-glass water, as if it was our audience – pretty good metaphor, when you think about it.

After we taped versions of the songs we'd brought, we wrote no new ones. We tried jamming, but it was all about animosity – fucking up the other guy's groove before he'd had a chance to get into it.

What we needed was Syph to get his heart broken – to think he'd gotten his heart broken. Not too seriously. That would incapacitate him. We needed some yearning, some *saudade*. Then he would write lyrics for Instrumentals $^{\#}1$, $^{\#}2$, $^{\#}3$ for 'Slightly Wonky Song', for 'Hooping Coffin' and for 'Stray Bridge and Maybe-Outro'. But he'd convinced himself he was so happy for ever.

Her name, and I hurt myself by remembering it, was Forest. Only child of some serious California hippies, she followed her name wherever it took her. She said those very words, when we met her, 'I follow my name wherever it takes me.' We laughed, she didn't, Syph didn't.

Hello, new feud.

Forest wasn't shitting us, though. She had followed it. First off, aged about fifteen, she became convinced she had to be both deep and dark. So she took drugs, to help with deep, and most of all heroin, to ensure dark.

Second, in her twenties, she got badly lost within herself. The polite way of putting it was 'periods of hospitalization' – friends (she still had a couple, and they leeched onto us) elaborated: 'Oh, she'd started to bite children.'

'Where?'

'Wherever she could get to. Mostly ears. Lobes. She nearly chewed a couple of those off, before they locked her away.'

Thirdly, she did silence. For two and a half years, she said not a word. This coincided with being mental. If a tree falls in the eponymous, does anyone hear it? Well, Forest seemed to be listening.

In the middle of it all, somehow, this complete loon got hold of a cigarette lighter and, predictably enough, if anyone had been following the name-logic, tried to set herself on fire.

She started with her toes, which I never saw but which Mono swears were still black.

Luckily, one of the other patients told on her – and was believed. Imagine that: if they'd thought, 'Napoleon's just hallucinating, *again*.'

Then, amazingly, showing a forest's powers of regrowth after decimation, she returned to the world – green, springlike, smelling strongly of damp earth, ready to circle back round to deep dark drugs.

Syph picked her up and for some secret reason of his own refused to put her down. I don't even know where they met, some S&M club somewhere. He'd been hanging out a lot in San Francisco. All the times we'd wanted him to settle, and then when he does it's with a woman who makes Nico look like a fitness instructor. (*Instructor* not *instructress*.) I can only think that Forest's hopelessness was what did it for him.

(By the way, if you ask him, I'm sure he won't be able to remember any of these little details. When she wanted, Forest was still pretty good at extended silences. I, fool that I am, tried to befriend her – and so her friends befriended me. In return for my company, they became selectively indiscreet. I feared, even then, the things they didn't say. What Syph knew from Forest was the myth – *I follow my name, wherever it leads.*)

Syph wasn't built for monogamy, so they did three- and foursomes. These were surprisingly difficult to arrange, given Syph's past history – but this was fucking (non-fucking?) Switzerland. I'm sure there were orgies where whole mountain villages took part, after christenings – we just hadn't been invited. Perhaps it was Forest who put the other girls off – those ear-biting stories got around. I'm not saying who spread them.

Crab and Mono tolerated her. Mono had brought Major over, so they fished the lake whenever they could. But whether in a boat or not, Major took no crap from anyone, and Forest, she could see, was fundamentally founded upon crap. This, too, caused problems in the studio.

Just because someone can *hold* a tambourine doesn't mean

they can *play* it. Just because you're *fucking* someone doesn't mean you should give them a *tambourine to hold.*

Syph even kept the assistant engineer behind one early morning and laid down some of Forest on backing vocals. It sounded like an operatic cow yodelling in a mineshaft, after falling down the mineshaft. To try to save things, the engineer had put on enough echo to satisfy even the Seven Dwarfs.

Hi-*ho*!

When the engineer guiltily and reluctantly played us the tape the next morning, Syph nodded along as if the presence of a cow-yodel in our mixes was quite usual.

The argument began, nothing strange in that, but Syph insisted early on, 'If that track goes, I go.'

Then he left, with Forest.

He *left* but he didn't *go.*

We all knew the difference. Industry lawyers had explained it to us on numerous occasions, at our own expense. Vast.

For a couple of days – yes, we started working while it was still daylight – for a day or three, we added overdubs. Cow-yodel track was left untouched, though we did listen back to it with Forest faded out. True to historical precedent, the best song on the album was the one we were in the process of majorly fucking up.

Me being me, I thought we could sort it out. Get Syph to listen to the song without Forest in the room. Ask him his honest opinion. Suggest we do two mixes. He and Forest had been inseparable for a month, but I didn't let that deter. I got the engineer, who had somehow kept his job, to rip me a copy – then I took a limo to Syph's house.

He was staying separately from the rest of us. They had checked out of the large, new and admittedly soulless corporate tower-hotel on the first night. He needed something a bit more *funky*, he said. Later I heard that it was Forest who craved funk, and so got them thrown out by urinating on the lobby couches. Not one couch, several.

What they'd found was a two-room cottage with a steep roof and a garden of thick mud.

The driver who most evenings brought Syph across to the studio was able to drop me there.

Europe, I love you. Why don't you love me back? Why do you always make me suffer?

The tinfoil covering the windows was a not-good-thing. The last time I'd seen this was during the so-called Thin White Duke breakdown. Since then, Syph had been if not *clean* then only mildly grubby.

I knocked on the door. There was a bell, an actual bell, but the rope had been pulled off the clapper – I saw it lying in the snow.

Did I say this all happened during early winter?

Knock, knock harder, and still no response. Knock once more, then, deep breath, try the door. It opens – in I go, to face whatever.

Or nothing.

The room was without furniture. But there was a huge fireplace. I looked in the other room, also empty, then came back to see if the ashes were still hot. Fallen out onto the floor was a chair leg. A couple of charred CDs, too. Syph and Forest must have moved on when they'd burnt everything there was to burn.

I tried the neighbours. All they gave me was grief. In French. Did I know those terrible people? Had I ever heard of the law? Of decency?

Back to the hotel.

At the three-quarter-band meeting I called, we voted not to search for Syph.

The decision-making process went like this:

Me: I think he might be in genuine danger . . .

Crab: Fuck him.

Mono: Yeah, fuck him.

Me: Fine.

I set off to search for Syph as soon as the others left.

When I say *set off*, I didn't actually leave the room. These days, the best way to find someone, or something, is to ask a few thousand strangers to help.

At first, I ghosted through the fansites, looking for sightings. News that we were recording a new album had been officially announced – after being widely leaked. It had taken Yoyo (hi Yoyo!) about three hours to track us down to Switzerland. Her contacts at Canadian airports are *astonishing*. Two Swiss fans helped her identify the studio, our hotel and were even able to give her a rundown of our bar tabs that evening. All this was up there for the world to see dot com.

I'd hoped one of the true faithful had been hanging around outside Syph's lovenest. No.

I was sure they'd have been spotted in whatever new hotel they were trashing. No.

I used my lurking identity, posted the question, sat back to wait.

No.

No-one had seen Syph or Forest for forty-eight hours. The fans knew of Forest. Many were infuriated by her. Many, particularly our monosyllabic or entirely giggly fifteen-year-old Japanese girlfans, believed Syph was, by rights, *theirs*. They had constructed elaborate shrines of on-line hate to Forest. Some were hilarious. Some were terrifying. I learnt things about her I didn't need, just then, to know. When I said *genuine danger* to the other guys, I thought I'd been exaggerating; I hadn't.

I wondered whether or not Syph had burnt their passports along with everything else in the room.

Trying Yoyo's approach, I called the airport – tried a couple of Syph's favourite airlines. They were so tight-lipped it was hard to get them to admit they even knew what a plane was. I slammed the phone down.

Then I thought.

Thought like a detective.

Addicts.

Therefore.

Drugs.

Therefore.

Dealer.

How many could there be in Geneva?

So, off I went to buy heroin.

I thought I was thinking like a private dick but really I was just thinking like a dick.

In the first bar I went to, I was arrested.

I've stayed in hotels that were less amenable than that Swiss jail cell: so clean, so well designed, and with a great echo. Even Forest's cow-yodel would have sounded bearable in there.

My phonecall brought record-company lawyers down, and I was bailed within six hours. They told me I'd have to leave the country, probably the next day.

Back in my hotel room, feeling a real idiot, having fucked the whole investigation (and whatever was left of the recording sessions) up completely, the phonecalls started. *I heard you had some problems*, they said. *I can help.*

Getting arrested had been an act of detective genius – now every dealer in the country knew I was looking to connect.

Few of them were informed enough to know I'd been in town a month already. If I hadn't scored before, I'd either have kicked or died.

I asked each of them whether they'd sold to Syph or Forest – and on number five I got lucky.

Yes, they'd purchased this and that from him. No, he wasn't going to divulge on the phone exactly what. No, he hadn't encountered them in a couple of days. Yes, he was sure he'd have heard if they'd gone looking somewhere else. Yes, he'd used a gofer. No, he couldn't put me in touch. No, not for anything would he put me in touch. Yes, for X amount he would put me in touch.

The gofer came.

The phrase 'pissholes in snow' almost covers it – but piss with lots of blood in it.

Otherwise, he was pale, thin, quiet, obviously close to dying.

He was also a blessèd angel sent from God – sent to collect Syph and Forest from their house and drive them to the airport. They had no bags to carry but, starstruck, he saw them onto a flight for –

– Stuttgart.

(Germany has always been one of my favourite countries.)

Stuttgart? What was there? A few minutes on my computer told me. I was so *dumb.* I should have followed the name-logic. Forest was taking Syph to herself.

Notorious junkie that I was, I had to fly out of Switzerland – disgraced, never to return – the next morning. Mono and Crab knew I'd been looking for Syph. I'd never scored drugs myself: it was one of the reasons I'd hung out with them – right from cigarettes up. Me getting busted was the funniest thing they'd *ever* heard. In Switzerland already!

I told them about Stuttgart, the Black Forest. Get it, guys? Forest? They said they might follow, if I found a. Syph, b. two decent songs and c. a small and unostentatious recording studio. Oh, and I had to get rid of that fucking talentless bitch, too.

It took two weeks. I don't know if you know this but the Black Forest is big. The fansites were no help – Syph and Forest had gone underground. Our management refused me access to his credit-card records. I let my instinct guide me – my instinct for Syph's instinct for the sordid. I looked for black-eyed underage girls crying in the darkest corners of bars. And when I found them, I talked to the barmen, the boys at the bar and, finally, the girls themselves. One of them, number fifteen or sixteen, had heard something from a friend of a friend. A story. A bad story. Her English was good. In the taxi over, she told me she liked our music. Some youth

84

cultures interpret what we do as Goth or Emo. Which is distressing but not un-understandable. The friend was amazed it was *really* me. 'Is it really you?' she kept asking. She would have done *anything* for me, and was clearly *dying* to, but I just asked to speak to the next friend. The one with the story. I was touched by the sight of friend two's bedroom: dolls which had been blonde subjected to re-dyes and dressing up in homemade vamp outfits; posters of bands half my age on the wall; an autograph book with the names of all their teachers in it – no-one famous before me. Her parents were out for the evening. The friend phoned the next friend (friend three) and the next friend came straight round. Perhaps she had been boasting about Syph, perhaps she hadn't really met him, but, no, there were lots of bracelets on her wrists to cover the bruising. More than that, her eyes were a decade older than those of her friends. (Please, not heroin. Not that.)

'Do you know where they are?'

Her English wasn't as good as friend one or two. Friend two translated. Friend two would do *anything*. Because, unlike, friend three, she hadn't already had to do it.

'She knows somewhere they were, yesterday.'

'Can she take me?'

'She can take everyone. We also will come.'

Another taxi. The longer we spent together, the more fanlike the three girls became. Friend three noticeably less so than the other two. She'd brushed up against the object of their awe – brushed and been bruised. I didn't ask directly what had been done to her. Her nails were black and bitten. I wondered, *If I had a daughter, would she be a Goth?* Thank God I didn't, if Syph hadn't fucked her, it would have been all her friends and most of their moms.

We tried one bar. They weren't there. The taxi driver almost refused to take us to the next place we wanted to go. Money persuaded. The girls told him I was famous. His eyes in the mirror looked me over, thinking: *famous kiddy-fucker.*

I was no longer doing this for the album. (When you say we didn't put enough effort in, Mr Music Critic, did you ever think of *this*?) I certainly wasn't doing it for Syph. Over those two weeks in the forest, I'd had enough time to think about what I'd say to him when I tracked him to his lair. No, I was doing it because I had decided it should be done; as a detective, I wanted to solve the case.

They weren't at the next bar, and the barman said he didn't know where they had been staying, but the owner overheard our conversation, said *hi*. He really was a fan. His bar was odd – Goth but in a very German way. (They should be experts at Goth, shouldn't they?) Lots of antlers and assorted wildlife-heads. Then a TV screen showing American sports. And paintings of stormy mountains.

In return for a promise that one day we'd play a concert on his pool-table of a stage, the bar-owner said he'd take me to Syph. I tried to ditch the three little gothlets but they insisted on coming.

We got in the owner's SUV. He told me stories of small-town excess. I laughed when I had to. He wouldn't tell me where we were going, but he *would* tell me that he wouldn't tell me where we were going, and also that he wouldn't tell me why he wouldn't tell me. That was the best joke of all. As far as he was concerned. And that was all that mattered. As far as he was concerned.

We arrived.

They were living in a treehouse. That was the punchline. My arm was punched. A treehouse, yes!

The owner's drug dealer had one at the bottom of his garden – for him, not his kids. In fact, to get *away* from his kids. A treehouse, the dealer told me, equipped with electric heating, sound system, widescreen TV, satellite, phone, bathroom. There was no tinfoil in the windows. Then I realized how dark it was, beneath the branches of so many trees.

'Go up,' said the owner.

'Yes, go,' said the dealer.

Girls one and two looked excited, three showed signs of fear. I thanked them all.

Climbed the ladder, lifted the trapdoor, pulled myself up into the room, looked around.

There were blankets on the bed, a fleshy spiral lump of pale white in the middle of them.

It was Syph, foetal, sobbing.

I said, 'I quit,' and it felt good – *I quit.*

'She's gone,' he said.

'I've had enough,' I said.

'She's left me,' he said.

'This is the end,' I said. 'I'm not coming back.'

'Didn't you hear me?' he said. 'She said she couldn't stand me any more. I disgusted her. I was so corrupt, so impure.'

A head came up through the floor.

'Please go away,' I said.

The trapdoor dropped.

'I need her,' Syph said.

'That's your problem.'

'She took her stuff this morning. She was gone before I woke up. I love her.'

'She was a total bitch. You're much better without her.'

'I love her.'

'Look at you.'

'She was . . .'

'She sang like a cow,' I said. 'And you wanted that on our album.'

'She was beautiful.'

'Goodbye, Syph,' I said and turned to go.

'You have to help me,' he said. 'You have to help me find her.'

So I did.

(I *know.*)

With a little help from the Baden-Württemberg police, and a man out collecting firewood.

Forest had handcuffed herself to a tree. Hypothermia. The

keys were found stuck into an apple, kicked out of reach. Not that she'd tried to reach them – forensics told us that. No, Forest just sat still and waited. I wonder if she sang to herself. I wonder if she liked the sound of her own voice.

The interrogator asked me where I thought she'd got hold of the cuffs. *That* made me laugh.

Home in Canada again, at the second studio, we mixed the album. We left Forest's vocals on the best song, 'So Holy', made it a Track One Side A, finished the rest of the good songs, added some filler, put it out, got slaughtered by critics worldwide, split, re-formed.

I play the drums.

FANS

They gave us an award, the fuckers.

No, I better be exact: we were offered the chance to accept a lifetime achievement award on not-quite-live-because-someone-might-swear Canadian TV, and we accepted *without hesitation*.

Not without discussion. *That* went like this –

Syph (manic): Fuck, yeah.

Mono (imitating): Aye aye, Captain.

Crab (slurred): Yessir.

Me (blah): Hey, shouldn't we at least talk this thing through?

Syph: We just did.

What it meant was, we stayed in an over-luxurious Toronto hotel, were driven to an atmosphereless air-hangar, sound-checked, were driven back to the hotel, hung around, showered, got dressed up, were driven back to the air-hangar, hung around backstage exchanging friendly greetings with members of the rock'n'pop community for whom we once expressed nothing but contempt, went out to watch the show begin, drank our table dry in competition with the adjoining tables, won (thanks to Crab), were mentioned, applauded, praised ludicrously by two talentless no-wits, watched a montage of our greatest misjudgments, were applauded again but *louder*, strolled to the stage through a crossfire of eat-shit glances and I'll-call-you gestures, made it to the microphone stand and said –

I know I wasn't the only band member to give thought to the question of what we really *had* achieved in our lifetime, so far. I was merely the only one of us to become radically depressed over the answers I came up with.

When we started out, we wanted to make a record. Our dreams still had the oil-slick sheen of vinyl. Simple. Make a record – prove everybody wrong. See, it's been worth all the sacrifices.

Well, there weren't *that* many sacrifices. The main one, respectability in our parents' eyes, only applied to Mono and me. Syph's funky mother even packed him a lunchbox before waving him off down the road he's been following ever since. The lunchbox contained some very powerful weed.

Crab's father was never sober enough to take a stance one way or the other, or, in fact, any stance but monged out on the couch of rancid. His greatest moment of clarity came the first time we appeared on TV. He thought Crab had been fucking with his video-player, about the only sacred object in his house, so he crawled over, picked it up with both hands and rammed it straight through our screen images – electrocuting himself.

Not seriously but not hilariously, either. He had a minor stroke two days later, which the doctors told Crab was completely unconnected.

The loss of control in his right side meant Crab Senior had to change his beer-can hand but not a whole lot else.

He stopped off on the way back from hospital and bought a new TV. Video-players, he's never trusted again.

So, what was our achievement there? Performing our first single on a local chatshow (you've never heard of it) or part-killing one of our parents? (Though Crab's father is still alive and mine isn't.)

There has always been collateral damage. So much so that *collateral* is clearly bullshit. *Necessary* damage, *required, essential, without which* . . .

I have a terrible ringing in my ears. Tinnitus. It's a minor thing, I know, but it never goes away. Have I told you about this before? The only time I really forget about it is when we're playing music – or I'm listening to something else. Rock, mostly, I can still hear it over classical. It's like someone has leant a guitar up against a still-on amp, right in my head. But feedback would at least change, warp, tie itself into a knot of a note. ('I Feel Fine' by The Beatles.) This is the sound of a television after the channel goes dead and before they put a continuity announcement up. A *beep* with an infinite number of *e*'s. The *b* was way back when. I'll know I'm dead when I reach that *p*.

'First off,' says Syph, lifting the award to head height, 'we'd like to thank our record company – everyone at Colombia – you've worked so hard, over the years . . .'

We suck corporate cock. That's what Syph's saying, and not even in code. We take it and we lovingly suck it.

As usual, we're letting Syph be our spokesperson. Always a mistake but no-one else wants to do it, and he'd throw such a tantrum if they did.

I am standing far back from the podium – any further and I'd be in our dressing-room toilet. At the end, I'll probably do the usual drummer-thing and lean too close to the microphone, boom out a word that sounds like *Hanks* and try to exit stage left without, please, falling on my ass.

When we started, we had principles. It was almost a manifesto: Never say what we were doing was rock'n'roll. Treat the people who liked our music with respect, as the intelligent and sensitive individuals they had shown themselves to be (by liking our music). Put halfway-decent songs on the B-sides. Split the publishing equally four ways. Don't exploit women as sex-objects in the videos – and try as hard as possible to exploit them as sex-objects on all other occasions. (Oh, that last bit was Syph's contribution.) What else? No guitar solos, drum solos. No lighters-aloft moments. No cocaine, no heroin.

Then we went on tour, and what happened to all mid-way successful bands happened to us. It's such a cliché, listening to some group who put out a delicate and well-arranged first album start talking about how the songs really only came alive 'in a live context' after they took it on tour and rambling on about how the second album was all about 'catching some of what this band's really about – which is the live show' and how that meant it was really important to keep a 'live vibe' in the studio and how they can't wait to get out there again and play these songs 'live'. All of which means turn the motherfucker up to eleven and rock the fuck out!!! And that's what happened to us on tour.

Gradually. Not the first time out. Our second album was still pretty un-rock. But after three or four years, we began to realize the *Why?* – the *Why?* of Mick Jagger's minstrel show, of Roger Daltry's wire-act, of Robert Plant's silk trousers.

Why?

It fucking works – makes a good night great, a great night transcendent, and a bad night survivable.

So, we ditched our trademark suits. Syph's posing became more extreme. Crab's solo grew four bars every other night – and had bastard offspring. The lightshow stopped being monochrome and became just a touch heavy metal. We haven't stooped to dry-ice, not yet.

'And we'd like to send a big thank-you out to our management team – Tony, Jordan, you guys – you really bring it on home, man – you're the best . . .'

We are pretentious no-lifes. It doesn't matter that Tony and Jordan, or whoever is managing us that month, despite being utterly unscrupulous, achieve the almost impossible task of keeping us idle enough to write and record songs. It doesn't matter that Cindy, their assistant, never gets mentioned but does at least 70 per cent of the real work. It doesn't matter that Clarissa and Maggie, who do publicity and marketing, are the truest friends this band has ever had. The fact that we're even able to use the words 'management team' puts us in that group of abysmal sell-outs who shift (not make) product (not music).

'And last, and most important, we'd like to thank the fans . . .'

We do have fans, and it is entirely correct that we thank them – also, that we blame them, hate them, fear them, feel infinite contempt for them.

If it weren't for the fans, we wouldn't have a reason to keep on keeping on. We do, some of us, quite literally owe them our lives.

Crab was married for a while to the woman who runs the Canadian branch of our Appreciation Society – named back when we thought it was patronizing to call fans fans.

Mono was introduced to Jesus by Shirley from Lubbock, Texas. Thankfully, he excused himself and went and hid in the spiritual bathroom a short while afterwards. But Jesus, thanks to Shirley, straightened him out at a difficult time.

And at least three female fans have saved Syph from overdosing.

The best fan-related story/worst fucking nightmare took place in Moscow Russia.

We'd just finished a gig and were relaxing, each in his different way, in the dressing-room.

The venue was an old theatre. Syph was sitting in front of one of those mirrors surrounded by bulbs. He also was surrounded by a bright halo of dyed-blonde heads.

Into the middle of this walks Irina. Very confidently, she pushes a couple of lanky, high-cheekboned beauties aside and says, 'I hov drogs. Gokaine. Yeroin. The byeast.'

Syph, whose eyes have been wandering, and not over the fans' bodies, says, 'Well, what are we waiting for, baby, let's go!'

I think about following them. The ease with which Irina gained entrance to the dressing-room is suspicious. She's no looker, not in comparison. Short, muscular, savage mouse-brown bob, shiny black boots. And usually there's five minutes whining-pleading with security – promises according to the old contract of no head, no backstage pass. As far as I can see, Irina's just waved straight in. Perhaps it's the drugs. Perhaps they are the best.

I think a second time about following them. But then I opt for an early night, alone if possible. I made a mistake in Sweden, the week before, and I'm still regretting her.

'Later,' says Syph, halfway out the door.

What happened after this has been stuck together from various sources, mostly deeply unreliable.

Syph's version, for what it's worth, runs thus:

'How was I to know something was wrong? She says she has drugs. She does. We go to the toilets in the theatre and do a couple of fine lines. Whammo. But the heroin, she says, is at her apartment. So the limo takes us there and, you know me, I waste no time. Next thing, I wake up in hospital. Only it's more like a prison. I feel like shit and I'm in a cell with a locked door. There's mould on the walls. I think I hear rats in the corridor outside. Someone tells me afterwards it used to be a KGB mental hospital. Now, I've been in a lot of fucked-up places . . .'

At which point, he'll lose the plot and start telling you about the English castle which still had a fully operational torture chamber or the brothel in Greenland where you could fuck a strapped-down bear. But we've got most of what we need from him. If pressed, he'll add two further details.

'I didn't really think anything much at the time, but outside the girl's apartment an ambulance was parked. I wondered who was ill. And when we go upstairs, two men are in there playing some faaassst game with shooting on her computer. I don't even ask who they are – or why they're wearing white coats.'

The first we knew about it, three that morning, the management get a phonecall saying Syph has been taken into a very exclusive private hospital – after overdosing on heroin. The hospital, in fact, is so exclusive that some clients have objected to the high fees charged for their world-class life-saving work. Syph is recovering well and is perfectly safe, but will remain under doctor's supervision until the sum of Z has been paid.

(Z, to put it in proportion, was our gross takings on gigs in Moscow and St Petersburg, plus Vilnius, Tallinn and Riga.)

Tony and Jordan stall, ask for a number. The hospital administrator (Irina, I think) says she'll call back in the morning.

Jordan calls the promoter who is handling the Russian tour. 'Ah,' he says, or words to this effect, 'so they're still trying that old scheme.' He doesn't want to talk on the phone. He will come to the hotel.

Tony wakes me, Crab and Mono. We join them in their suite. Boy, are we pissed.

When the promoter arrives, he is nothing but business. There are two options, which he proceeds to lay out. First, pay the ransom – that's what it is, a ransom. Second, let him (the promoter) hire a small army of former KGB operatives, supply them with weapons of choice, pay a few people off to find out where Syph's being held, storm the place. With surprising calm, he then mentions the upsides to the courses of action. With the first, we're guaranteed to get Syph back. The promoter had dealt with these people before (naming no big names) and believes them to be trustworthy. With the second, we'll be greeted with a lot of respect if we ever come back to town. Then he gives the downsides. First option costs probably twice as much as the second (killing is cheap) and, quite frankly, isn't the Moscow way of doing things. He would much prefer it if we could sort this out with the maximum number of people getting hurt. Second option could leave us with a dead lead-singer, thirty years each in a Siberian jail and the Russian mafia after us and our loved ones for the rest of our (short) lives.

When the management say, after due consultation (a series of nods around the room), that we'll go for option the first, our promoter does something very odd: he pulls out his phone, speed-dials a number, says, 'Da,' and then smiles very broadly.

Yes.

That old scheme.

Syph, two hours after the financial arrangements have been concluded, which takes a day and a half, is delivered safely to the hotel lobby.

As a farewell gift, Irina has injected him with a full dose of the premium Afghan brown she used in the sting.

Before she did this, though, we eventually find out, she has him sign copies of *all* our albums, singles and even some majorly obscure bootlegs.

Irina is a true fan, you see.

'So, thanks for supporting us all these years,' Syph says. 'We love you. We couldn't do it without you.'

I step up to the microphone, lean in too close, boom out a word that sounds like *Hanks* and exit stage left.

BEADS

Rock'n'roll is dead.

Thank God.

But God is dead, too.

Thank Whatever.

Whatever is whatever.

Everything, as someone once sang, is everything.

But nothing is never nothing.

I'd given up – I'd given up not *everything* (I can't quit breathing; eating I've tried and failed), but *everything I can.* And on top of that, as much as I could, I'd given up caring about having given up. No longer did I live my life, my life lived me – and it was more of a lifestyle, to be honest. We were mid-way through an American tour, with only two weeks' holiday afterwards before we had to go to Europe and Asia. I was doing unspeakable things in rarely thought of States of the Union. And, looking ahead, I feared for the integrity of 22nd London, 23rd Cardiff, 24th Glasgow, 25th Belfast, 27th Dublin ... I feared for myself because I hadn't managed to give myself up: I still cared about the fact that it was just conceivable someone might possibly care about me – and, in my tourbusting state, I would probably have thousand-yard-stared right through them. Lost – but not enough – in America, I spent a lot of time with Syph. (Words of doom.) I didn't try to rival him, that would have been suicidal, but I did do my best to *accompany* him. For the first time in quite a while, I stopped saying *no.* One or two afternoons, as we emerged into the lobby or climbed onto the bus, I was the one to be lauded for my squalour of the early morning hours, for outrages committed. I even sunk so low, back then, that I earned the affectionate respect of the roadcrew.

In the middle of the beginning of the end of all this, I met a Buddhist monk in San Francisco.

Religious types are particularly skilled at gaining access to dressing-rooms of all sorts – more adept, even, than slutty High School girls. Many a rock star has found himself down on his knees before a visitor saying 'OH GOD PLEASE FORGIVE ME FOR THE SINFUL LIFE I HAVE BEEN LEADING.' (An unusual situation for rock stars, who are much more used to having visitors on their knees in front of them – for contrary purposes, though the kneelers may also say 'Oh God,' occasionally.)

It was before the show. The monk had a bright saffron robe, a nice smile and wanted to give me some beads.

That was it.

He didn't have a speech to give me. I'm not even sure if he spoke English, though he may have been fluent in six languages for all I know. He may have been live-and-direct from the Potala, Lhasa, Tibet.

After handing me the beads, he pray-bowed like they do, smiled once more, nodded as if something had been understood between us and then left.

I put the beads down somewhere and went back to what I'd been doing, which was long, narrow and snow-white. All around my brain.

We got the gig over with.

I forgot about the monk's visit and gift until the next morning when I found the beads on my bedside table.

There was only one rational explanation: the girl I'd been with the night before had picked them up from the dressing-room, had maybe worn them or kept them in a pocket (but she had very few pockets, as I recall) and then, when she was about to leave, had felt guilty about taking them, so put them where I'd find them.

This made me feel guilty, about the beads and about her. She'd been a nicer girl, I now saw, than I'd taken her for. I hadn't appreciated that, and was getting old-style Clap-

feelings of regret. Annoyed, I left the beads where they were.

It took less than twenty-four hours for them to catch up with me again. The hotel we'd been staying in was monstrously efficient – and it was their policy to FedEx everything a VIP guest left in their room (everything including suspiciously might-be-valuable items in the trash) either to that guest's home address or, as in my case, their next hotel. A gold-leafed shirtbox was sitting waiting for me on the counterpane – inside, the two unused condoms, a copy of *Wire* magazine and the reincarnated beads.

I did not take this as a sign – I was *resolute* in *not* taking this as a sign. A sign was not what I needed, right that moment. The minibar, however, was.

Soundcheck, hotel, gig, hotel.

We had a rest day the following day. I had a choice of fishing with Mono or drinking with Crab or drugging with Syph. I followed my heart – it wanted to beat as pointlessly fast as possible.

We were staying every night in another one, another link, in a chain of hotels. I knew that if I left the beads here, including in the trash, they would follow me to the next room, the next city.

But there was always a chance, my decelerating heart told me at 3 a.m., that they wouldn't.

So began the secret game of a week. Day one, I left the beads under the pillow. Day two, in the safe. Days three, four and five behind the bed, beneath the bed and between the bed and the mattress. Day six, under a pile of bloody tissues in the bathroom bin. Day seven, in the cistern.

HOTELS 7 – ME 0.

Or maybe that should be BEADS 9.

I found out, later on, that it was part of our management's deal with the chain that our rooms be subjected to an FBI-style search every time we left. I'm not sure if this was the direct cause, but we'd once been forced to cancel a show because Syph wasn't able to find his lucky guitar pick. His paranoia had gotten to the point where he believed, if he didn't play with it, he would forget all the words to all the songs in his solo acoustic set.

At the time, though, because I didn't know this, I put the beads' pursuit of me down to a bizarre combination of the supernatural and the corporate. And so I decided to have one final go, a real good one, at getting rid of the little danglers – I threw them out the window of the tourbus, the toilet window.

They almost killed a 6' 4" biker – hit him full in the mirror-shaded visor. He turned his big old Triumph around and went back to collect the evidence, always knowing we in the bus weren't going fast enough to get away. It was a lonely stretch of freeway in East Texas. I'd tried to ditch the beads in the driest, dustiest part of the desert. Once he'd found the projectile, the biker got back on his silver machine and in about two minutes pulled up alongside us, made some easy-to-interpret gestures, flagged us down.

'I should sue you,' he said. 'I'm going to sue you.' Sue was a lot better than kill, but the fact he spoke with a Brooklyn accent and didn't once swear made him a terrifying figure.

No-one confessed to having thrown the beads at him. I mean, I was too scared to confess.

The management talked him down – explained who we were. Girls tied things to our bus all the time, and this love-gift had probably been there for a while and just worked loose. The biker was interested. 'A band?' We were charming. He was charming. We made friends with him. He was a lawyer. International copyright. We knew people in common. Lawyers, mostly. He liked some of our music. He thought our international legal set-up was *risible*. I never thought I'd hear a biker say *risible*. We invited him to our next show, and his girlfriend. Ah. That would be *boyfriend*. He went off almost happy, with a story. He left us the beads. 'As a souvenir.'

Which, of course, immediately turned them into the single most desirable thing on the bus – and that included eighteen-year-old Lula-Maybelline from Fort Worth and twenty-four-year-old Honey from All Over. When I said, 'But they're mine,' no-one believed me. Everyone now claimed them. I explained about the monk. No-one remembered him. Following the laws of physics of the *okay* tourbus, the most desirable thing always ends up with Syph – and Syph always ends up getting bored of it (them) and discarding it (them). But for some reason he took an unusual liking to the beads. He began to wear them on-stage. I was afraid they would become his lucky beads, replacing the lucky pick.

I needed them back, and there was only one way to get them: ante up and rejoin, after five years' sabbatical, the perpetual back-of-the-tourbus poker game, catch some strong cards, go heads up with Syph, put him all in, win, bankrupt the motherfucker.

This took ten afternoons and cost me approximately twenty thousand dollars, Canadian (we have some loyalty). I'm a better poker player than Syph, not than the roadies. And Syph had some astonishing luck. When it came to it, he was reluctant to put the beads into the pot, but with no more cash left, he had no choice. Full house beats three of a kind every time. As soon as they were in my hand, I cashed myself out and left the table.

'There *was* a monk,' said Syph, getting up to hound me. 'I remember now – there was a monk, in a robe. He gave you those beads.'

I got in my bunk, pulled shut the curtains.

Although he really wanted to harass me further, Syph could not break Bus Rule #2 *If a band member wishes to be alone he may signal this by drawing the curtains on his bed-area shut. It is absolutely forbidden to disturb a band member who wishes to be alone – unless the bus is on fire and the fire is getting close to them and you give a shit.*

I held the beads in my hand. They were a little scuffed from hitting the highway – Syph's stage antics with the mic-stand had probably done some damage to them, too. But the night in the cistern didn't seem to have adversely affected them. I stared at the beads. Why had I tried so hard to get rid of them and then so desperately to get them back? I put the beads on.

Nothing changed. I didn't become an insta-Bodhisattva. My behaviour, truth to tell, worsened – but only because the tour was continuing and, by then, all sensations were null.

Syph stole the beads a couple of times. With some help from my buddies the roadcrew, I got them back. They'd seen me win the beads – and although Syph was their blow-and-pussy God, they refused to let him resort to theft. They wanted a God they could respect. (Don't we all?) Eventually, Syph lost interest. Still nothing changed.

Nothing changed and the beads stayed the same. I wore them all the time, even in bed, even in the shower. They became a still-point in a tumble-dryer world. During radio interviews, I silently counted through them, just numbers, not prayers. There were twenty beads before the two separated by an elastic knot. I wondered, vaguely, if twenty *meant* anything.

I began to think about the monk – not about trying to track him down, ask him the meaning-of-life question. No, I began to think about him as a thing, a living thing, giving thing. He had come to see me and hadn't wanted anything from me – not a conversation, an autograph, a handshake, not even a thank-you. Which was lucky because I hadn't given him any of those. Not even a thank-you. And that was what made the gift so amazing.

They were cheap beads, I knew – I thought I knew. He probably gave them away by the dozen. He was probably famous for it, in San Francisco.

But when I asked around, no-one on the scene had heard of a monk who handed out beads.

I began to wonder if they really were worthless.

On the next free day, I took them into a pawnshop.

The guy (who looked like the kind of pawnshop guy you'd buy from a pawnshop) offered me ten dollars. I told them that wasn't enough, that I wanted a hundred. He offered me fifty. I knew then they weren't cheap giveaways. I said I'd give him fifty dollars if he told me what they were really worth. He looked at me strange, then told me they were antique ebony – black all the way through. Their monetary value was high. He'd have to check. That was enough for me. They were expensive. But maybe he'd been a rich monk.

The beads were working on me. Just by being a pure gift, they had made me realize quite how cynical I'd become – always looking for undeclared motives.

You could say, the monk *did* want something from me. He wanted to make me a Buddhist, convert me.

But that's not how Buddhists operate. They're not out on the street corners telling you their way is the only way, and any other is a sure-route excursion to hell. (Oh, Texas, I remember your million churches.)

The monk wanted only one thing from me, the acceptance of what he had to give.

It was a beautiful gesture – like writing a song you know people will really love, and not fucking it up in the recording studio.

By this time the American tour was coming to an end, glorious and debased.

A one-night stand at Madison Square Gardens . . .

I was in bits.

Nothing meant anything.

Rock'n'roll was dead.

Thank God.

etc.

I could count up to twenty.

People congratulated me. It took a second to figure they meant a sold-out night at Madison Square Gardens, not owning a set of elasticated ebony beads.

There were lots of fans in the audience. Full house. A saffron-wearing monk was not among them.

What I had around my wrist outweighed the adulation.

Retrospectively, I was grateful to the Frisco girl who'd picked the beads up from the dressing-room table. Or floor.

I was sorry I hadn't confessed to the biker.

Ebony is a very dense and dark wood.

Encore, encore, encore, curtain call, off.

I caught the red-eye to Vancouver, skipping the end-of-tour party.

It was necessary for me to be alone with the fact that I was alone with the beads.

Back in my apartment, I took all my clothes off and then, for the first time in weeks, took the beads off, too.

I put them in the very centre of the circular glass dining table, clearing away a bowl of fruit someone had left for me.

Then I went and had a short shower, unable to relax for the thought they might be gone when I got back.

The water could not wash away what I had done, but it could give the illusion of starting to do so.

When I emerged, I felt morally a little less repulsive –

– and the beads were still there.

I put them back on, starting from them, originating a new self – a self that had pursued and caught me, though I had tried to evade it – a self more like my old self than my current self – an attempting self.

In my bedroom, such a strange room in its familiarity, I carefully chose clothes – un-tour clothes: a good black suit, a pressed white shirt, a black silk tie, patent-leather shoes.

Dressed, overdressed, I went for a walk.

It was towards dawn.

Nothing happened during the walk.

Let me repeat that.

Nothing happened during the walk.

Let me repeat that.

HER

I met her, finally.

Her.

I met *her.*

My long-awaited.

She isn't a fan. It didn't happen because of who I am or what I do. It happened, you could say, in spite of those things.

This is how:

You join a band to meet girls. Then, after a while, you realize the girls you're meeting are the kind who want to meet men who are in bands.

For *meet* read *fuck.*

And usually not just one band but a series of bands. Which suggests, maybe-maybe, that what they're looking for ain't the Chapel of Love but the House of the Rising Sun.

In my experience, boys-in-bands react to this discovery in different ways: some punish the girls for being so screwed-up and needy, some try (and fail) to rescue them from themselves.

Myself, I've been through many phases, from mild abuse to all-out rescue missions. My ground rule with contempt-fucking was: Leave no permanent physical scars. But niceness, as I've learnt, can be the most murderously cruel thing.

What you come to realize is that, when you arrive in town, you probably look to them very like the solution to all their problems *but* that all their problems have been living with them in that town (which is probably the main problem) since whenever – and anyone who seeks a cure-all is probably on a deathtrip, anyway.

Now, there's a big difference between aspiring to be Casanova and joining the end of the gang-bang line.

And so musicians on tour are just as likely to hit on the

forty-year-old mother-of-five waitress refilling their coffee as the swimsuit calendar model in the booth beside them.

Because the waitress, unlike the model, hasn't advertised to them just by *being there* that seduction is unnecessary.

Syph had one girl who, at the moment of orgasm, cried out, 'Oh, Mr Horowitz!' The fact she was underage only confirmed his suspicions. Horowitz was her surname.

But he told this as *a funny story*.

If you can't see it as *a funny story* then it's whatever the opposite is. Beyond unfunny. Maybe not quite reaching tragic. An anti-funny story.

Anti-fun, I've had a lot of that. It becomes pornographic. A matter of stats, not flesh even. Sweaty accumulations.

I wanted this to end.

By myself I managed up to a month of self-imposed (and freakish, to Syph) road-celibacy – then I got bored, drunk, lonely, curious, all of the above.

You see, I couldn't make it alone. I needed a reason to believe –

I needed *her*.

Her, whose name turned out to be Esther Cloud.

There's that Liza Minnelli song where she goes on holiday, hoping to meet a man, heads for Dubrovnik, and *does* meet a man – who turns out to live in the very next-door apartment to her in New York. Norm Saperstein, his name is.

It wasn't exactly like that. For a start, my mother was intimately involved. But there was something of Liza's haplessness.

Since my dad died, Mom has become manically social. Not that he ever used to repress her or hold her back. His company most of the time was all she wanted. They call it *happy*. With that gone, there was a need for the making of new friends (widows, mainly) and for the collective avoidance of loneliness.

Hence, antiques.

She goes to these talks by visiting lecturers, sometimes

from as far away as England and Russia. A whole set of suave silver foxes, who tell the assembled ladies about ormolu, Louis XIV, bureau bookcases, pewter or Toby jugs. (She has books by said foxes on her shelves, from which I took these details.)

I even went to one of these hoedowns. Got stared at a lot, and learnt more than I'll ever need to know about commodes. Throughout three whole hours, no-one mentioned what they were *for*. I felt about twelve. 'Is that for taking a dump?' I wanted to ask. 'Do you ever find antique poop in them? What's a really high-quality, original-condition piece of eighteenth-century do-do worth?'

After the talk, coffee was served. Everyone tried to get talking to the commode-fox.

Everyone except my mother, whose sneaky reason for persuading me to come along was suddenly revealed.

'This is Joyce Cloud,' she said. 'She has a wonderful collection of antique lead-crystal glassware.'

'How fascinating,' I said, half twelve-years-old and half imitation silver fox. 'What attracted you to that in the first place?'

Mother gave me a mother look. You might be famous and all, but I can still . . .

'She also has a *beautiful* daughter.'

'Really?' I said. 'Are you collecting those, too?'

'Her name's Esther,' Mrs Cloud said, ignoring the rudeness. 'Your mother and I were talking last time, and we thought it would be a wonderful idea if we got you two together.'

Mrs Joyce Cloud looked like every other woman there. Grey-haired, well turned-out, cool and calm in the way of widows with enough in the bank to start antiques collections. Mrs Cloud looked like every other woman there, especially my mother.

Of course, I was trying to work out from Joyce what Esther The Beautiful might look like. All that kept coming into my mind was a picture in one of our family albums of me being breastfed. There was my mother, at twenty-two; there, as far as I was concerned, was Esther.

I turned to, or more accurately *turned on*, my mother: 'You're matchmaking me?'

'We think you and Esther would get on splendidly. She's thirty, single, likes music. You'd have a lot in common.'

Really, I thought, I should go to the bathroom, check I wasn't unexpectedly circumcised. Since when had my mother become so Jewish, already?

'You could come round for coffee,' Mrs Cloud said.

Was Cloud a Jewish name? Perhaps she was influencing my mother – who had never, through all my adolescence and later youth, *ever* tried to fix me up.

Just then the silver fox came over and asked for my autograph. He'd heard from one of the other ladies, who'd heard from my mother, who I was and what I did. In that room, we shared a vague celebrity – and it was enough for a few moments' conversation.

A second or two later, we were sharing something else, in that Mrs Cloud was trying to matchmake us both. The fox, it seemed, had met the new Mrs Fox – my mother.

Although he must get this all the time, he seemed more than a little fazed.

I realized why as the minutes passed. The Fox had come over not to talk to me but to get an introduction to Mrs Cloud. Sly is not the word.

My mother mentioned Joyce's glassware.

'How fascinating,' said Mr Fox. 'Do tell me more.'

Have mother will travel – out the door, into the parking lot and over quite a large emotional distance.

'I appreciate the thought but I don't need your help to meet women.'

'Yes, you do,' my mother said. 'You're back here, on your own, living in that messy apartment. You don't have many friends.'

'I do.'

'You say you don't like them. You complain.'

'Do I?'

'Let me be honest,' she said. We were talking across the roof of her SUV – I could see the top half of her head. I think we both felt that if we actually got *in* the car, this would become a real proper argument. 'I'm fed up waiting for grandchildren. There's only you, and it's possible you've become a father several times over –'

'Mom.'

'I know what goes on. But I'll never get to meet those kids.'

'There aren't any.'

'Right now, even if they turned up with a lawsuit, I'd welcome them. You don't realize the effects of your rock'n'roll lifestyle on those close to you.' This stunk of prepared speech. 'My friends all have the interest of another generation following on from their children. I like your music fine, for what it is, but it won't fill a photo album.' I waited for the phrase *those long winter evenings.* It didn't come. Matchmaking might have been a novelty but the central accusation of my relationship with my parents has been unchanging, probably as far back as breastfeeding: *You're so selfish. All you ever think about is you.*

'And you'd like me to meet this young woman, fall in love, get married and have babies by when? By Hanukkah?'

'Would it be so awful?'

We were doing okay for a real proper argument, even without getting in the car.

'What are the chances I'll like this girl?'

'Well, I like Joyce.' (Oh, the logic of mothers!)

'And what are the chances I'll fall in love with her?'

'Probably better than you think. I've seen her photograph, don't forget.'

I was rolling – I wasn't going to be halted by brute curiosity. Not just yet.

'And what are the chances, after I *do* fall in love with her, that she'll fall in love with me enough to want to marry me and have my children?'

'Perhaps you're right,' said my mother, wounded and intending to wound – a rarity with her. 'No-one else has.'

Antiques ladies walked past us to their SUVs. 'Bye-bye,' they said. And there went Joyce with Mr Fox following close behind.

The drive home was the most silent, ever. More silent even than the moment after Mom interrupted band practice by stepping up to the mic and singing along with a fifteen-year-old Syph.

Still, the next day, on reflection, I continued to refuse to meet Esther Cloud, the future love of all my incarnations (I hope). It was now a point of principle. What if I did like her? The lifelong humiliation of a relationship based on maternal interference. And then the farce began. Or maybe it was just a romantic comedy.

'If that's what you want,' said my mother. 'Loneliness.' And put the phone down on me.

There was just one thing: My mother had said she'd seen Esther. And I wanted to know exactly what she'd seen. But I knew, given the phone slamming, that I could never risk asking.

So – guiltily, after midnight – I went online. I googled 'Esther Cloud', checked her name in White Pages, scanned High School records. Cloud is an uncommon name.

And this is what I came up with:

No photos.

(I like to discuss with Esther what would have happened if, at this point, I'd got a look at her. She says I would probably have left the country rather than risk meeting such a monstrosity. Esther is photogenic but won't believe it. Personally, I think I'd have been visiting a very high-class 24-hour florist's on the way to my mother's – or romantically stealing flowers from someone's front garden. Peace offerings would have been required.)

Esther Cloud. 32. Originally from small-town Manitoba. Good qualifications. Currently working in the paediatrics department of Vancouver Hospital. Specialization: Autism, Asperger's Syndrome, Behavioural Disorders. Co-author of several papers with titles involving the words 'outcomes', 'therapeutic', 'recent' and 'positive'.

If my mother was looking to send me messages, they couldn't have been much clearer.

Esther did good. I was evil – and infantile.

I made up with my mother – did, in fact, visit a florist's, though not late-night.

But she's a stubborn woman. I arranged to go round for dinner that weekend, to demonstrate our reconciliation. (I didn't even pretend my many friends, who I liked, wanted me elsewhere that Saturday.) And, in the kitchen, when I arrived, helping with the vegetables, was Mrs Cloud. With her, offering his worthwhile opinion, was the Commode-Fox – these days my father-in-law, so I should be a bit careful.

Esther passed unmentioned until the end of the evening.

'She'd like to meet you,' Mrs Cloud said, on the porch, touching my arm. 'And, after getting to know you a bit, I'd be happy to introduce you to her. I was a little reluctant before, but you're nowhere near as wild as I'd expected.'

After they'd driven off, I turned to my mother and said, 'Could we just consider that argument as *had*?'

'What argument?'

'The one we could have now.'

'You apologized. I can invite who I like to my house. What have you got to lose?'

I didn't say, 'My dignity, in front of *you*.' And I didn't add, 'And any sense of running my own life.'

We kissed warmly because otherwise we'd have kissed coldly.

Back in my messy apartment, I remembered how corny the Fox's chivalry towards Mrs Cloud had been. Pushing her chair in behind her, helping her into her coat, flattering her intelligence and taste whenever the inevitable subject of antiques came up. But I also remembered the way he looked at her. Through his eyes, I distinguished her from the crowd of his audience. Mrs Cloud was whatever the female equivalent of a silver fox is. Although she still looked a bit like my mother – this sentence is going badly wrong. At eighteen-years-old, Mrs Cloud must have been . . .

At thirty . . .

During the following week, I found the car had started to want to drive me past the hospital. Somehow, the internet had decided to tell me where the Paediatrics Department was located.

I seriously considered heading for Dubrovnik.

My mother felt that Saturday's dinner had been such a success (she believed she was bringing Joyce and the Fox's romance on apace) that we should all meet again the following Sunday – and bring Esther into the party. Mom's deal – she offered one – was that the Fox would be inviting a blind-date for her, so the embarrassment would be shared 50/50 between us.

Sure, I wanted to meet someone. But I'd sat at that table with my father since my father had bought the table, thirty years ago.

Other false excuses occurred to me. I didn't bother making them. I thought about saying I'd be out of town for the weekend. I considered agreeing to turn up then not. Too childish. I don't like being estranged from my mother, even for short periods. What if she dies during one of them? You hear people talking about this, on TV.

I was watching a lot of TV.

'No,' I said. 'I'm not meeting her at our kitchen table.'

'We've thought about it.'

'We?'

'Joyce and I. You can take Esther out for a meal – on Sunday night. Then bring her round.'

'For what? The post-mortem?'

'So she can get a ride home.'

'No,' I repeated, until the message was through.

Then came the killer admission. Mom: 'I've already told them you're coming. And Esther's already accepted.'

'You will not win,' I said. 'You have made a big mistake.'

Sunday night, I watched TV. I couldn't work up the energy to go out of town.

And when the phone rang the first time, I didn't answer. (No message.) Nor, half an hour later, the second. (No message – maybe a sigh.) But on the third, I picked up – and found myself speaking to Esther. She said her name straight off, after the words *Listen, you, this is.*

Esther Cloud was angry.

'I'm insulted. Who do you think you are?'

'Where are you calling from?'

'What business is that of yours?'

'You're not at my mother's house, are you?'

'You must be very arrogant. My mother is quite upset. Your mother told her what you said.'

'I said nothing.'

'About me.'

'Believe me, *you* are not the issue. What did I say?'

'Even if she asked again, why would I want to meet an arrogant, selfish prick like you?'

'Don't worry. You don't have to. Why did you call?'

'I don't know. To see if you were as hopeless as they said.'

'You've talked to my mother about me?'

'A girl's got to do her homework. How do you think I got your number. She's very disappointed in you.'

'So you know who I am?'

'Yes.'

'Did you know before?' I asked. 'Before our mothers started –'

'I'd seen your face around. Don't flatter yourself, you're not that famous.'

This was a conversation. We could never meet, but we were talking. I wanted to ask what she thought of my face.

'Why are we still talking?' I asked.

'Because it's funny,' she said, and she sounded amused. 'You are now the person I must never meet. It would be too terrible if I liked you.'

'We have *that* in common,' I said. 'If I ever went on a date with you, my mother would have won. Total annihilation. I've been fighting her since —' I didn't want to say breastfeeding.

'Where do you live?' Esther asked.

'Why?'

'So I can avoid it.' She laughed. 'So I can never go down that street again — in case we *meet*.'

I told her the address. Then said, 'But you knew that already, didn't you?'

'How did you know I knew?'

'More homework.'

'So, where do I live?' she asked.

'How should I know?' I said, then felt the conversation begin to tumble. I didn't want it to hit the floor, smash. I made a grab for it. 'I'm not a stalker . . . But I did admire your paper on the proven links between artificial sweeteners and ADD.'

'Bitch!' she said. 'You total bitch!'

'I was curious,' I said. 'I know that I can never have children in this city — we cannot *meet*.'

'Never,' she said.

Something in her voice told me what to say, it was echoey with the boom of the future.

'Not next Friday,' I said.

'Definitely not.'

'Not at eight o'clock.'

'Never going to happen.'

'And not in complete secrecy, so no-one ever knows if we don't get on.'

'Uh-uh.'

I named a French restaurant I wasn't going to reserve us a table at.

'I would rather die than be there,' Esther gleefully said.

Later, a lot later, my mother told me she, Joyce and Esther had sat around on Saturday morning discussing the best way for her to trick me into asking her out. Scripted it. They *knew* I wouldn't make the dinner.

But on Friday, at eight, finally, innocent of my dupedness, I was there, in the restaurant, waiting. We'd talked on the phone every day in between. For hours. Laughing. Cackling. And, by the time she sat down opposite me, it didn't matter she was beautiful.

KID

I have more observations on the subject of heartbreakingly-heartbrokenly beautiful young women, but not here. (Enough has been said about that.)

Also, I have much I would say regarding – and *to* – their fathers, but not now. (Not enough has been said to them.)

Men is what I'm interested in: men – alone – together – travelling. Because that's what the whole *okay* experience has really been about.

For every hour we've spent in the company of women (and Mono's marriage to Major certainly boosts our average) we must've spent ten with each other.

Truly, we would have known more of female-kind had we become hair-stylists.

Casanova, Don Juan, Screamin' Jay Hawkins, Syph – they *leave*, that's the point of them.

Most women pretend to hate this. They fuck the going-men in a desperate attempt to make them stay – or so we're meant to think. Probably, they use faking an attempt to make them stay as a way of getting the really desperate sex they crave.

It's only recently, since the Buddhism, that I've realized how much what we do is about departure. We wanted to get out of Vancouver, sure. But to be always leaving is a weird state to achieve – to start seeing yourself as a going-man, and then to stop being able to see yourself as anything else.

That's why the practice of meditation has been so difficult and so rewarding for me. It means stopping.

And from the centre of that stopping, I can see the whole *okay* thing with much greater clarity.

We all – as kids – had problems, and those problems were

similar enough to bring us together. (Boredom, misery, hate and lust, if you really need to know.) We formed a band. We became successful. We still had the same problems.

Sometimes, in order to write the next album, we had to make those problems worse. Syph has trashed perfectly good relationships for the sake of a dozen song lyrics.

I suspect that if we had no problems, we would also have no fans. Us being emotionally adolescent keeps us emotionally relevant to adolescents. Who aren't, as you might have noticed, very together people, on the whole.

Of course, as you get older, you start lusting after the moms, not the daughters. Or as well as the daughters. But now it's the values of *our* moms I've started to yearn for. Not in a sexual way – in a way that yearns for a lack of sex.

Ultimately, I want an end of all yearning. That's a stage which resembles age not youth, wisdom not enthusiasm, grandmothers not groupies.

(Oh God, what's going to happen when people around the band read this? If the roadcrew got hold of it, they'll be bringing candyflossy ladies backstage to meet me and joking about how much I must be looking forward to Florida.)

But I'm still more on the subject of women than of me and the other guys in the band.

It's not that we love each other in a gay way, although living as we do there have been occasional kissings, gropings, suckings and more.

No, it's this: after so many years, we still find ourselves objects of mutual fascination.

Take Crab – an infinitely less charismatic creature than Syph. Yet it's him I look to for the truth of the matter in hand: I watch his face for grimaces of commentary. Even when soaked, he has a strong instinct for exactly what to reject. In this, Crab has remained the most Canadian of us – the quickest in quietly ditching the extraneous. He is mostly drunk, these days, and I think it's because that, too, fascinates him. Sober, he bores himself; sober, he knows the drunk in him would reject him; sober, he believes intellectually that he *should* be rejected.

And Mono. He's more of a fucking Buddhist than I'll ever be. He squats on lakesides, waiting to catch fish which he knows he'll put back – teasing them with the prospect of death and reincarnation. In Major, he has found someone truly stalwart. She won't allow him to ruin his life. Out of all this shit, they have a relationship that is as indestructible as a tank in cloudcuckooland.

We thought we formed *okay* for the music, but it was for the escape – the escape with one another. When we re-form, it's for the return to one another. Sadly, it has very little to do with the music any more. Even the money is irrelevant, except that it allows us to spend long periods of time in company.

There is an enjoyment, still, in thinking – from some hotel bar somewhere – how far we've travelled, how much we've accomplished.

This isn't *said*. I'm talking about the talk of men.

Our success materializes at the table, a fifth band-member. We all acknowledge he is there (our success is male, too) but without even a nod.

Perhaps it's in the carelessness with which we order drinks and food. No bill will ever touch us – the amounts are irrelevant.

Crab pays for his drinking, pays a stupidly high and every morning increasing price, but he'll be an elegant wino for the rest of his life, never a penniless street bum. If he gets into life-threatening situations, liver-wise, our fifth member will come to rescue him.

So what is it that *is* said, between us?

Not a great deal. Nothings that are sweet because uncruel. We have such vicious armouries of ammo, if we wanted to go to war. There is the mellow-illusion to be maintained: the illusion that things have always been this cool.

Untrue that.

Syph doesn't know but Crab once tried to arrange a hit on him.

That's not the story I'm interested in right now, though.

There had been a couple of quick cut'n'paste jobs, but never before the full vanity of a book.

What is it about pages of paragraphs without the relief of pictures that makes musicians go so pretentious?

Syph tried to seduce the writer, then to impress her, then to scare her – finally, he ignored her. This was where Crab and Mono had started, but only because they were desperate to maintain mystique. They knew that silence and distance were all they had going for them. A single face-to-face interview and they would have to confront, in print already, the terrible fact of being ordinary.

They weren't always ordinary.

We all started out as odd – marginally odd fish, within a small bowl (Vancouver, apart from Syph). But time passes, you leave behind your first, second and third set of contemporaries, you travel, maybe you become famous, someone invents the internet, you go online – and you find out that, all along, there were others just like you, that your odd wasn't.

Everyone is an average, if you have a wide enough range of standards by which to judge them. Average serial killer. Average conjoined twins.

The most terrible thing is finding out that The Parents were right in some of what they said. They understood, all along. Their questions weren't really questions; their questions were sewn seeds – were preaching-in-disguise.

'It's very loud, isn't it?'

'Yes.'

'Why does it have to be so loud?'

'It just does, okay? Look, could you step out of my room?'

'But do you enjoy it?'

'Yes. It's the best. Now –'

'Won't you get bored of it, eventually?'

'No. Never. Absolutely not.'

'Why don't you consider getting a proper job? Just in case –'

'Fuck you.'

But the you of *Fuck you* comes closer and closer to being the true you. And that you can't avoid post-adolescence for ever – and when you become unmistakably middle-aged, you realize you can't avoid saying the words *kids today* and that you're doing so as a non-kid.

I've watched many documentaries about the birth of rock'n'roll. Read quite a few books, too. And what I'm starting to realize is, those who opposed it weren't without their reasons.

Things were lost, because of it.

For us, it's easy to mock the Viennese-accented psychologists who were coaxed blinking into bright TV studios to expound on the *inzezzant chunkle ryzzms of zis rocking and rolling music*. But the Herr Professor *vasn't hrong*, the rhythm is the thing you can't get away from.

I know – I've lived a life almost exclusively in 4/4 time.

Faster, slower, a little breakbeat influence creeping in around 1996, incessant.

'Won't you get bored of it, eventually?'

In the end, yes, it gets a little dull.

I remember an interview with Yoko Ono, about when she first met John Lennon and heard his music. (I have been rude about Yoko in the past. I followed the party-line on her being the archetypal band-breaker. Yoko, I apologize.) What she said was that she found it difficult to listen to The Beatles because, unlike both the Japanese classical and New York avant-garde stuff she was used to, it neither slowed down nor sped up. *Thump*-and-*thump*-and.

And that's me. That's my home address.

Yoko and the Herr Professor knew something that, at twelve, when I made my pact with the Devil of Garage Rock,

I was ignorant of: life, unlike *okay*'s music, slows down and speeds up. Mostly, it slows down.

Rock music is a fight against that. An insistence on excitement and a battle against entropy.

But constant excitement is boring, entropy is inevitable.

The battle is worth it (The 1956-vintage Parents were wrong about that) – the battle *is* worth it, for a while.

Ten years.

Ten max.

The battle is not worth it for twenty – twenty years of road, of *thump*-and-*thump*-and – not on into your forties – not when you are about to become a parent – not when you are me.

I intend to surrender.

I want to enjoy slowing down.

McCartney was wrong: the Road (the Rock Road) may be Long but it is far from Winding.

Life slows down and speeds up, sweeps left, cuts right, has switchbacks, breakdowns, crashes.

The Road of 4/4 is a straight line from rainy windscreen to flat horizon. Cover of Springsteen's *Nebraska*.

For a drummer to leave a band and cite *musical differences* would be ridiculous, or so you'd think. The differences are in the melodies and harmonies and styles and influences, not in the positioning of the *thump* and the *and*.

When I announced I was leaving *okay*, I cited musical differences – I cited my deep desire for them.

I had been listening to classical music and feeling like a savage in the jungle, *shtuck wiz my inzezzant ryzzms*.

Percussionists are such untermensches within the orchestral Reich – except in something like *The Rite of Spring*. I wasn't quitting to join the Vancouver Phil. I was quitting because maybe I'd made a mistake, back at the beginning.

I had no talent for anything other than basic rock drumming. Maybe I didn't have enough talent to be a musician at all. I should have done what The Parents – in the person of my parents – wanted: become a professional. My mother wanted me to be a doctor, my father a lawyer. I tried to imagine myself as either. Couldn't.

Esther, the one, was seven months pregnant.

I told the band I was leaving.

We were at Band HQ. No longer an ironic reference to the small office from which our first managers operated. This was a company employing twenty, and looking to expand. Tinted glass, a woman on front desk who doesn't know whether to treat us as The Boss Times Four or as the Coolest Cats in Town, Man. Not a fan – a fan would make really bad front of house.

More specifically, we were in the unironic Boardroom – around the long black table that I couldn't help but see, the second before I opened my mouth, as a coffin-lid.

'No!' said Mono.

'You sure?' said Crab.

'See you,' said Syph.

They should have known it was in the post. At the previous couple of rehearsals, I'd tried to introduce some musical differences. Changes is what jazz musicians call them, though I didn't try anything of that complexity: I'd have been kicked out, not quit. What I attempted just confused them.

I think they thought I'd lost my ability to keep time – and maybe I had.

Or maybe it was that I'd lost my will to 4/4 discipline. I was outmoded. A drum machine did what I did, and so much better. There was a glory to Mo Tucker, my favourite skin-thumper – there was something transcendent about the strictness of her tempo. Half an hour of 'Sister Ray', undeviating. Each beat that didn't miss was a brick in a Great Wall of Rhythm. I loved Mo. She was motorik before krautrock. She danced to the machines. She found joy in repetition, like a true American. I would never be Mo. I didn't dare keep it simple, stupid. I had to have my fill of fills. Sorry, Mo.

I'd discussed it with Esther, before I quit.

In the kitchen.

She, give her credit, thought I was making a mistake. In all the years I'd been in the band, I'd initiated nothing, musically. (Had I initiated *anything*? In the mid-eighties, I got Syph to try sushi. The thought was terrifyingly sad.) She said it was time I brought something to the table – thought the others might be receptive to it. They knew we'd gone stale. How could they not? I tried to explain what stupid and stubborn bastards they were. I implied their contempt for me. She had more faith. It was justified.

'No!' Mono had said.

My lack of faith was also justified.

'See you,' Syph had said.

What to do next?

I didn't want to travel but I did feel a need to explore. I put on big fat headphones and set off into the deep north of the string quartet: Haydn, Mozart, Beethoven, Schubert, back to late Beethoven, Debussy, Bartók, back again to Mozart to hear what I'd missed, Janáček, all the way through all of all Shostakovich (to the death), Webern, Cage, Messiaen. The end of time. It sounds pretentious. It was wonderful. I was a postulant – a junior monk. I wanted to be allowed to kneel at the temple gates, in the snow and rain, in the mud, in the hammer sun, for a year, until they saw my faith, until they let me in, until they started to show me what enlightenment really was.

Mono came round and found me with the big fat head-phones on. He hadn't had to travel far – he and Major kept an apartment in Kitsilano, as well as the house in Northern Ontario. They stayed in each for six months of the year. Best of both.

Mono was as close as *okay* comes to a deputation.

'We want you back,' he said.

'I don't even understand it any more,' I said in honest reply. 'I don't understand how I ever did. I'm lost.'

'We can get you into a programme,' said Mono, kindly.

'Like the one Crab went on last year. It worked – for a while.'

For Beethoven's 'Grosse Fuge'? A programme?

'How's Major?' I asked. 'You should come round to dinner.'

'Are you on downers? What is it? We can help.'

'I'm trying to understand everything I haven't been doing.'

'And you're taking them, one by one. A drug encyclopaedia. I get it. Just tell us when you're finished. Where you up to?'

'It's *not* drugs.' The painkillers were beside the point – they were for rheumatism, in my kick-drum foot, in my snare hand. 'It's . . .'

I almost saw the continuation dots float out into the air, and I knew that, right then, I was unable to chase them down with any meaningful syllables.

'Tell the others – tell them what you like. That I've had a breakdown, got religion, Catholicism this time, not Buddhism. Tell them I've lost my nerve.'

Sad-faced, Mono picked up one of the records. The Alban Berg Quartet. I was listening to everything on vinyl – warm analog, through a valve amp.

'You really like this stuff?' he asked.

'I do,' I said.

That was my marriage vow, right then and there. Mono didn't even know he'd spliced me and Ludwig, until death do.

'They're really pissed, the others. We've got an album to record – that's fine. We can get session drummers in.' I wasn't even offended. 'But then there's a tour.'

The thought – the thought of the repetition.

'Never,' I said.

Mono stood up. 'You'll be back,' he said.

'Not as me,' I replied. 'Not as the me I now am. I will have to be different.'

'You're crazy, man.'

'Tell Major to bring you round to dinner.'

Amazingly, he did.

Esther cooked. Big rich beef stew. It was midwinter. Thick red wine. French cheese. I chose the background music. I was respectful – only music the composers would have expected not to be listened to: divertimenti, minor stuff. No-one noticed, just as I wanted. We talked about the old days. Esther was amused. Major asked for the stew recipe. I felt civilized. Mono looked awkward. I think he thought I was trying to be something I wasn't – domesticated or European. I felt such love for him, across our dining-room table. What I wanted least of all was for him to lose his musical faith like I had. Like I had when I had a breakdown, got Catholicism, lost my nerve and married Beethoven. It would be too cruel to wish these changes upon him – wish him away from what had brought him such a good life.

He told the story of the kid.

We were on tour in America. Some city. He said it was Pittsburgh. I thought it was Detroit. I'm sure Syph and Crab would have added two other cities. 'Heavily industrial,' we agreed upon.

'And we finish the show, get back into the dressing-room, and there's this child there.'

'A child?' asks Esther, interrupting but only to keep the story moving, not annoying.

'A boy,' Major adds.

'About seven or eight,' Mono says.

'Or six,' I joke.

'Maybe six,' Mono concedes. Six makes the story better. Six makes the story worse.

'Yes?' says Esther.

'You're awful. Tell the story *properly*,' says Major. 'Describe him.'

'He was small.' Major goes pah! 'Dark hair. Flat, not spiky. Pale skin. A little weak-looking, but intense. Bright. He seemed older than he was.'

'Five, maybe,' I say.

'Six.'

'Yes,' says Esther.

'He's there, eating peanuts from our rider. He has an *okay*

T-shirt on. Now, we didn't make them that small. But it looks perfect. A miniature version of the tour before that's T-shirt. And the kid looks at us when we come in, and he says –'

I join in on the chorus: '"Hi, guys."'

Mono continues, solo: '"Where's your mother?" asks Syph. I think maybe he sees the kid isn't too bad-looking, and wonders if she's worth checking out. Is she in the bathroom? No. "I don't have a mother," says the kid. "What about your father?" asks old Clap over there.' The women look at me, with approval. 'And the kid says –'

'"I don't have a father."'

'So I ask, "Then who brought you here?" And he says, "I came by myself. You guys are great. I'd like to hang out with you." "Are you a midget or something?" asks Syph. "Fuck you," answers the kid. We all ask his age, but he refuses to say. He just wants to talk about the set we've just played. He says he thinks we played too many obvious songs – should be more rarities in there, for the real fans. He names some old ones even *we've* forgotten. And however old he is, these were written and recorded before he was born. "How old are you?" we keep asking. The kid just won't say. We're amused by him, now. But we also want to move on, get something to eat, go to a club. The kid wants to come. We say no, he shouldn't even be here. "But I am here," he says. "And I was there in Minnesota, too."'

'"Detroit,"' I say.

'Whatever,' Mono says. 'Location isn't the point of this story.'

'And what is?' asks Major.

'Destination,' says Mono, quick as that. 'And I'm getting there as fast as I can. We're impressed by the kid. If nothing else, he's a great liar. People come to take us away. We wave goodbye to him at the stage door – and he's there to meet us outside the restaurant. Swear to God. The kid gets there *before* us. Our limo didn't drive slowly, either. And he's *in* the restaurant. "How did you get here?" we ask. "You tried to dump me," the kid says. "That wasn't fair." We figure he's earned a meal. The management at the restaurant don't seem to mind. Probably think he's a son or a cousin. We eat. The kid talks. He's very confident, and witty. He flatters us by being cleverly critical of our last couple of albums.'

'It's all true,' I say.

'I think you're right,' Mono says to me. 'I think he was probably six.'

'From the mouths of babes,' says Major.

'We give him autographs. We buy him food. He's offered burger and fries but has, get this, asparagus followed by veal. He is this evening's amusement. Again, outside the restaurant, we try to say goodbye. The kid gets upset. "I thought we were friends." "We are," Syph says. "But where we're going, you cannot go." Into the limo. Wave, wave. Halfway to the club, we decide to go somewhere else – just in case the kid has heard our plans and taxied there. We ask the driver, take us somewhere funky. He understands. Spins the wheel. Does a 180 there and then. It's a little hole in the wall place, when we get there, and –'

'The kid!' says Esther, wowed.

'– is in our booth. Behind the ropes. In VIP. We ask how he got there, he won't say. Crab is starting to believe the kid's a ghost, or a group hallucination. Syph has other ideas. Secretly, he's paranoid that he might be the kid's father, and this is some bitter mother's way of introducing them – before the lawyers get involved. We ask the doormen how he got in. They say they never saw him before. "Are you a millionaire?" I ask. "You've got a helicopter outside." "I just want to hang out with you guys," the kid says. "Quit trying to ditch me." "Can we be arrested for this?" Crab asks. "Only if we buy him drinks, I think," I say. "It's okay," the kid says, "I'll have *Coke*. I don't want to get you into trouble." So, we're amused. We let him stay. We have a great time, talking. It ends about three. He doesn't reappear back at the hotel. He's called it a night. But he's there after the next gig, backstage. He follows us from city to city.'

I am privately thinking of the beads around my wrist, but I say nothing.

Mono concludes: 'He follows us for the rest of the tour. We give up trying to escape him, after a few more switch-backs. He's too much. He's a phenomenon, even if he isn't supernatural. We joke about whose kid he is. On the last night, Hollywood Bowl, he says –'

'"Thanks, guys. It's been great."'

'And he hugs us around our middles and walks out of the dressing-room. And we've never seen him again.'

The women look at me. 'It's true,' I say. 'Every word.'

'And you have no explanation?' Esther asks.

'None,' I say.

'Zero,' says Mono. 'The kid is the strangest thing to happen to us, any of us, in almost twenty years.'

'How old would he be now?'

'Sixteen?' I say. 'Or a bit more.'

'Wow,' says Esther, my beautifully pregnant one.

'He's told me the story before,' Major says. 'And the details are remarkably consistent.'

'Why would we make that up?' Mono asks.

'What do you think?' I ask everyone. 'Ghost or millionaire or . . . ?'

'Ghost,' says Major.

'Millionaire,' says Mono.

'A friend,' says Esther. 'A true friend.'

I don't want to have to decide.

After this, the evening dies slowly. No story can compete. But it's been great. I kiss Major on both cheeks. She is Mary Magdalene and more. (Esther knows about my worship.)

When they've gone, I talk a while longer with Esther about the kid. Like I said, she is seven months pregnant, and we've done a lot of talking about kids, recently.

'What if he's this one?' she says, holding her big tummy. 'Come from the future to take a look at his daddy.'

'But he didn't single me out. He loved us all.'

'That should tell you something,' Esther says.

'This isn't a point of argument,' I say.

The next day, I put the big headphones back on – I listen to opus 133, to Deutsch No. 810, to Köchel 465. But I can't forget the kid. He is incessant. His image keeps repeating, thumping.

I made the right decision in leaving.

Two months later, I call Mono and tell him to tell the others I'll do the tour.

We meet. They say no. I explain. They say yes.

Not millionaire. The other.

Oh my little son, my lost son.

FUCK-UP

It wouldn't be me if I weren't alone, lonely, lovesick and forlorn – a long long way from home.

I fucked it up, bigtime.

Deliberately.

With Esther.

Well, kind of deliberately.

Esther has short, thick, very black-but-not-dyed hair with – when she doesn't pull them – one or two lightning-slashes of silver. She likes to paint her toenails a particular shade of damson which she can only achieve by mixing two cheapo brands of nailpolish. At a Chinese restaurant, she will order Peking duck; in Starbucks, decaf latte grande with nutmeg on. Born in the year of the Aardvark (private joke), Esther is Bette Davis the Second, Field Marshal Monty Python, the Queen of the Tambourine, Sexual History 101, a tigerskin mouse and a moon-harpoon (all private jokes).

As Elvis put it, I've forgotten more than you'll ever know about her.

She didn't ask for faithful, just truthful.

That was the motto in our imaginary sampler up on the real wall in our actual dream home.

NOT FAITHFUL,
JUST TRUTHFUL

But this nineteen-year-old girl had come all the way from Osaka Japan, just to see me. She'd spent her savings since she was twelve and first heard one of our records ('Sea-Song $^{\#}3$'). I felt some responsibility, you understand. I also felt horny. Esther was out of town, visiting her parents. I was drunk. She was cute enough. There is no excuse.

Esther minded that I lied about it, when she asked. I have no idea how she found out – perhaps it was in my face, the fact that I was trying to keep out of my face the fact I was trying to keep anything out.

I fucked it up. I tried testing it. I couldn't believe the sampler was telling the truth about not faithful. So I did half the opposite of what I should've.

Esther minded enough to push the big red button.

I thought I'd get more than one strike.

'When trust is gone,' she said, 'it very rarely comes back – ever.'

I was out.

She left the apartment, but I was the one in the cold.

And so I did bad things, to make it seem to myself like I wanted it to be over.

For example, I went to Osaka. And not for the seafood.

That lasted all of five days. Awe is not an appealing quality, not for more than three days. Awe so huge that the feeler can't make sentences. I'm very good at taking my feet of clay and moulding obscene objects out of them, firing them, presenting them as gifts – gifts which no woman could possibly ever want. Ceramic atrocities. Besides, none of our songs were there on the karaoke machines. (She hated karaoke, my visited visitor. I had to force her to go. She wanted romantic walks over meaningful bridges in small parks.) When I met her parents, I was older than her mother by exactly one week. There was steam on the windows of the kitchen as I ate a week's wages. I could touch the ceiling with my elbow, at a stretch. In her eyes, still awe. Even after a particularly fine clay figurine of a drunken drummer, vomiting down a demure Japanese girl's back. Her parents' acceptance of me was heartbreaking. They were far from Canadian.

Day five, I bought her a wedding ring, arranged to go out for dinner that night with her grandparents, and left for the airport. Only hate, I believed, could make her sell the diamonds and get back the money she'd spent on airfare.

How wrong I was.

Three days later, seen through the fisheye lens of my front door, her whole family, including grandparents. I never quite got the details straight, but someone had sold a fishing boat to book their tickets.

She looked at me with awe, because I played drums on some songs she loved.

The ring was on her ring-finger.

I could see only one solution: I introduced her to the rest of the band. Syph, at my request, stole her from me. (He'd probably have done it anyway – for free.) I took her to the rehearsal studios, without accompanying blood relations, and she cried for joy. Syph said he would write a song about her, because she was so beautiful.

The wedding ring was returned to me – such a beautiful red box, and tightly wrapped in black paper with delicately drawn marigolds.

When I asked at the hotel, the family had checked out.

But what if I'd made a mistake? Perhaps what my sordid soul needed above all things was innocence. That awe, it was almost as good as grown-up love, wasn't it? No-one else would ever want me. I was throwing away the only –

Another trip to Osaka.

I made it as far as the staircase of her apartment block before I realized that, so far, I'd messed up ten people's lives, but, right now, I was one cheery doorbell-chime away from destroying them altogether.

So there I was, again, alone, lonely, lovesick and forlorn – a long long way from home.

I turned around, and awe was standing in front of me, her mother to one side, her father to the other. Just as if my guilty conscience (I discovered, through her, that I still possessed one) had got action-figures of the three, and posed them.

'I came to apologize,' I said, to her father. 'I am very sorry,' I said, to her mother. 'Please translate,' I said, to her.

They invited me in for tea.

('Wouldn't the coolest thing now be to be Japanese?' as someone once said.)

I accepted.

We had what amounted to a business meeting. The daughter took no active part, merely translated the terms of my attempt to make up for lust, folly, vanity and cruelty.

'A bigger boat,' I said. 'With an icebox.'

We bowed for a very long time – my feet on the concrete of the stairway, theirs on the tatami of their hall.

The taxi took me to a nearby monastery, where I asked the Buddha, *Please, no suicides – no deaths of young girls who deserve better than me.*

Go home, the Buddha told me to tell myself. *Go home and try to do no more damage, to yourself or to others. Sit still.*

His voice was golden, like his face, like his toes.

I skipped the in-flight meals, fasting already.

There was a message from Syph on my answering machine, wondering if he could get that Japanese girl's number. 'She was cute,' he said.

There was no message from Esther.

I wanted to know how I could become good enough to deserve having her back. Until I was close, I daren't ask directly.

Sit still.

I couldn't.

I tried the Japanese way – went to visit her parents, mother and stepfather. They had moved back out to rural Manitoba. In penance, I set off to drive there. From Vancouver.

'I came to apologize,' I said, three days later. 'I'm very sorry.'

Perhaps something was lost in the lack of translation.

'Go away,' said her mother, Mrs Cloud. For a moment, when she opened the door, I'd thought it was Esther – aged by sadness.

'I've come from Vancouver to see you.'

'You've seen me. Now go away.'

'I brought you something.'

'How do you think she'd like it if I went accepting presents from you? I'm not going to say it again.'

'Please tell Esther I'm trying.'

'I will do you the favour of not mentioning this at all. Say hi to your mother. Poor woman.'

When she shut the door, the antique knocker on the outside rat-a-tatted about five times.

I got into my car, stared at the curtains for a while to see if any of them twitched in a way that I found totally loveable.

In the first motel I came to, I watched TV.

Actually, I watched a battle between TV and the Buddha. It was very like a Godzilla movie. TV hurled a series of beer adverts at the Golden One. He replied with universal love and compassion. TV countered with the bubble booty in a couple of rap videos. Buddha sidestepped this, offering a lotus flower in response. TV escalated to a full-on grunting treble porn-channel assault. Buddha said, 'Catch you later,' turned a sandalled heel and walked off into the haze of the empty minibar.

When the management refused to send any more drinks to my room, I tried to buy the motel.

The only thing that prevented me was, it being Sunday, there were no lawyers available. During negotiations, the keys to my car went missing (they were returned to me when I checked out, two weeks later, not having slept in my room again).

'I'll walk,' I said.

'Be my guest,' said the owner, a good man, with my car keys in his pocket.

'I *am* your guest,' I said. 'And there are rules of hospitality. If this was Japan –'

'This is Canada,' he said. 'And you are drunk.'

'Where's the nearest bar?'

This being Canada, he was polite enough to point me in the right direction.

'How far is it?'

'Don't worry,' he said. 'You'll still be drunk when you get there.'

He was right. When I got there, I was still drunk – but it was a day and a half later. In between the motel and the bar were two other motels, and I checked into, drank dry and got kicked out of both before I made it to what would become my regular barstool. It was summer, so I didn't even need a blanket to sleep in the alley alongside the bar. I slept on an old mattress I found. In the bar, there were beautiful neon signs in the dark between the mirrors. Four of our songs were on the jukebox. Maybe I could live there. The barman didn't believe I was who I said I was.

'Do you want to buy a car?' I asked. 'A good one.'

'No, thank you,' he said.

'Have you ever been to Japan?'

'No, but I've been to Thailand.'

'Japan is better,' I said. 'The people there are really decent.'

'I have no doubt about it,' said the barman. 'They have always seemed decent to me.'

Tuesday was a slow night. Wednesday, too. By Thursday, I was coming to suspect that it wasn't the nights that were slow but the town – more accurately, the outskirts of the town. But on Friday, people came and, if I hadn't been there already, I'd have had to fight for my barstool.

A drunk man coming through the door howled. 'Full moon out there,' he said, and perhaps saved my life.

I went to go look.

The sky was clear, horizon to horizon. Even at the edges, no decorative clouds.

Down the alley I walked. Up a dirt road. Through some trees to the top of the hill.

When I got there, I knew the Buddha had just left. I could smell the poems he'd been writing. Falling to my knees, I started to grub round in the grass. If I could just find a piece of gold leaf from one of his feet. I remembered Esther's toenails. I remembered the temple in Japan. I remembered the fog in Amsterdam or Rotterdam. I found something which shone, but the moonlight made it the purest, most beautiful silver. Next day, when I looked in my pocket, I found it was the wrapper from a stick of chewing gum. But up on that hill, I thought the Buddha was telling me to follow him. Leaving flakes. If I didn't follow him fast enough, all his gold leaf could come off bit by bit. Children visiting his temple would be disappointed by how dull he looked, though their parents would take it for wisdom. I would be responsible for the loss of glory. The way up and the way down are not the same. There is no bottom, and I was in danger of reaching it. If the flake wasn't Buddha-gold it was moon-silver. I sobbed then shouted to both of them: 'I came to apologize. I'm very sorry.' I was, very sorry. To show them how sorry I was, I pissed my pants. Or maybe I just didn't reach the zipper in time. 'I never wanted this,' I said, face down in the grass. After sleeping for a while, which I knew because the moon had moved further away from me, I tried rolling down the hill. This should be innocent. The grass was too long. I climbed back up, laughing. In the morning, there were deep cuts in my palms. At the very summit, I looked at the moon and howled. Waited. Howled. Someone howled back. It wasn't a wolf. How I would love to believe it could have been a wolf and not another drunk. They howled and I howled a reply and they did a very long howl and I tried to match them but my lungs gave out. 'Fuck,' I said, 'this is beautiful. This wouldn't happen in Japan.' The howling got louder, and turned into the man who'd come with a howl into the bar. He arrived friendly but when I staggered over to embrace him he thought I was attacking. I did have a rock in my hand, for some reason. He beat me but good. Saved my life a second time, I believe. I'd been doing too much relying on the kindness of strangers, this past week. How many people have heard the Buddha howl like a wolf? How many men have felt the moon's hard fists in their gut? He urinated, silver in the moonlight – not on my head but close enough so I could feel the warmth and taste the splash. 'Are you famous?' he asked, before he left. 'They told me in the bar you said you were famous. Well, I swam for the province – butterfly. Nearly got a trial for the Olympics. Next time, you be careful who you howl at.' I could see him thinking about kicking me. 'They know where you are,' he said, then walked down the hill. 'Thank you,' I said, pushing myself up into a sitting position. I wanted to howl but my wolf-spirit had left me. The moon was still there, lower in the sky, further away. Closing my eyes, I sat on a tatami mat of grasses. Sat still. Then I thought about the things I usually try not to think about. I was asleep within seconds.

When I woke up, the first thing I saw was the back of Esther's new stepfather's head – silver. It was the Commode-Fox.

He was driving me to hospital. I was in the back of his car, the car seat (a blanket under my sodden ass) holding me upright. The car's paintjob was gold.

'You awake, now?' he asked.

'Yes, sir,' I said.

'Don't give me that shit,' he said. 'How do you feel?'

'Like shit.'

'Good,' he said. 'I'm not doing this because anyone asked me to.'

I knew who *anyone* was.

'And I'm not doing it because I like you. I think you're disgusting.'

'You're right.'

'Agreeing with me doesn't make it any better. Do you want to die?'

I didn't answer.

'We were sorry about it. God knows,' he said. He didn't mean cheating on Esther. 'But you have to be stronger.'

'I can't,' I said.

'Then, please, if you're going to drink yourself to death, do it somewhere I won't hear about it. I don't want you on my conscience.'

'Thank you,' I said.

'For what?' he asked. 'I'm not doing you a favour.'

He left me without shaking my hand in the hospital lobby.

They took my credit-card details and gave me a room.

Just like with me, Esther was able to read what her step-father was trying to pretend he wasn't keeping out of his face.

She waited three days before she came to visit. I was shaky but part-way back.

Esther said, 'I didn't want to leave. I knew she was nothing. You gave me an excuse to punish myself. I hate what you've done to me. That was *our* baby. It was the most terrible thing. I blamed you even as I thought it was my fault. We did nothing wrong. We were unlucky. You didn't make it any better. How have you dealt with it? Like this? You stupid fucker. How annoying is that. Look at Crab – look at his life. I have something I need to say.' And then she said it: 'I *don't* trust you. I don't need you. But, unfortunately, I still love you.'

There were conditions.

I agreed to all of them.

In the black of Esther's hair, a real lightning-storm.

FAITHFUL AND TRUTHFUL
OR NOTHING, BUSTER

The way up.

GOLDEN

Twins.

Girls.

Non-identical.

Beautiful.

Which made a load of folks say *it must make up for losing one before* – which made us lose (fast) quite a few friends, or lose respect for them.

Sarah (11.33 p.m.) and Grace (12.12 a.m.).

Let me tell you *exactly* how wonderful they are.

Or, no.

You're pleased, but I can see you'll be even more delighted if I spare you the glorious details.

So I will.

Most of them.

On their birthdays, the world rebegan again – just as it's done on a trillion different days for a trillion different men. I was glad to join this great club of average transfiguration. I was glad to be so *normal*.

All through the pregnancy, all I'd asked for was *normally healthy*; I didn't mention *beauty*, *brains*, *athletic prowess* or even *being more like Esther than me* (which would be a cheating-way of asking for all the above).

What I cared about was that they emerge from the womb alive. After that, everything else was down to us, diapers to rehab.

Twin *daughters*.

Over the years, I've said and thought such terrible things about women. Let me take this opportunity to apologize.

Several revelations have come my way, since Sarah and Grace. First of these is –

Women are better than men.

And second, which I have to mention straight away, after that, is –

Women are nicer than men.

Men have meetings in restaurants and draw important arrows on important pieces of paper.

(Dear Esther, how can I ever...?)

Men are overcome by a sense of their own importance, when examining the arrows they have drawn in important restaurants.

(Dear Esther, I am more sorry than I can ...)

Women are different. They see things differently, and how they see things is a better, nicer, less arrow-dependent way of seeing them.

Women see differently.

(Dear Esther, I'll calm down soon.)

Jewellery taught me this, and the way Esther enters into it entirely. Women see it in greater detail than men, because they allow their eyes to change size. They look at a ring as if it were a building – as if the whole of the world might start again, from first principles, taking this small trinket as the beginning. Men stay as eye-giants, in comparison, lumbering, and are only impressed by cathedrals – which may be intricate but are never intimate. Except for God-the-visitor. (Cathedral-type buildings, I mean. Banks count, as do malls.)

A different hat; a different world.

This is the rule of clothes that women understand and men, most men, including me until recently – this is the rule men need to be told about and learn by heart.

If I wear this on my head, the atomic structure of Africa will alter. Not the butterfly effect, no. Avoiding chaos theory completely. Instead, there's a direct improvement caused by me (a woman) buying this hat and choosing the absolutely right occasion upon which to wear it.

Hence the horror, also never understood by giants, of turning up to a party and seeing another woman wearing the same dress, or hat; a parallel universe in which improvements overlap and so cancel one another out. Poor Africa.

To women, men are such a disappointment.

Why won't we rise? Women give us the utopian clues of their clothes. Silk as anti-war protest; pattern as plea for a more detailed and compassionate approach to human inter-relations. 'Don't rip the texture of the world – the textile of the world.' Jewellery to say to men: 'Stop and examine more closely *everything*. Me, especially. Beautiful me. Because if you find me attractive, you are less likely to do harm (to me but also, somehow, to others). And so, by my being beautiful, I save the world.' Distract the beast even in the moment it threatens to go berserk. As a justification for beauty, it is beautiful.

'No,' said Esther. 'You're being reckless again.'

She is so beautiful, as I've said before.

Women have always tried to save me, by being beautiful. One of them succeeded, temporarily. And now she's brought in two reinforcements. Sarah. Grace.

This was where I had reached, about a month ago. This was my new world-view. I was outlining it to Esther, and she was gently telling me how wrong I was, when the phone rang and Syph weighed in unwittingly on my side.

'Man, you gotta come over – you gotta come right over right now because I've got some weird shit I gotta tell you, I mean, this is some fucked-up shit, man, you're not gonna fuckin believe ...'

Etc.

Come right over is easier said than done, as our house is almost an hour from downtown – where Syph bases his operations.

I knew better than to try and deal with him down the phone. When I've tried before, he's smashed the receiver at his end – resulting, once, in him being unable to call for an ambulance when his latest girlfriend OD'd. Which was what he'd been calling about.

She survived, luckily. Someone visiting the building (not a neighbour, they were used to weird noises) heard Syph's ranting and called the cops to report a domestic disturbance.

It was early evening by the time I made it to Syph's door. I hadn't been to his apartment in maybe half a year. He'd redecorated twice, or so I'd heard.

Around Christmas, Syph had a sudden revelation that anyone who didn't live in a cave or tent was pissing away their soul. So first the place was done out as a Neanderthal dwelling, with finger-paintings of buffalo on the walls; built-in cupboards for the entertainment media, however. And then, around Easter, this was re-done into the circular layout of a Mongolian yurt. Syph set up an ancestor-altar in the Northern corner – framed photograph of his dad at a Canucks game. Sitting on rugs, he sipped milk tea and told my informant (Crab) that he felt centred for the first time in his life. Reincarnation explained everything. Particularly the guilt. (A word I had never known him use before – not in reference to himself, at least.)

'Enter,' said Syph, who was wearing a kaftan of metallic pink. Above his forehead was a shiny disc, like a cartoon dentist might wear, only this disc was gold. Overall, he looked disturbingly like Sun Ra's honky flugelhorn player.

Behind him was something which, at first double-take, I took to be a high-end 1970s roller-disco. Then I realized that the flashing red and yellow lights were in fact control panels, and that the hallway closely approximated to the bridge of the *Starship Enterprise*. (*Star Trek: The Next Generation*.)

'Welcome to the *future*,' Syph said. His voice was very different to when he'd called me on the phone: calm, fruity, British-accented.

I was freaked. It was as if, when speaking to me before, he had done an impression of his usual untogether self in order to lure me to his space-lair.

Syph, who smelt strongly of rosewater, led me through into what he called 'the Receiving Area'. Here, the encircling

144

walls of the yurt had been upgraded to include windows out into what, apparently, was deep space.

In the middle of the room was a circular rug populated by circular throw-cushions. Mono sat cross-legged on one, Crab lay with his head resting on another.

Approaching, I could see no sign of drugs, drink or even cigarettes – the usual accessories to Syph's chosen sitting-place. There was, however, a lime-green Ovation semi-acoustic guitar spangled all over with decal stars.

You bet I sensed danger.

'Thank you all for coming,' Syph said. 'I expect you're wondering why I asked you to join me here.' He sounded *just* like Lord Summerisle in *The Wicker Man*. 'I won't keep you in suspense any longer.' Obviously, the others had been hanging round till I got there. From the deep pockets of his kaftan, Syph drew out a TV-remote and pressed one of the buttons.

'Planet Earth,' he said, just as a beautiful image of said planet appeared on the twelve huge window-screens. 'Six billion people, and counting. I have received word from my Masters that this situation is what they call "unsustainable". An intervention must be made. And soon.'

Syph walked over to the lime-green guitar, picked it up and strapped it on. He then began to sing a song whose chorus ran:

> Hail, the beloved starchild!
> Hail, you harbinger of dawn!
> Clear our polluted earth-senses!
> Let us know we've truly been born!
>
> We are born to a destiny
> To un-iver-siality
> We must leave our home planet
> We can do it, if we but plan it.

'That's the opening track,' he said, almost as an aside. 'Me. Solo. Acoustic. Then there's an orchestral interlude, which I've got worked out already. And next comes . . .'

Next came:

> Message from the cosmos
> Knowledge from the gods
> Can we survive? Can we endure?
> Against such overwhelming odds?

And then:

> Confusion
> Illusion
> The Masterpiece of Doubt
> Come faster
> O Master
> And show us the Way Out

And so on, through all four sides of the album. Here is the planned track-listing:

SIDE A

Star-child (Brilliant Love)

Cosmic Wager/ 1000–1 at Least

Astral Travellers' Cheques

Madness! Sadness! (Possible duet with David Bowie)

The Wink of a God in Waltztime

Teeming Masses

SIDE B

December Morning (The Battle Begins)
Roundelay of Afternoon (The Battle Continues)
Yellow Interlude
Bad Metal Boogie (The Battle Reaches Its High Point)
Devastation Groove (The Battle is Tragically Lost)

SIDE C

But No, There is Hope!
Golden Music Teacher
Golden Section of Resurrection: Comeback Kings
Perfect People, Perfect Peace
Brilliant Love, Reprise

SIDE D

The Love Suite (parts I–VIII)
Rain of Hopeful Promise on Children of the Stars

'And I think *that* could make a good single,' Syph said, when the final chord (C major) had died away.

'What do you call it?' Crab asked.

'*The Masterpiece* colon *Message from the Golden Music Teacher* subtitle *Tales of Demographic Explosions.* I hear it as kind of "Ride of the Valkyries" meets "Ride a White Swan".'

'Hmm,' said Crab, and nodded. I have never witnessed a more sublime demonstration of deadpan. It was only awe which prevented me from pissing myself. 'What do *you* think?' Crab asked Mono.

'Yeah,' Mono said, playing along. 'I really like the riff for, what was it? Something Interlude.'

'But it's the whole thing,' said Syph. 'That's only a leitmotiv. The three-note structure is repeated emblematically throughout the piece, and it modulates from minor to major through contrasting keys.'

Personally, I thought it sounded like the 'Moonlight Sonata' as played by a doorbell.

'What about you?' asked Crab. He was focussing the full beam of his straight-man genius upon me.

'The Plan,' I said. 'The lyrics mention a Plan. Could you tell me, what *exactly* is the Plan?'

'I, as the Golden Music Teacher, must ask the world to change its ways. The perfect children *can* make perfect peace, but the imperfect children are the battle-bozos. We must gently rise, together, towards the light of intergalactic under-standing. We, by which I mean, "the Bright Ones", must prepare the planet for the journey to eternity. My Masters have told me this. Our feathers must be washed of the clay that holds us down. We are mired in conflict. This is because not enough of humankind is perfected.'

'Who isn't perfect?' I asked, dreading.

'The small yellow races,' replied the Golden Music Teacher. (I was trying very hard not to think of him as my old friend, Syph.) 'That is revealed in the lyrics to Yellow Interlude.'

148

'Aren't the, er, small yellow races more golden than us?' Crab asked.

'No. We are white gold,' said Syph. 'We are the pure.'

'Do you mean Chinese people?' Mono asked. 'I don't have any problem with Chinese people.'

'Chinese. Japanese. Korean . . .'

'Mongolian?' asked Crab, indicating the yurt.

'Yes,' said the Golden Music Teacher. 'Them, too.'

'And you want to kill them?' I asked.

'No. I want to allow them to die. Give them a generation or two. Make it humane, you know.'

'Why *allow* them?'

'They want to, really,' the Golden Music Teacher said. 'That is their purpose, galactically speaking. They make way so that the race of white gold may prove its worth to the Watching Ones. Then the Watching Ones will beat us into beautiful ornaments to adorn their breasts. The Watching Ones have large and shapely breasts.'

'What happened?' I said, looking at Crab and then Mono. 'What happened to him? Where did he go?' I didn't mean outer space.

'No idea,' said Mono.

'It's okay,' said Crab, oddly serene. He was still lying on the circular carpet. 'I can handle it.'

'The Golden Music Teacher will not be handled. I have called a press conference for tomorrow morning –'

'Fuck,' I said.

'I will announce *The Masterpiece* to the world.'

'Do they know about the' – I could hardly say it – 'small yellow part?'

'Of course not. For maximum impact, the Higher Knowledge must be injected directly into the media bloodstream.'

'Exactly,' said Crab. 'You *read* my mind.'

'They read *our* minds all the time,' said the Golden Music Teacher. 'Then they beam us back to us.'

'Like a superpowerful laser,' said Crab.

'I am like a lens,' said the Golden Music Teacher. 'Or a prism. Or a diamond. I can change shape at will.'

'Like a shaman,' said Crab. 'Like Jim Morrison.'

I couldn't believe what Crab was doing, encouraging the lunacy.

'You're going along with this?' I shouted.

Crab gave me a *shut up* look. 'Of course we must spread the great wisdom,' he said, rolling up onto his feet. 'Perhaps we should retire for a while, to let the Great One commune once more with the cosmos.'

'I do feel like I should check in,' said the Golden Music Teacher.

Crab grabbed my arm and pulled me towards the door. Mono followed. 'See you, man,' he said to the Golden Music Teacher.

'It's suicide,' I said, as soon as we were in the elevator. 'It's not even just career suicide. It's *actual* suicide.'

'Don't worry,' said Crab. 'It's never going to happen.' His amazing calm was, I figured, entirely due to not having taken in the absolute shitness of our situation.

'What if he mouths off to twenty music journalists about humanely exterminating China –'

'Relax. Just relax. I'm going out to pay a few visits –'

'To who? To the Masters of the Universe?'

'Yes,' Crab replied. 'You could say that.'

'We have to get him put away,' said Mono. 'He's not well. He can go to that place you went, Crab. Where was it?'

'Later,' said Crab.

'What's your plan?' asked Mono.

The elevator had reached ground-level.

'Trust me,' said Crab.

I drove home.

Maintaining trust in Crab took so much effort that twice I almost drove into oncoming traffic.

When the girls were safely asleep, I told Esther the whole thing, including track-listing – it was scorched into my brain. In reply, she told me to trust Crab.

'But . . .' I said.

'You are safe,' said Esther.

That night, I was never going to sleep. I walked around our house, looking at all the things that were soon to be taken away from me. Although I had spent a lot of time and money trying to overcome my materialism, the thought of losing *everything* still terrified me. When I stopped in on the girls, their sleeping bodies seemed so unprepared for the tsunami of hate they'd have to face, later in life.

I went outside and looked up at the stars – fuckers.

The press conference was set for 7 a.m. The Golden Music Teacher aimed to hit all the morning bulletins.

I got to our management's glassy offices early. Just as I arrived at the front door, a secretary I only vaguely knew was sticking a notice up:

> Today's press conference has unfortunately been cancelled due to ill health. The band wishes to extend its sincere apologies for any inconvenience this may cause.

'What's happened?' I asked.

'Crab just called,' the secretary said. 'From the hospital. He didn't sound all that ill.'

'How *did* he sound?'

She thought for a moment.

'Happy.'

I was there within half an hour.

In a very expensive private room, I found both Syph and Crab lying, side by side, on drips. Crab was awake, watching a breakfast show that – due to him – made no mention of a well-known rock band's cosmic concept album, or its ultra-racist message to the planet.

'And . . . ?' I asked.

'God bless cocaine,' said Crab. 'And God bless acid. And God bless heroin. The Masters of the Universe, who many mistake for humble drug dealers, came through. Cocaine. LSD. Heroin. In that order. Too much, but not *really* too much.'

'Is he still the Golden Music Teacher?' I asked, nodding towards Syph.

'We'll see when he wakes up. I kind of doubt it. We stayed up until four, listening to the Zep and Sabbath. I think by about three a.m. I'd brought him safely over to the dark side – temporarily, of course. Satanism's so much more respectable, in music circles, isn't it?'

Back at home, drained, I tried to apologize once again to Esther for the stupidity of men.

'But it was Crab who saved the world,' she said.

Three weeks later, sitting on a throne of plastic skulls, Syph claimed to have no memory whatsoever of the Golden Music Teacher. His apartment was black as hell. I thought it felt kind of homey.

Mono turned the 'Yellow Interlude' riff into a song called 'When I wasn't Me'.

I still think women rule.

I feel old.

My daughters are – of course of course – a different generation, and things young-me couldn't help but find new and exciting (the first Compact Disc in its display cabinet on the record-store counter – slice of silvery, rainbowy future) are relics that, to them, might as well be Victorian.

I will find it difficult not to try and impress upon them the importance, and even worse the superiority, of these bits of junk.

Not the CDs. The songs on them.

I love pop culture, still, but what if everything I've invested in it was a mistake?

Wouldn't it have been better for me to learn Latin and read the classics, or become an archaeologist and develop a relationship with the *really* old?

They will think me uncool, my daughters, probably using a less uncool word than uncool. Today, if they were tweens, I'd be *so over.* (Unless *so over* is *so over* and something new has popped up to take its place.) It's terrible to know that, because I have a bit of money, they'll end up speaking like spoilt Californians. Everyone speaks like that at the good Vancouver schools, that or like gangsta rappers.

Spoilt – not a concept the kids spend time worrying about.

One night four or five months ago, when they couldn't sleep, I was trying to come up with a new lullaby for them. There's only so many times you can sing Leonard Cohen's 'Suzanne' – and Esther had banned 'Chelsea Hotel No. 2' because of the oral-sex reference. I wanted something long-lasting, something folky – a tribal gift. Halfway through 'Rock-a-bye Baby' I realized how it ended, and stopped dead. I couldn't remember more than the first couple of lines of

'Lavender's Blue'. Is this my culture? What kind of heritage to pass on! Pop and fragments. I couldn't remember what my mother used to sing to me, so I called her up. It was only just gone ten. She told me she couldn't remember, either – then phoned back to say she'd remembered something. 'When you were about five, you used to love "I'd like to buy the world a *Coke*".'

Boy, that dates me. Man, that depresses me.

What do I have? What do I *own*?

Is Leonard Cohen it? The real thing?

Mom called back again, to say that when I was little I'd liked 'Nights in White Satin' and anything by the Mamas and Papas.

'Thank you,' I said, 'that's great. If you think of any more, please don't tell me.'

'I thought you wanted to know.'

'I did. I don't any longer.'

'You sound tired.'

She was right. Tired is how old people sound, because the young are exhausting them. They use us. We buy them stuff for them to lose interest in, quickly.

It's not that I don't want my daughters to make the mistakes I did. It's that I don't want them to make the mistake I *was* – to go with a guy who is the contemporary equivalent of the guy I used to be.

So, should I send them to violin lessons, ban rap music, have a *no tattoos no piercings until 18* rule? Should I install a smoke detector in their bedrooms?

(They are going to be two next week.)

I decided to reconsider Leonard Cohen. What was so bad about him? He wasn't shallow – an advance on buying the world a *Coke*.

When I was thirteen, Cohen was my God. His biography didn't mean much. Born Montreal, 21 September 1934 – that detail-crap. Author of esteemed books of poems with ornate titles, ahem, *Let Us Compare Mythologies*. Not important. All I cared about was the *Songs from a Room* long-player, and the clues it offered a lonely boy of a possible future. I know now that it's bad art whose greatest achievement is to make you envious of the life of its creator. Biggest clue was the back-cover photograph: a bare-bottomed blonde, dressed only in a white towel, seated at a typewriter, at a desk, in a white-painted, shuttered, pale-floorboarded room. Also present were a table, some books, a chessboard, a burnt-down candle-stick, a sheep's skull and a white-sheeted bed. To pick out the important details was not difficult. Here was a woman and here was a bed. The two things could be linked. The woman might get into the bed. The woman might just have gotten out of the bed. And then, above the desk, typed out life-size, perhaps even by *that* typewriter, were the ten song titles. One of them, 'Seems So Long Ago, Nancy', contained a woman's name. Yet somehow the information had reached me that the blonde at the desk was Marianne, not Nancy. On another album, his first, Cohen had bade her farewell – so long, so long ago. This was Cohen's *ex*-girlfriend! Once upon a time, they'd had sex – probably in that bed. (And this did seem distant enough, from me, to be a once-upon-a-time fairy story.) I gazed at the back-cover and was all envy. If Marianne stood up and pulled at that towel, it would drop to the pale floorboards. (Women in Cohen's early songs are more likely than not to get naked, even nuns.) Perhaps, after the photograph was taken, that's exactly what she'd done. Cohen had then placed the camera down on the table, along-side the skull, and they'd had sex – or made love. At thirteen, I was still working on that fine distinction. Cohen, I knew, must have taken the photograph: there was a credit (John Berg) for the cover photo but none for this. To be in that room with that woman and that typewriter and that bed, holding a camera! I wanted it all. It was an injustice that I didn't live Cohen's life. His *ex*-girlfriend! There is no express-ing the glamour of such sadness, when it seems so unattain-able. So long. Past-tense Marianne wore a white towel she could drop, and I wanted that sexual availability for myself. To live in the scent of women no longer girls, women with children by other men. (I'd learnt this information, too: Marianne's son, not pictured, was called Axel.) Emotional complications far beyond those available in my suburb, to thirteen-year-old me – although my parents' generation was deep in the blue tangle of them. Being young is all about wanting to be older. I wasn't Leonard, eye watching shutter go click and Marianne reappear, still smiling, towelled. What more could life hold? What else could I aim for? One thing: to have had it and lost it. Typical for an envy-artist, Cohen's song of total ownership was one of renunciation. With great contempt, 'So Long, Marianne' wasn't even *on* this album. The photographer was already gone from what I might never have. At thirteen-years-old, not confident in my looks, it seemed entirely possible that no woman would ever tell me she could take no more betrayals. I was so far from female embrace (not my mother's), and I missed it so much – the fragrance and softness and cold burning of it. This was where Cohen's other renunciation song, 'Seems So Long Ago, Nancy', came in. That the young woman addressed had worn green stockings was neither here nor there. Bohemianism, in my future lover, would be desirable but I wasn't going to make it a without-which. No, what *really* got my attention was the line saying that Nancy had slept with *everyone*. And if she really *had* done that, then, if *I'd* been around, she would have slept with *me*. This seemed an epic promise. All I had to do was put myself in the vicinity of such women and it would happen. Listening to 'Nancy', I felt a new hope. Pre-viously infinite distances became at least imaginable, astral. Sex, as far as I was concerned, was the moon. Men had been there, young men, some of them I even knew. Romance, however, was Alpha Centauri. And regret, erotic regret, was probably a parallel universe. Yet, learning from my envy of Leonard Cohen, I desired erotic regret far more than I did sex or even romance.

And I sing these songs as *lullabies?*

Not any longer.

Not after I'd thought it through, done a little research.

My daughters weren't called Marianne and Nancy, but imagine if I'd subconsciously insisted.

As a father, what I felt nostalgic for now was my ignorance and my idealism. I longed for my longing because all I had now was *having*. Unless I started having something else: affairs. Which would be having it all and more. I didn't want more. Esther and two daughters was more than enough. I idealized my earlier lacks – and that's what Cohen had done, too. He was such a fake, such a schlockster. It was all a line. He was saying *so long* to Marianne in the hope that, after writing such a sad and catchy song, he'd be attractive to a huge number of new women – all hoping he'd love them and leave them and immortalize them. Poet and novelist wasn't enough. He wanted the more I didn't. And I'm pretty certain he got it: singer-songwriter, modern-day troubadour, ladies' man.

The Cohen of the photograph was, I now knew, the Cohen of the Greek isle of Hydra, 1961–1965. That came before Cohen the Rake. But I wasn't interested in him: I'd been him, stroked the acres of smooth female flesh until my hands were calloused with it. Maybe his total *was* greater than mine; I knew the scented territory. No, it was a different, later Cohen that fascinated me – and almost as much as photographer-Cohen had: monk-Cohen.

In 1996, the cocksman retired up Mount Baldy in Southern California. He went Zen. Entered the monastery.

Now, his biography began to fascinate. Born Montreal. Father dies when he is nine. After a lifetime's sensual indulgence as a touring musician, gets Buddhism. What happened? Someone visit his dressing-room and slip him some beads? He renounces it all. Is ordained as a monk. Is known, get this, as Jikan, 'the Silent One'. And a couple of years later, he's back on the angelic streets of Sin City. And enlightenment? What of that? Carried in his suitcase or left behind?

I wanted to talk with him. People I knew knew people who knew people he knew – Canadians in exile, snow-nostalgists. Messages were sent. Was I sure it wasn't Joni Mitchell I wanted? Two weeks passed. Jikan stayed true to his name.

I wrote Mr Leonard Cohen a letter. One of my people had slipped me his email address, but what I had to say needed heavy laid paper and a smooth-flowing fountain pen. Courteously, I sent it via his management, marked personal. Then, a month later, I re-sent it direct to his home address, an address given me by one of the more sympathetic people my people knew. It was a letter about sensuality and Godhead. He had come down from the mountain. Was there any point me starting to climb it? Flesh of my flesh, daughters two. I live with three women, am outnumbered and loving every hysterical second. Had women, in the end, been a greater nirvana for monk-Cohen than the empty mind?

Jikan remained Jikan.

I took silence as my answer and was content.

Until I happened to find myself in LA with an afternoon free.

I went to his house, which was modest, and looked at the lawn out front. For the first time in years, I felt what fans must feel when approaching me: nerves like I was going to puke through my arse and shit out my nose.

Getting back in the rental car, I tried to calm myself down enough for a second try.

I could see the door, plain enough. There was the doorstep, where I would stand.

But I knew I wasn't capable.

I'd opened my door often enough on People Looking for Answers – opened it whilst thinking maybe this was the pizza delivery boy, or Fed-Ex with those new cymbals I ordered, or anything but fronting up as myself.

How could I expect Lenny shirt-sleeves to be Leonard '*Songs from a Room*' Cohen, on demand?

I of all people should see the unreasonableness of this.

I started the car.

And then I saw him.

He came out the door, let it close and lock behind him, patted his jacket pocket (keys? cigarettes?) and didn't break stride until he'd reached his ride. Leonard fucking Cohen. His eyes were behind dark glasses. This was the ex-monk. Those eyes had looked upon Marianne, through the view-finder. He hadn't replied to my question, my letter. Sincerely, L. Cohen.

The car started up and he pulled past me down the street. Without thinking, I turned the ignition and began following him.

A left, a right, another right, onto the freeway.

Has he seen me?

LA is not a place you want to be tailed.

I'd been followed, too, plenty of times, by People Looking for Answers, and People Angry for No Clear Reason, and People Who Think It's Funny to Follow Minor Celebrities, and People with Cameras and Kids to Feed, and all sorts of other People.

Whatever he did, wherever he went, I'd be disappointed. Unless it was right back to Mount Baldy. Unless he'd just that afternoon thought, *I've made a terrible mistake.* Unless I'd caught the issue of the epiphany. He was probably gone for groceries.

I slowed down and took the next exit ramp.

What if I'd tailed him to Wal-Mart? Would that have been more crushing than if he'd wound up at a fantastic little kosher deli? Or a titty bar? Or his record label?

Soberly, I completed my business in LA.

When I got home, among my mail was a short handwritten note from Leonard. In it, he politely thanked me for my letter. These were deep questions. They took a lot of time, and he was a slow thinker – and an even slower writer, if that were possible. He was sure that when I needed to I'd make the right decisions. How wonderful to have twin daughters.

He liked my band. Good to see some fellow Canadians flying the Old Maple Leaf. If I was ever passing, please to drop by . . .

This was a good man, a man whose songs any father could sing to his daughters.

Again, I sang them.

(. . . drop by, but call first.)

I don't even know if I should record this next bit.

A few weeks earlier, my thoughts had become so Cohen-saturated that I even remembered him whilst changing my daughters' diapers.

Infant sexuality is what I was probably thinking about, really. Their little slits look like boxer's eyes, closed up so much the fight has to be stopped. But although they seem swollen they are not bruised. As I cleaned the mustard-poo off, wiping the cotton-wool in one direction, I thought of whether I would be happy for a young Leonard Cohen to witness the nakedness of a grown-up daughter of mine.

No, not whether I would be *happy*, whether I could *bear* it.

When they were just born, Syph came over and I gave him them to hold, took a few photos. 'So beautiful,' he said, like everyone else. Such an unholy terror, I felt. Those hands of his, and where they'd been, and what they'd done when they got there. Was this fatherhood? It was so violent.

My daughters' cunts. Here, in future, young men I distrust and older men I fear will trespass – or be invited. It's possible the older men may even be older than me. Imagine that.

We don't take bathtime photographs any more, even digital ones, for fear that if someone official gets to see them we'll be arrested as paedophiles. None of that smut on my hard drive. Looking at them, even as I wiped away their practical poo, my eyes felt guilty. I've thought such terrible things about women. The girls who slept with me, the underage-ish ones, wanted to – at least in the sense they were never drugged or physically compelled. But maybe larger forces were angry with them. Maybe it was a sky-high father with thoughts of previous wrongdoing.

Being Jewish, Cohen is big on atonement.

I try to be good, singing.

???

I saw it in a desk-calendar – one of those chunky ones with a quote for every date:

NOVEMBER 26th
Everything not given is lost.

And I was embarrassed to find it so true.

I've read some very respectable books, great works of world literature, which moved me far less.

Forget the fact that the 25th said *Smile and the world smiles with you* and the 27th *A journey of a thousand miles starts with a single step.* I know these both for clichés of corporate spirituality – just the right sort of uplifting sentiments for the hungover office worker, ripping away another yesterday and hoping for some hope. And November 26th – *Everything not given is lost* – is probably no less of a cliché. But, and here's the thing, it was one I'd never heard – that I came to fresh as a new-mown daisy on crisp white snow.

Felled me, that's what it did. Like the good old tree in the forest with no-one around to hear.

For what have I not given? What have I tried to keep on keeping? What have I sought to bury away, and ended up just burying? What have I still to lose?

The date this happened wasn't November 26th, it was some time in May. I had been left alone in one of the offices of our record company, and there was nothing else around to read – apart from other bands' gold and platinum discs, on all four walls.

What I wanted was a quick laugh at some sentimental trash, a little superiority-buzz.

I confess: I ripped November 26th right out of that calendar.

Only afterwards did I wonder what effect this would have on the record-company executive who'd been keeping me waiting. It wasn't that I *liked* him – quite the opposite. He was a knob. Plus, he wouldn't leave one of his real top-selling artistes alone for a second. If he couldn't be there personally, he'd send the most attractive girl in the department across to keep them amused. But maybe the very words he needed to begin the long task of extracting himself from the samsara of knobhood were the ones I'd stolen from him. Eventually, I got to feeling so guilty about the possibility that he would suffer the continued damnation of being a complete knob, however rich, successful and handsome, that I photocopied November 26th and sent it back to him – along with an apology for secretly removing that day from his desk-calendar. I did this, I should say, before the end of October.

Next I heard of it, our management were on at me, really pissed, for carelessly 'if amusingly' interfering with the delicate process of contract renegotiation. Mr Executive, you see, had taken the motto as a coded warning that we felt we weren't being paid (*given*) enough untaxable cash, and that if this situation didn't change then we'd soon be gone (*lost*).

Knob.

I kept November 26th in my wallet, behind the photographs of Esther, our daughters and Ringo Starr's 1964 Ludwig drumkit – all of which are there to keep me honest, keep me safe, and remind me of what I love the most. Faithful *and* truthful.

. . . not given . . .

What did that mean? If I didn't want to lose my family, I had somehow to give it away? To whom? Or didn't Esther and my daughters count, not being *things*? But 'everything', I knew, included things which weren't things. Everything, definitely, included me. And I'd given myself to them. Maybe not enough, though. Esther and I had talked about getting married, after the girls were born, but I never formally asked, and I think Esther was waiting for that. I'd tried to make it so she could be sure of having me, for ever. She and the girls were the only beneficiaries of my will. And, in a way, by giving me children, Esther had given herself to me. But I couldn't be sure I wouldn't lose all three of them.

Gifts are so terrifying.

There are shows I've played where not one single beat was for the audience, for the music itself or for my bandmates – money is what I wanted, and if the promoter had been fool enough to let me, I'd have taken it and left without even *seeing* the stage.

There are relationships I've entered with my exit strategy not only planned but already put into operation. Two-timing two perfectly nice women, as a way of being simultaneously discovered, dumping both and ensuring that neither would come back for more. (Okay, I did this once.)

There are prayers which I thought would make me look good, in front of Buddha. Like I really *did* feel that generous to the rest of the violent world, rather than pleading again and again for those I love to be spared the worst of it. *Oh-mani-padme-humbug.*

. . . is lost . . .

As a young man, in fact as a handsome young prince, the Buddha did something usually done only by bastards: he walked out on his wife and kid.

What he said to them, in no words at all, was *I am more important than you.*

And he *was*, because he was the man who would become, after some while of wandering, the Buddha. But . . .

I never understood this, not properly. That each seeks

enlightenment entirely alone – fine. That the Buddha had to give up everything – okay. That that *everything* included his family – hold it right there.

This was an undeniably cruel act.

I've never read anything about how his abandoned wife got on, or what happened to his disowned baby. Did they gain from the harsh lesson of him leaving? *Unless you give me up, I will be even more lost to you than I am now.* Is he saying that? *If you love me, let me go.* Surely he should have given them his life, as he had pledged to do.

Whatever – it makes it pretty hard to forget that the Buddha, like all men, was from time to time a fucker.

Perhaps that's the point, exactly.

Of course, this took place when he was an unenlightened being – but after he sat under the Bodhi tree and became enlightened and saw whatever he saw, did he go back? Did he apologize?

No – because he must have realized there was no reason to. He had given them his absence; cosmically, seen from the point-and-no-point of view of an enlightened being, this was as good as his presence.

I guess.

But I'm still troubled. What sort of religion would his wife have started? Or his son? Or wouldn't they just have gone off and started a war?

Crab left his family, too, and this isn't the only thing he has in common with the Buddha.

He often sleeps in the open, under trees. But the Buddha's main hang was balmy India/Nepal. Crab is out there for Vancouver autumns. (He's not so dumb as to freeze to death November through February.)

Whenever Crab manages to gather together some material possessions, he ends up giving them all away. Sometimes I accept some of them, just so I can try to give them back when he realizes he's left himself with absolutely nothing.

And most importantly, Crab is a teacher. I don't just mean

guitar lessons, though he has always been humblingly generous with his time – never too busy to show some kid the
tuning for 'Honky Tonk Women' or 'Gimme Shelter'. In
comparison, I have been a miser and a recluse. Making that
Indie-Rock Drumming for Beginners video was no equivalent.

I try not to sentimentalize Crab, or sanctify him, but he
has given everything – not just to the band, to *everyone*, to the
world, to (more accurately) the universe.

He has been our teacher.

I am, in the language of that great neglected band, The
Minutemen, *boozh* (translation: bourgeois). I do not *jam econo*
(translation: travel light), as they would have put it. This
means that, at some point, I must have sold out and become
mersh (translation: commercial).

Every morning, without fail, the fact I own an extremely
good espresso-machine makes me feel suicidal. And it does
this by reminding me that Crab, because he doesn't own
anything, doesn't own an espresso-maker. If he requires coffee,
he steps into a diner – and *if* he requires coffee, it is usually
because he has a definite objective he wishes to achieve, for
which he needs to be sober.

Otherwise, beer. Otherwise, bars and parks.

One average everyday evening, not November 26th, after
the girls were in bed, I tried to explain to Esther about the
desk-calendar. I went the roundabout way, and began by
saying, 'Esther, would you marry me?'

'Of course,' she said, without missing a beat – conver-
sationally, she keeps better time than I do. 'Any time you
want to ask.'

'I thought I just did.'

'Try again.' She said this with a true smile. Her words look
harsh, written down, but didn't sound that way.

'I don't get it,' I said.

'Yes, I *would* marry you. Under certain circumstances.'

'What circumstances?'

'Well, first you've got to ask . . .'

'Would you be my wife?'

'I *would.*'

'Do you want to get married?'

'I do.'

'So, have I asked you yet?'

'No. But you're closer than you were. I'm sure you'll get there in the end.'

I understood.

'Esther, *will* you marry me?'

'That's right.'

'Will you?'

'In the right circumstances.'

'What circumstances?' I asked again.

Our main downstairs living room – the family room – is in a style Esther calls 'please God anything but minimal'. One wall is framed photographs of people we like, the opposite is pieces of fabric that Esther likes, which leaves the mantelpiece with the large painting above it and a wall of glass leading out, when slid back, into our garden. The large painting is by me, as Esther thought I should try it at least once. (Once is exactly how many times I'm going to leave it at.) We have a big squishy sofa which is guilt-makingly leather. And I am half-responsible for choosing it. On either side of this, to make things worse, are matching chairs. Mostly, I graduate towards the left-hand one. Esther, without wishing to pun, is usually seated in the right.

Esther asked, 'Do you want to marry me?'

'Of course, or else I wouldn't have asked.'

'But why are you asking me *now*? Have you been having an affair?'

I don't know why I hesitated before saying, 'No.' I hadn't even flirted with the idea of another woman since the girls were born.

'There's something . . .'

And finally, as I'd known all along it would, the conversation came round to the desk-calendar. (This is how compatible Esther and I are.) I pulled November 26th out of my wallet. It was the first time I'd shown it to anyone. 'Don't laugh,' I said.

Esther read the words carefully, then laughed. 'Sorry,' she said. 'I was really trying not to.'

'I am terrified by this, as a thought. I don't know how to work my way around it.'

'Through it, I think you mean.'

'Are we still getting married?'

'Because of this?'

'You could say that.'

'Terror is not a good basis for marriage.'

'Isn't it the only basis?'

Esther stood up and went into the kitchen. For one terrible moment, I thought she was heading towards the espresso-maker. I didn't want to complicate matters even further by mentioning my feelings about that. But, no, she was just running a glass of water. In this way, with great simplicity, and also giving me time to think my way a little further *through* my stupidity, Esther answered my question.

She waited until she had sat down before she provided a gloss. 'I'm not in the least bit scared.'

'You're not?'

She shook her head and took a sip. For some reason, it was the sip which made me believe her.

'The girls could die,' I said.

'Yes,' Esther said.

'They could die horribly.'

'Mmm.'

'And it could be my fault.'

'That is true.'

She was forcing it all out – every last bit.

'It could be *your* fault,' I said.

'I'm still not scared.'

'How can you not be?'

'Because you are.'

169

'What? So, you delegate the existential angst to me. I sub-contract –'

'No. Because if we both were, life would be unbearable. I made a practical decision. Your angst is more productive than mine. It makes you a better drummer. It makes you a drummer period.'

'You can't just *decide* not to wake up pissing yourself with fear. I think of horrible things . . .'

'So do I. But I don't let them horrify me. I go on.'

'Could I . . . ?' I asked, meaning take a sip of her water. My sip was more like a gulp. Afterwards, I said, 'You're protecting me.'

'More myself. And even more the girls. Enough horror in the house could probably kill them.'

'It's like we're already married, and you're doing what I should really be doing.'

'You do more than enough.'

'What do you think of that, then?' November 26th was still in her hands – she'd carried it into the kitchen and back.

'It's cheesy, a little simplistic.'

'How do I *not* lose you?' My tone was unashamedly pleading.

'You keep me.'

'But how do I do that?'

'You've done it so far.'

'If we get married, things won't have to change.'

'*If* . . . ?'

'*When*, then.'

'I still haven't said yes.'

'I thought you did.'

'We don't *need* to get married.'

'We just want to,' I said. 'I want to.'

'Yes,' said Esther. 'I think you probably do.'

She picked up the glass of water and put down November 26th.

'Does that mean the conversation is over?' I asked.

'No,' said Esther, and walked out into the garden.

There was moonlight. We have a very big lawn. Strangely, this doesn't make me feel as bad as the espresso-machine does. I went to join Esther. We strolled.

After a while, she said, 'If the girls die, I will mourn them.' And then, after a significant pause, she added, '*If.*'

I put my arm around her. It fit.

'You mean don't mourn things which aren't dead. Don't mourn your own life.'

'Now *that* would be a good thing to put in a calendar,' she said.

'Tell me how I should ask you to marry me.'

'Oh, I think you know well enough,' she said.

And it turned out that I did.

The next day I was checking, for the third time, that I'd strapped the girls safely in the back of our station wagon.

'Yes,' said Esther, coming up behind me. 'I will.'

It took me only a moment to realize where I was: engaged.

We found the nearest marriage commissioner, phoned them, asked for the next available date.

Crab was best man.

I gave him November 26th, framed, as a souvenir. He kept it, of course – by giving it away to the first person he could find.

There is still an espresso-maker in our kitchen, but I had one of our lawyers draw up an extensive document assigning the full moral responsibility for it to Esther.

She drinks water.

SCOTLAND

I went to Barcelona, Bucharest, Hong Kong, Melbourne, Perth, Buenos Aires, then returned home.

Esther believed I was the same; I knew I wasn't, but didn't know exactly how I'd changed.

Nothing had happened during the promotional tour – no significant encounters had taken place; no story-worthy incidents; no more girls or kids or monks.

But something changed in me.

What it was only became obvious when they asked me to go away again: I'd finally had enough.

Enough Club Class passenger-lounge complimentary aromatized wafer biscuits; enough last-bag-to-arrive-on-the-carousel; enough misspelt versions of my name awaiting me just beyond immigration; enough radio interviews where the hairy DJ has been deludedly expecting and heavily trailing Syph; enough tipsy PAs telling me how they envy creatives like myself – how that's what their boyfriend does, when he's not designing corporate websites; enough eyes of expectation in faces of delight wobbling on bodies with which I am familiar, typically if not specifically; enough phonecalls long-distance to tell Esther where I've been; enough of Sarah and Grace crying in the background, and not coming to the phone to talk to me; enough of how good I am at so many things my younger self would have hated my present self for being good at: meet'n'greeting, recording stacks of station idents for W-ANK and K-RUD, jamming with local percussionists (well, that's not so bad), accepting well-intentioned compliments which are actually vicious put-downs ('I really love the B-side to your second single – I think it's the best thing you'll ever do').

I'd had enough of that goo-goo stuff, enough already, enough *enough*.

Not enough for the moment, enough for good.

When I told Esther, beautiful known wrinkles at the corners of her eyes, my home in this world, she was delighted and terrified. (She was also standing at the breakfast bar with a mouth full of yogurt and granola – I picked my moment.) The cause of both emotions was the same: I'd be around the house a whole lot more.

I called a band meeting, usual place, usual booth, early enough in the day for Crab to be conscious if not sober – and they didn't take me seriously. (It wasn't like it hadn't happened before.)

'Anyway,' said Syph, across a double espresso, 'I want to go back to Japan next year. My rope-mistress is expecting me.'

'Don't believe me,' I said. 'Just watch. I'll be the empty seat on the plane, next time you fly out. This is it. I'm done. No longer participating. Over.'

'And the new album,' asked Crab. 'What about that?'

'As long as we record it at a studio within driving distance of my house – and I don't mean Seattle.'

'That's cool with me,' said Mono, who hated to leave Major in either Northern Ontario or Vancouver.

Syph gave me a look of dominance.

'Just watch me,' I said. 'I'm not there.'

And three months later, I wasn't. An air-ticket to Tokyo was in the trashbag at the bottom of the drive. The answering machine was flashing like a cherry-top cop-car in hot pursuit. I'd given my cellphone to the girls to play with. 'Hello, this is Barbie,' they said, to anyone who rang. 'What would you like to wear today?'

When the management arrived, I spoke to them through the front door.

'Well, get another drummer. Good-bye.'

Twenty-four hours later, they'd flown in Yoyo (hi Yoyo!) to plead from the fans' perspective: a sneaky trick.

I gave her coffee, bagels and a long explanation, which she posted on the website: 'He seems to be full of strong decision. Very proud, like a man. We must respect him even as we are sad too. See you soon, drummer boy.'

After a week, the management faxed me a grossly shitty legal document, fifty pages of it, which they'd had some mafia lawyer draw up. They claimed to own my Vancouver house – and have stakes in both my other properties (New York apartment, log cabin up North). My marriage, they stated, was in breach of contract – because I hadn't informed them of it in advance. If I didn't fulfil my obligations, see Coda A, paragraphs 1 to 33, they would be left with no option badda-badda-badda but recourse to the judicial system.

I called Syph and told him how disappointed I was, slowly and calmly.

'Come back. It solves everything,' he said. 'We miss you. This new guy, he's technically way better than you, but – just come back.'

'I haven't *gone* anywhere,' I said. 'You have.'

'That's a lie. Moving is our staying still.'

Wasn't that the truth?

'You saw the empty seat,' I said. 'Did you believe me then?'

'We believe you – we believe you. You are a strong, powerful, independent-minded motherfucker. Now fall in line.'

'I love you,' I said. 'Use a condom. Goodbye.'

Then I paid a visit to the most expensive lawyer I'd ever heard of and instructed her to terminate with extreme prejudice.

Her secretary had ordered me an infusion of mint leaves, whilst I waited. It tasted so delicious it was almost worth the fees for an hour of the woman's time.

'You have nothing to worry about,' she said as I sipped.

'I know that,' I said.

She smiled and offered me another drink.

When I got back home, after a long, happy trip to the

record store, there was a message from Syph on the answering machine. He was sobbing. Counter-suing, for some reason, had always upset him. 'You didn't have to start fucking World War Three,' he said.

A fax came through from the mafia lawyers. 'The band *okay* has dispensed with our company's services.'

If I wanted to, I could grant myself the illusion of being free at last, free at last.

For a couple of weeks, the girls climbed all over me on the couch and told me that everything I thought was wrong and everything I said was stupid, and I agreed.

'Let's go away,' Esther suggested, when she'd taken a good, assessing look at me and my TV-eyes.

'I can't fly,' I said. 'They'd crucify me.'

'Fine,' she said. 'We don't fly.'

Brochures arrived.

We took a Caribbean cruise, after a flight to Florida: I compromised.

On board ship, the girls invented their own new game, under-the-table-tennis – which kept them happy all day.

The map of headless-legless-chicken-shaped Barbados showed a place called Scotland. We drove up there in a rented Moke, drinking *Coke*. It was quiet – a shaggy craggy hillside. There was a shack available. If we stayed, the girls could consumer-detox (no more pink purchases), I could gibber in my own sweet way, and Esther could walk round in bare feet looking holy. So we ditched the cruise and bought more insect-repellent.

Sitting on a deckchair looking out over the rough Atlantic, where surfers were patient and sometimes rewarded, I tried to relax.

Couldn't.

Two days went by.

Still couldn't.

'Come and talk to me,' I shouted to Esther after she'd put the girls to bed.

But when she sat down, cross-legged in the doorway, we stalled after about five minutes.

'Does my life have too little resistance?' I asked.

'With those two?' she said.

'Shall we try for a boy?'

She hesitated but then said, 'No.'

'Why not?'

'I like the gender imbalance. I like seeing my feet – and eating anything.'

'You eat hardly anything.'

'But I can eat whatever of it I want.'

'You are beautiful.' And then, a little later. 'I feel wrong. My head feels wrong.'

'You need to do something – you can't do nothing.'

'I have no transferable skills. When the world ends, who's going to want a drummer?'

'The world has ended. Here we are.'

'Really?'

'Well, you seem to think so,' she said.

Grace started to cry in her sleep, and Esther went to comfort her. She always did this. I'd tried, failed. When the girls were learning to be comforted, I wasn't there to learn how to do it.

Twilight came and we resumed our conversation, drinking white rum – brewed less than nine miles away (that's how long the island is).

'You want a challenge?' said Esther. 'Be a good father.'

'Shalom,' I said, my usual greeting to her Jewish mother persona. 'Am I not trying – by quitting touring?'

'Don't congratulate yourself too much. That decision was mostly selfish.'

'If we had another baby, it might be a girl.'

'You'd probably leave us.'

'Always outnumbered, always outgunned.'

I got up from the deckchair and joined her in the doorway – it was just wide enough for our two sets of hips.

I asked: 'Is it inevitable that as we get older we get sadder?'
She didn't answer.

'I feel I did things better when I didn't know so much about them.'

The sky was the colour of amethyst. Around us, the shadows were making noises of insects as big as small animals. In one of the shacks a little nearer the water, music started up. It was not by *okay*. Neither was it surf music. And neither had it been made on the tropical island paradise of Barbados. It was American hip-hop. We sat and listened. After a while, they turned the volume up full.

'It'll wake the girls,' Esther said.

'Hold it,' I said. 'I recognize that.'

'Will you go and tell them to shut it off?'

'It's me,' I said. 'I've been sampled. They've sampled me – my beats.'

'Really?' Esther said.

'"Holding",' I said, naming the track off our second-last album. I'd been pleased with that break – it sounded like I was playing backwards, even though I wasn't.

'Oh yeah,' said Esther, and smiled. I love her – she's my happy. 'Go and introduce yourself, then ask them to turn it down.'

She went inside to check on the girls.

I picked up the bottle, still half full, and ambled down the hill. My limbs moved in a more Barbadian way. Hey, I wasn't some washed-up indie honky – I was down with tha mutha-fuckin' MC Whoever.

The surfer shack was smaller than ours, funkier. Up five crooked wooden steps, the door was open and a low light shone amber.

'Hey,' I said, and rapped my knuckles on the threshold. 'Hello?'

Through a beaded curtain I saw buttocks rising and falling, female hands cupping and pulling; I saw beaded dreadlocks swaying and bright blue fingernails digging; I saw very young firm smooth tanned Caucasian flesh, dark brown above and golden below.

'Oh, I'm sorry,' I said.

Their rhythm skipped.

I turned away, wanting to get into the dark before they made it to the door.

'Whu?' the young man shouted. But I didn't hear him coming after me.

I decided to take the long way back to our shack. The music went quiet whilst I walked along the beach, feet in the cold sea.

Esther was asleep when I got back.

Next morning, down on the beach, I saw Dreadlocks carrying his board out of the waves. Blue Fingernails, who looked about eighteen, was sitting in the shade of a tree, watching him and breastfeeding a tiny baby. There was a burnt-out campfire beside her, with crushed cans encircling it.

Esther and the girls came down to join me, and I knew I wouldn't have to make any introductions myself.

'How old is the baby?' asked Sarah, running straight over. 'Can we hold him?'

'Sure,' said Fingernails, 'when I'm finished.'

'How old is he?' Esther asked.

'Two months tomorrow.'

'Hi,' I said, and shook Dreadlocks' hand. 'Congratulations. These are ours. Sarah. Grace.'

His hand was still salty-wet. He undid the elasticated band linking his leg to the board. Then he said: 'Craigie, Jenny and Boo.'

'He doesn't have a proper name yet,' said Jenny.

'Your accent,' said Esther.

'Scottish,' Jenny said. 'That's one of the reasons we're here. Who wants to hold him first?'

They both did, but we made them take turns. The baby's chin was still milky and Jenny took her time about putting her nipple away.

'Look at him stretch,' said Grace.

'Was I like that?' asked Sarah.

We became holiday-friends.

I could tell that Esther thought Jenny was wonderful; I envied Craigie – envied him his body, the surfing and Jenny.

They came round for dinner that night, bringing warm rum (no fridge) and baby Boo.

After we'd finished eating, I put the girls to bed. They resisted, wanting Mummy tuck-in, but this was the new fifty-fifty regime. In the end, after a yowling half-hour, sleep took them.

'We heard your music last night,' said Esther, doing my detective work for me.

'Was it too loud?' asked Jenny. 'I said it was too loud.' The baby was asleep in her arms.

Neither of us wanted to say anything.

'Sorry,' said Craigie, 'we'll keep it down.' He was very young to be a father – a good father, better than me. But they lived in a shack without a fridge, and he surfed all day long. How good a father was that?

There's always an atmosphere of sweet panic around very young parents, even if they themselves don't feel it. *Keep life away from them*, everyone thinks, *keep them safe from realizing what they've lost*. For the first time ever, I felt grandparental emotions.

'What album was it?' Esther asked. 'Only . . .' And then she explained who I was and what I did. Tssk-Boom-Tssk-Tssk.

Jenny looked doubtful, but a moment later said: 'I recognize you.'

'It's not an album,' said Craigie. 'It's a mix-CD someone gave us in New York. Doesn't even have a track listing.'

'Can I borrow it?' I asked.

'I can burn you a copy,' said Craigie.

I must have looked surprised.

'I have my laptop,' he said.

'No fridge,' said Jenny, 'but email.'

'Satellite phone,' Craigie explained. 'If you want to call anyone ...'

'Definitely not,' said Esther. 'But thank you.'

Boo started to wake with animal stretches. Jenny fed him. I saw Esther's look. I was not mistaken.

'I've been thinking about that baby,' she said, when we were in bed later on.

'The boy?' I asked.

'The girl,' she said.

'As long as it's not twins,' I said.

We tried to keep it quiet.

The CD was slipped under our door the following morning.

I borrowed the girls' CD-player and listened to myself coming out of the pink speakers, via who knows where.

'Don't sue them,' said Esther, meaning the rappers.

'What makes you think I'm going to sue them?'

'Mint tea?' she said – I'd told her all about it.

'Not even for that,' I said.

I listened to the track again. It was good enough to be a hit. Perhaps it already was, underground.

'I'm the new funky drummer,' I said, buzzed.

'It's good,' said Esther. 'We're going to the beach.'

I listened a couple more times then went to join them.

When Craigie came out of the waves, after catching a couple of monster rides, he sat down beside me and accepted a beer. I could feel his coldness and salt-wetness.

'I saw you,' he said quietly. 'The first night when you knocked. Don't think I didn't see you. There's a little mirror at the top of the bed.'

'I didn't watch for long.'

He looked at me sideways. 'But you watched,' he said.

'I watched,' I said.

He went back to looking at the sea.

We stayed another two weeks. Craigie and family moved

on before that – the surf, they'd heard, was up off Hawaii.

As soon as I got home, I had someone start tracking down whoever had used the 'Holding' sample.

In a week, they came back to me with a name and a cellphone number. I made my plan, checked with Esther, dialled.

'Yo-wassup?'

I explained who I was, why I was calling – that I was flattered he'd liked my beats enough to sample them. I stressed that I wanted nothing from him.

'How much you don't want?' he asked.

'No, truly,' I said. 'I'm just pleased I'm still relevant in some way – however tangential.'

'Yeah,' he said.

I'd lost him already.

'Can we meet up?'

'Sure, man.'

He lived in Manhattan.

I suggested a place I thought we'd both be comfortable, Starbucks near Times Square.

'Four o'clock, Thursday.'

'Yeah, sure.'

I knew he wouldn't show, but I flew down, stayed Wednesday night in a hotel that made me feel incredibly white and unstreet.

At four o'clock precisely, a man walked up to my half-hour-occupied sofa in Starbucks. He wasn't the man I'd spoken to on the phone. I knew because that sweet, light voice would never come from this body – from his *amount* of body, vertically and horizontally. They call them body-guards but his was a body-weapon, tactical, nuclear. Big Boy.

'You him?' he asked. 'You him the drummer?'

He was carrying a new briefcase.

'Yes,' I said.

'He ain't coming. This here's for you.'

The suitcase was placed in front of me.

'Don't be calling him again, or we come and take it back. You got yours, now.'

'I just want to say thank you,' I said. I knew what was in the briefcase – pretty sure. To within the nearest ten thousand. 'That's all I want. I don't want this.'

Big Boy kept going, and when he went out the door it was as if the room had lost a wall.

I cracked the briefcase.

I'd been right, to within the nearest ten thousand. It was a very generous settlement, though infinitely less generous than the handshake and smile and musicianly conversation I'd been hoping for. I'd needed that so much more than I needed this.

In sadness, I walked out of Starbucks, taking the briefcase. I could have left it behind, to change a barista's life, but I didn't. I could have given it to the next needy person I came across, but I didn't. I took it to a large bank where I have an account.

It was only when I was standing in line that I looked down at the carpet and realized what I should do. This was the same pattern carpet as in our record company's corporate headquarters.

Outside the bank, I gave half the dollars to the first needy person I saw and the other, with the briefcase, to the guy working the till at Starbucks.

Two months later, the song made it to Number One on the Billboard Hot 100.

okay's highest position was seven, and that had been six years previous.

Big Boy was there in the video, sipping Cristal, enjoying a slo-mo lapdance, nodding sagely to the beat.

My beat.

Maybe I'd made a mistake by quitting.

LA

There's this moment – and if you're lucky enough to be in a half-decent band, you'll know it.

It comes when you're playing a gig, can be near the start but never right at the start, can be during an encore, but usually it comes halfway through the second verse of one of your best songs, for some reason not your *very* best.

You stand there, playing whatever instrument you play, and at the same time you're able to sit way way the fuck out towards the very back of your mind – and you're able to watch everything around you.

The music isn't exactly playing itself, but during that moment it feels as if it could, possibly, with one more push.

And sometimes, just then, when this is upon me, someone else in the band will feel the exact same thing at the exact same moment, and they'll turn their back on the audience, and we'll exchange a glance that says it all.

And after this moment, whether there's been a glance or not, what I always feel is best is to look out into the audience – if the lighting allows – and find someone there who saw the glance and understood just what it meant: that this, for us, isn't just another gig, this is the very reason we go through all the other shit.

There is a moment – I know there is a moment; I remember it pretty well, it's just, it's been so long since I've experienced it, since I've made any kind of eye-contact with another member of *okay*. (Our image doesn't exactly require us to be chummy-chummy. I know that certain fansites have compiled lists of the gigs we broke off halfway through, after throwing our instruments at one another's feet or heads.)

This, the above, is why I thought it was time to tour again – not, I repeat, not for the money; there is enough of that, given our back catalogue and the eventual decision to let them use 'Sea-Song $^{\#}3$' to advertise that cranberry juice.

No, I wanted to feel the moment, be in it, and then do a little dance around its precinct.

I'm thirty-nine now, and I've only got a limited number of little dances left – or a limited time in which to dance them, without loss of dignity. (Dignity, surprisingly, is important to me – even the controlled loss of it: children bring this upon one.)

When I dance these days bits of me move that never used to, because they were never there, or because they were more securely attached.

I don't want to be an embarrassment to anyone, least of all my daughters, who will see the footage when they grow up, and already like some of our records (the early ones, the little bastards) – but I do need, for what feels like the last time, in California-speak, to reconnect.

And so I called Syph, and I called him, and I called again, and after a week, when he probably thought I was his dealer, he picked up.

'Hey,' he said, a *Hey* which seemed to go on for at least ten seconds.

Although we are famous together, and I am one quarter of the reason he is ten times more famous than I am, it took me a minute to get him to show any comprehension of who I was.

'Oh,' he said. 'Hi.' He wasn't unfriendly, he was just speaking long-distance, and not to me, to his own mouth: I could tell; I knew him and his drugmoods well enough. It was antidepressants with God knows what layered on top: drugs of focus, drugs of obliteration – a careful balance that no longer worked, certainly not for me, probably not for him.

I explained what I was thinking – a tour of smaller venues – and Syph didn't say no: whether he'd still remember this conversation the time after the next time he lost consciousness ... I decided to fax him a reminder, then called the others.

Mono was out of the house, probably fishing with Major. Since she quit the cosmetics counter and moved into his lakeside shack, that's mostly what they've done. I left a message on his machine, faxed, emailed and wrote him a letter on fluorescent paper, just so I could be sure.

Crab wasn't easy to get, either. I tried calling but his phone just rang and rang. Eventually, I went down to his neighbourhood bar – and there he was. Getting his agreement wasn't hard. He lives for the road and dies without it. 'I'll be there,' he said, before I'd even said where.

LA – two weeks later. Crab having taken the red-eye, gone to hang out with Syph and try to get him both straight and in the mood. Mono having had the letter, and the fact that he owned an answering machine, a fax and a computer, drawn to his attention by the delightful Major. Perhaps she wanted him out of the house. Now I see what made Syph fall for her – she's a solid woman. She'd put any man right, even Syph.

Not like the matchstick I found him with when I arrived at his off-Mulholland (please, don't do it, Syph – but I just love the view) mansion. I can never remember who it used to belong to, but they were very famous and waited till they'd moved out before drinking themselves to death. Syph wasn't intending to make the same mistake. The windows were painted black, I saw from the outside, and also covered with tinfoil, I saw when I cleared a space on the couch and sat down – very grateful not to have spiked myself on a needle, of which there were many. I hadn't known it was this bad. Crackhouse chic – burns up some of the walls, Jackson Pollocks of dried blood, a sea of takeout containers, mice. It can be a terrible thing, when the cheques keep coming in without you having to leave the house. Syph was wearing the darkest pair of glasses I've ever seen.

I remembered wanting the moment back, but I also wanted to save my friend from himself, from the matchstick girl, the Mexican with the Virgin of Guadeloupe white-sparkling on his chest.

Crab had got Syph onto the JD, so he was at least not raging. Whilst I talked, he did what passes with a lead-singer for listening: wait for the sentences that include his name and then follow the content from then until the next period is reached. I had long known how to deal with this, and so began every other sentence with, 'If Syph agrees . . .' or 'Syph, of course, is important here for . . .' This pisses both the others off, but they know it has to be done – otherwise decisions are reached that Syph later claims never to have been consulted about. Legally, this causes problems; worst of all was the cranberry juice ad.

I told Syph that Syph had been really fired up by the idea of a small-scale tour, first time I called Syph, and Syph seemed to believe me. The other two knew I was lying but didn't mind; checking with them later, I confirmed that, seeing the state our old friend was in, they'd decided to join me on my mercy mission: get him road-ready, get him away from all the jewel-encrusted amigos and matchgirls.

'We'll just turn up in a van,' I said. 'Let the college radio station hear about it, accidentally, a few hours before. Appear under a different name, play covers, or hardcore versions of our songs, or whatever the fuck we want.'

'Whatever the fuck we want,' said Syph, with a smile, then nodded off. I'd forgotten to include his name in those last few sentences.

We had made a start. The following afternoon, the band reconvened. Syph was very different – completely lucid, focused, aggressive and wanting to be in charge. From what he said, it appeared he now believed that he'd called us together, that the small-scale tour was his idea and that, out of the other three, I was the one being obstructive.

'Er, Syph . . .' said Mono, but I shook my head at him. Although he was delusional, this was fine – I didn't mind Syph beating up on me; better that than dying before our eyes.

Syph had been up all night. Our management, who I was interested to find were still interested in us, had taken an early morning flight over from New York – were due to arrive within an hour. Good old Tony and Jordan were long gone. This latest pair were far worse – straight out of *The Matrix*.

'They'll deal with all the shit,' said Syph, who hadn't sat down once since we arrived. 'The bookings, the fees, the equipment.'

'Of course they will,' Mono said. 'That's their job.'

'And we can just . . .' said Crab. He closed his eyes, nodded and mimed a descending bass part that I think I recognized.

'Fucking *exactly*,' screeched Syph. 'They can talk, we can rock!'

I remembered a time, long ago, when we only used the work *rock* ironically – verb or noun, it didn't matter; the word referred to something bands did to please fans who made evil fingers back at them. When I looked at Syph, now on the point of raging, I realized what a Monster of Rock really was. I also realized exactly what kind of price, in terms of personal humiliation, I was going to have to pay to save Syph's life – or temporarily delay his death, long enough to give him a choice to choose it, again. The management should be doing all this.

The management arrived. They talked almost exclusively to Syph, and once they were over the disappointment of not making the maximum amount of money possible, they began to agree with everything he said. Weirdly, Syph gave them my speech of the day before, about why we should do this tour – word for fucking word. I didn't think he had that kind of memory left. Mono looked at me and shook his head, Crab didn't. They nodded and smiled and said *absolutely* and sipped drinks that contained no caffeine.

'We need somewhere to rehearse,' said Syph, and one of them made a note in his palm.

*

Five days later, we were in some purpose-built rehearsal facility with everything we might want – especially everything Syph might want. Heavy men with devotional jewellery came and went throughout the afternoon, and Syph spoke to them in a unisex toilet with more horizontal than vertical mirrors.

'It's comfortable,' said Mono, lying on a long leather couch. I didn't know whether he meant the couch, the studios or our life in general.

'How's Major?' I asked.

'Pissed,' he said. 'But I had to come. It's what I do, isn't it?'

'I thought you caught fish,' said Crab.

'Or not,' I said.

'Or not,' said Mono. 'How are the girls?'

'They rock,' I said, ironically, and was glad to see the other two smile. It was bizarre we hadn't had this conversation the moment we saw one another. Since the last meeting, we hadn't hung out much; we knew that, if we were going to be touring soon, time alone would be a rarity.

'How's Ginger?' I asked. Ginger was Crab's on-off girl-friend. On when she was out of rehab.

'In a wheelchair,' he replied.

Just then, Syph banged out of the bathroom. 'Okay,' he shrieked, 'let's rock'n'roll!'

We picked ourselves up and moved slowly across to our instruments. I have to say, it was good to be reunited with our old equipment. It had been a year and a half. My kit had been lovingly treated by some hi-grade drum-tech – the last I'd seen of it, it was scattered across the stage of some arena. I've never trashed my instrument before, but it was the end of the tour and God did I need the release.

From the moment the bass intro to the first song started up, we were *okay* again. No matter how many sessions I do with other musicians (it pays well), there is something fated about how we work together – as a rhythm section, as a band, as a sound. I looked around for someone to make eye-contact with, but Mono and Crab were entirely heads-down no-

nonsense boogie – and Syph was working an imaginary audience.

We played through our setlist, with smiles, jokes and sips from *Cokes* in between. Syph only went to the bathroom twice, and we accommodated this by jamming whilst he was away and kicking into fast numbers the moment he came back through the door, raging. That's us: part-band, part-nurse.

I tried to ignore the management, who stood somewhere off to our left – nodding, as if they liked music. We sacked our first manager because he wasn't getting us bookings on television, and never since had we dealt with anyone in possession of an undamned soul, not even Tony and Jordan. Oh, we made so many mistakes – and this, I was beginning to feel, was another of them.

'Come round to my room,' I whispered to Mono and Crab at the end of the rehearsal, 'about one o'clock.' We were all staying in the same hotel, so they didn't have to cross town or anything.

'What is it?' said Crab, who joined me and Mono around quarter after two. Mono, thank God, hadn't asked me anything – I think he knew already. We had just sat and watched a movie, buddies.

'I don't think we should tour,' I said.

'The fuck, man,' Crab said.

'It won't help,' I said.

'I agree,' said Mono.

'The tour was your idea,' said Crab.

'It was,' I said. 'But this' – I gestured around the tasteful beige interior and out over the grid of LA lights – 'this wasn't.'

Crab said, 'Yes, but –'

And Mono said, 'Clap is right. We're not helping Syph. This isn't what he needs. It's turning into a monster already.'

'*He's* turning into a monster.'

*

After the rehearsal, we had gone back to Syph's house to celebrate. Without him making a single call, people began to arrive for the party, none of them had to ask where the bathroom was, and by the time I left, about a hundred were there. I was surprised Crab had remembered our meeting, or thought it urgent enough to attend. Perhaps there was something still in there.

'I don't care,' said Crab. 'I just want to play.'

'So do I,' I said. 'That's why I started this – if you remember. But we've lost that before we've even started. We can't just do anything any more.'

'We're not real,' said Mono. 'We've stopped being real. This isn't real.'

'It's true,' I said. He had put it too well – it was the sort of comment that changes your life. These days, I tried to avoid hearing those. It's been changed enough already, thank you very much.

'Well, fuck, yeah, hey, man, we're keeping it real for our brothers on the street.' Crab was more drunk or something than I'd noticed. 'We were never *real*.'

'We tried to be,' said Mono. 'At least, I thought we tried. What have we got left to be true to?'

Crab said: 'The music. The fans.' Because it was something he would say in an interview, we knew it was a lie.

'Each other,' I said. Mono had been saying everything I'd meant to say, and better than I could have said it, right now. Major had trained him well. I needed to put in at least one comment that went in advance of him.

'We are,' said Crab.

'Syph needs help,' said Mono. 'He doesn't need more drugs and fun. He needs to lead a very boring life, supervised by people who are paid lots of money to make him forget he's bored.'

'We can talk to him,' said Crab.

'God can talk to him, perhaps,' said Mono. 'He won't listen to anyone else.'

'So it's all over. We just pack up and go home and wait for this to happen again in a year's time.'

'No,' Mono said. 'We stay here – at least, one of us stays here to be around Syph. We try to get him through.'

'Yes,' I said. 'That's what we should do.'

After a long while, Crab said: 'I disagree.' Then he walked out.

Mono and I stayed in my room and decided to do what needed to be done.

The management had been partying with Syph, or pretending to party, but they were up and bright at ten o'clock when Mono and I made a surprise visit to their LA office. We explained our position to them, and watched them cope first of all with the idea that we might be important enough to interfere with their plans (a three-month itinerary already roughed out on the wall), then with the fact we were asking them to behave like responsible adults and finally that there were very good reasons, even of profit, why they had to admit we were right. They agreed to nothing, formally – but they said they'd see what they could do. We left, aware we'd have to fire them pretty soon, and that it would take money and lawyers and more money.

We went for lunch, then drove to the rehearsal rooms together. Mono had rented a Mustang of some sort, I don't know cars. It was red and made a boom of blissful bass. The sun was shining in a blue sky on grey roads and off-white buildings. I wasn't tempted for a moment.

In the parking lot was an ambulance. We ran towards it, expecting to find Syph in a coma.

We'd only got about halfway there when two men got out of the cab, walked round and opened the back doors of the ambulance.

It was Syph, on a gurney but fully conscious – raving. Beside him, crying, was the matchgirl.

'No,' she said.

'What's this?' asked Mono.

'Hi,' said Syph, pushed up onto an elbow.

'He refused to go to hospital,' Matchgirl said. 'He made them bring us here.'

'Rock'n'roll,' Syph said, and grinned – his eyelids were twitching, there was no flesh on his face.

'Is this true?' Mono asked one of the ambulance guys.

'He said to bring him here. He said he felt fine.'

'Half an hour ago, he stopped breathing,' the girl said.

'I think I'm going to write a song about it,' Syph said. 'I've got the chorus.'

The management came out through reception, followed by Crab. 'What's going on here?' the management asked.

'And you brought him here?' said Mono, very angry.

'He insisted,' said the same ambulance guy. 'And he promised us tickets.'

'What if he died?' I asked. 'Your tickets wouldn't be much good then.'

The ambulance guy smiled as if he knew better, which he probably did.

'I'm not going to die,' said Syph. 'I just want to go and play some music.'

'Hey, man,' said Crab, 'are you okay?'

'Never better,' said Syph. 'Breezy.' He sniggered. 'Can I have some more of that oxygen?'

The matchgirl put her huge face in her huge hands and her tiny body bounced with sobs.

I turned to the management. 'He needs to go to the hospital, immediately.'

'We need to think about this,' said one of the management.

'No, you don't,' said Mono. 'You need to make sure your number-one client doesn't die.'

'What do you want?' the other half of the management asked Syph.

'Like I said, man . . .'

The management took a step or two away, to consult in private.

It was then that the girl shrieked, 'He went blue! He

stopped breathing and I didn't know how to make him start again. I didn't know. He was blue all over.'

'I'm okay,' said Syph.

'I just hit him on the chest, like they do on the TV.'

'Thank you,' said Mono. 'We're very grateful. You did exactly what you should.'

'You'll definitely get tickets,' said one of the management. 'Backstage pass, too.'

The girl held Syph's hand. 'I love your music.'

'He goes to hospital,' said half the management while the other half made a call.

'Thanks, babe,' said Syph, to the girl. He lay back and closed his eyes.

'Do your job,' said Mono to the ambulance guys. 'We'll follow you.'

'What do you want?' the ambulance guy asked Syph.

'He's doing it again,' sobbed the girl.

'No, I'm not,' Syph said.

'Give him some oxygen, for Christ's sake,' I said.

'Are you taking him here?' asked the management making the call and pointing to the address on the side of the ambulance.

'Who are you phoning?' asked Mono, in the management's face. 'The *LA Times* or *Variety*?'

'The publicity department,' the other management said. 'They always handle this kind of thing.'

Mono turned to Crab. 'How fired are these fuckers?'

'Very fucking fired,' said Crab.

Management looked at me, their last chance.

'Third vote,' I said. 'You're out. I never want to see you or hear from you again.'

'You'll hear from our lawyers,' the management said, both together.

Crab got in the back of the ambulance and one of the guys closed the door on him and the matchgirl, whose name it later turned out was Celia.

Management walked away. The siren started up – and I wondered how much extra that would cost us. Didn't matter. It was worth it.

I looked at Mono and he looked at me, and that look said it all.

We walked together towards the big red car, although part of me felt like doing a shameful little dance.

ORANGE

When I arrived in Mexico City, the day before our seven-date arena tour, there was a vast bowl in my hotel room, containing apples, oranges, a bunch of bananas, some seedless green grapes, a single kiwi. A bowl of plastic wood – wood-effect plastic.

It was still there when I came back, two weeks later, although those specific complimentary fruit items had – I'm assuming – been replaced, once if not several times.

(I think about those lost, uneaten fruits, and where they might have ended up. On the spotless gingham tablecloth of some maid's grandmother's *apartamento* deep in the *barrio*? Pigfeed? Anywhere but the trash, I hope.)

The night before we flew home, I sat cross-legged on the bed in my hotel room and ate one of the oranges.

Here is the truth:

I remember that orange better than I remember any of those gigs – the whole of that tour, in fact. At some of the arenas, there was an attendance of forty thousand people. (*okay* is big in Mexico. We have just the right amount of melancholy for them, is my theory.) They came, applauded, screamed, screamed louder (when Syph told them to), waved banners that had taken them hours to paint, held lit lighters aloft, jumped up and down, hugged each other, wept, experienced the most profound emotions – and I forgot them.

Worse, I didn't bother acknowledging them even when they were right in front of me. My contact lenses out, I failed to focus on a single adoring face.

Let me describe the orange. Curving around and around so fully in the low lamplight, its delicately dimpled skin was shiny with wax and God knows what other crap. It was quite a bit larger than I'm used to at home. (Esther buys organic, when she can.) It was a display-case orange. Where the stalk had been removed, a perfect star-shape of green remained behind.

I don't know why I plunged my thumb in and began the laborious process of peeling. If I'd wanted a quick vitamin C fix, I would have gone for the grapes.

If you eat an orange with your hands, you know you'll have to wash them afterwards. That may have been part of it. I might have wanted to do something sensuous, sensual, one or the other, or both together, I always get them confused. I think I might have felt it a good thing to be forced to wash my hands. They weren't dirty, even symbolically. I hadn't slept with anyone I shouldn't have. Faithful and truthful, I'd called Esther and the girls several times a day. I was alone in the hotel room.

Since the twins came along, I have been much more enthusiastic about getting dirty. The visual isn't enough, and my ears are fucked. I want experiences which involve intense smell, touch, taste. As Richard Manuel of The Band put it, 'Can't we have something to feel?'

During concerts, I don't even *hear* the applause any more. It's like, I know it's there, but really it doesn't exist outside me any more than my tinnitus does. Intellectually, I know that the person in the back row – Juan, Juanita – clapping so hard, hands above their head, is thanking the four of us for choosing the life we did. But it gets to a point where that gratitude seems contemptible. And then it gets to another point, where it seems contemptuous.

People *envy* me.

I know this from the way they behave towards me (by paying me much too much attention, or ignoring me completely) and from the things they write about me, but most of all I know it from the questions they ask me.

They are what I call the Bob Dylan Questions – the ones he asks in his songs about where you are tonight and what you know and don't know and, mostly, how it feels?

And to them I give the Bob Dylan answer, which is to ask them once again what it was they wanted?

'You're the drummer,' that's what my questioners imply, and sometimes even say. 'You don't even write the fucking songs. How come you get to go along for the ride? You're not that good-looking. You're not such a great drummer.'

To be famous is to be put in a position where failure is your only option. And when you've failed, and fallen completely out of view, it's not too bad – you achieve total has-been status, and are ignored. But the way down is the roughest ride, not the same as the way up in reverse, not at all. Up is booster rockets and G-forces. Down is spine-jangling bumps and bouncing reality checks. They hurt, and you develop a soul-wince – a wince back in the direction of fame and its safety harnesses.

When I got home from Mexico, I walked through the front door and said to Esther, 'It's happened. We've turned into The Eagles. We are Corporate Rock Cocksuckers.'

'Say hello to the girls, why don't you?'

'Hello, girls.'

That night, I couldn't sleep. I could imagine them, out there – wherever *out there* is, these days; younger bands, all of them saying, 'We're never going to end up like *okay*, just touring fucking stadiums for cash. We're never gonna sell out.'

And some of them won't, the failures, and some of them will, also the failures. You cannot but fail if your true premise is this: *We're never going to grow old.*

I remembered a journalist – not from Mexico. From years ago. Finland, I think. 'You must feel very lucky,' he said. And I didn't want to tell him the truth, because that would have made us seem either a. grasping (no, we fought damn hard to get here) or b. ungrateful (yes, it's been a breeze). I referred instead to the loyalty of the fans – it was they who made the choice in favour of longevity. We exist by their good graces. Blah blah blah.

At least I wasn't talking to a fan. Try telling a group of

them that what you have isn't what they *think* you have – see how they react. Demented are go. They will destroy i-and-m. We exist as a projection of their desires, from the most mundane (*I hate my job and want to quit and tell the boss to go fuck himself*) to the most extreme (*I want to two-time Miss August with Miss World*). The trick is knowing which is which; navigating between.

I know. I started as a fan; if I betray anyone along the way, it's myself-as-a-fan.

How early did I realize it wasn't going to be what I dreamt it would be?

Dreamt here, isn't a figure of speech. I remember whole night-visions of me, blinded by the lights, counting the band in, 1–2–3–4, and then hearing an awesome crowd lift in recognition of our latest hit.

My dreams came true, they were very accurate predictions. And *so* many fans out there must be experiencing the same, night after night. But would you think I was lying if I told you the dreams were better than the reality? In the dreams you always think, 'Wow, this is really happening!' whereas in reality you think, 'This is just a dream – it can't be happening like this.'

In dreams you take all the credit and are fully present in the moment; in reality, the mind doesn't react well to dreamlike situations – mine doesn't, anyway.

Fans, though, aren't half as bitter as contemporaries. Early on, you learn the road has a wayside, and you see nine-tenths of your generation heading for that fall, and leaning frantic- ally away from it, towards the other side of the road – and you learn that there's a wayside that side, too.

How do we know what we're doing while we do it? We don't. How do we know the effects it will have on other people – not just immediately but in a future so distant that we too have become other people? We don't.

In late September of last year, three months after the orange, a fourteen-and-a-half-year-old American boy called

Otis Wallace-Benjamin committed suicide whilst listening to our first record. His big sister Caroline found him — he was hanging from one of the ceiling struts in his basement den. There was a note. In it, he said that he knew *exactly* how his future life would be, and didn't want any of it.

'Read my diary,' he said. 'Then you'll understand. I hate being me. It's a really shitty option.'

Option, followed by three kisses, was the last word Otis Wallace-Benjamin wrote.

The next day, sedated, his parents, Aaron and Jean, sat down together with the diary. What they found was nothing terrible; it didn't seem as if Otis had been abused or bullied at school. Instead, there were repeated mentions of *okay*, and how much our songs meant to him — how the songs kept him alive.

When Caroline looked at the Recently Played list on his iTunes, she saw that — for as far back as it went — Otis had listened exclusively to us. She told her parents and, taking an earphone each, they tried listening to a few songs. They thought it might help them to understand.

The following day, they called our record company, who passed them on to our management.

'We don't want to sue,' Aaron said. 'Don't worry about that. We just want to talk to someone.'

Syph was in rehab; Crab was on a bender; Mono couldn't be contacted; it fell to me.

Along with the telephone number, I was given what amounted to a briefing: 'Our lawyers have stressed that you should not admit to any kind of culpability or offer any form of compensation.'

Oh, take *off*.

Caroline answered the phone.

I told her who I was.

'Really?'

'Yes,' I said.

She called out, 'Mom, Dad! It's him!'

The next voice was an older version of Caroline's. 'Thank you so much for contacting us. We're so grateful you could take the time from your busy schedule.'

'We're both listening,' said Aaron. 'I'm in my office. It's on speakerphone. Jean is in the hall.'

I imagined my voice in their echoey house.

'I'm so sorry to hear,' I said. 'You have my, and our, deepest sympathies.'

I'd discussed with Esther what to say. All I could think of were clichés. 'If you make it too ornate,' she said, 'it'll come across as phoney. It's not what you say, it's just the fact that you're saying it – and meaning it.'

'But I feel phoney. I've never met them. I never met him.'

As it turned out, I started thinking about the girls as soon as I heard their parental voices. This is what I'd sound like, if Sarah or Grace died: disturbingly normal, but not – like a ghost pretending to be an accountant.

'Thank you,' said Aaron. 'We appreciate your kind words.'

I heard noises, clatterings.

'My brother thought you were way cool,' said Caroline, shouting into the speakerphone.

'Yes, I was told that. I'm glad.'

'The funeral is in two days' time,' said Jean. 'We thought we would invite you.'

'We're inviting you now,' said Aaron. 'That's what we mean. Could you come? We want to honour him . . .'

The father was crying.

'Of course,' I said. 'Tell me how to get to you.'

Chicago, then a two-hour drive. Iowa.

'We have a bright-blue front door,' said Jean. 'You can't miss us.'

I took Esther and left the girls in the care of Esther's parents.

I had tried again to contact the other band-members, but they were all hiding, in their various ways. Not hiding from this, just hiding.

'You don't think they want me to speak, do you?' I said, as we waited in the departure lounge. 'At the funeral.'

Esther said she was sure they didn't.

'I can't just arrive and take over. I'll distort everything.'

'I think that's probably what they want you to do.'

'I'm not being immodest.'

'I know you're not. This is one of the consequences of what you do, of what you are.'

'Of who I am.'

'No, of *what*.'

On the flight, I had time to listen back to our first album. Somehow the detail had got through to me that this was Otis's favourite, and the one he chose to kill himself to. And perhaps that was why, for the first time ever, I was able to hear the songs as if I'd had nothing to do with creating them. A couple, 'Click' and 'Sea-Song #1', I've played live at every concert since they were written. But still, I *heard* them.

They were satisfying, that's the best word. The melancholy in them was true. I couldn't really tell if they were good or not. That didn't seem relevant. They communicated. I recognized them.

'How was that?' Esther asked, when I took the earphones out. She knew what I'd been doing.

'Strange,' I said. 'Very strange. Maybe I see why he liked us.'

At Chicago, we hired a decent-sized car. I said that I would drive. I wanted something to do.

We got to their town mid-afternoon, and checked into a bed & breakfast they had recommended. There were images of lilacs on almost every surface, and it smelt of lilacs, too.

A man in a grey suit approached me when I went outside to get our bags. He had followed me from the B&B.

'I'm an uncle,' he said. 'Thank you for coming. It really means the world to Jean and Aaron.'

I shook his hand. He was undecided about whether to hug

me – I could feel that. I came from a world of common hugs, but held off.

'When you're ready, I'll show you over to the house, if you'd like that.'

'That would be good.'

'Let me help,' he said, taking Esther's case.

'You're Jean's brother,' I said.

'I am.'

'How is she?'

'You got kids?'

'Two.'

He gave a grunt meaning, *So* . . . Then, because that wasn't clear enough, he said, 'She's a strong woman, Jean, but you can't expect too much. These are the first days.'

The uncle carried the bag upstairs in front of me.

Esther was in our room.

'Chester,' said the uncle. 'I'll be at the funeral.'

'Esther,' she replied, and they both laughed sadly.

'I'll leave you to get ready,' said Chester.

We met him outside fifteen minutes later – and followed his car in ours. I felt self-conscious about my very expensive black suit.

The B&B was only five minutes from the house with the blue door. It was a small town. We drove past a church with a graveyard.

Aaron and Caroline were waiting at the bottom of the drive. I guess Chester must have called to warn them. Jean came out just as we stopped, a cloth in her hands.

There was a basketball hoop above the white garage door.

We got out.

Chester reversed until he was close to us.

'I'll leave you,' he said, and drove off.

We all shook hands.

'Well, come on in,' said Jean.

The house was as I'd imagined, perhaps a little smaller. A well-adapted American home, not built to last for ever. It smelt very clean. In the kitchen there were unopened bags of potato chips in bowls all along the counter.

'This is Marjorie,' said Jean. 'She'll be doing snacks.'

'Would you like to see the basement?' Aaron asked, from behind me.

'Yes,' I said.

I realized, as he led me through to the back of the house, that the basement was one of the main reasons I had come.

The next room was a utility room, with large white goods. A door to the left was painted red and covered in radioactive waste decals. Aaron opened it, flicked a light-switch, and I saw wooden stairs with a strip of shaggy orange carpet running down them.

'Would you like to go alone?' Aaron asked.

I looked round for Esther, but she had stayed in the kitchen.

I grunted a yes.

'Take your time,' Aaron said. 'We don't have to leave for an hour or so.'

He went straight back into the main part of the house.

I wanted a cigarette or something.

There was a bike on its side in the mud of the backyard.

I went down into the basement.

Part of me suspected this might all be a trick to get me here – and Otis, alive, would be waiting downstairs with a group of his friends.

The large room was unoccupied.

Around me, the walls were hidden by shelves, and the shelves were full of tools and toys.

I sat down on a couch covered in a tartan blanket.

When I looked up at the beams, there was no way to tell which Otis had used. One towards the middle, I guessed.

There was a low table in front of me. All of our CDs were laid out across it in a line.

There was an acoustic guitar on a stand.

At first I didn't play it, and then I did.

The guitar was still in tune.

When I finished, it was as if the room were suddenly filled with applause.

But for Otis.

C$_2$H$_2$OH

The first time Crab pissed his pants on-stage, I thought our career was over, right then and there.

Denver Colorado.

Second time, two gigs later, Sioux City Iowa, and I was able to take in the fans' reaction: abandoned screaming of wild delight.

Third was the same.

Fourth, he was showboating, and fifth it was an established part of our act – missed if not performed.

And get this: some of the audience, women and men, had already started to copy him.

(Word spread via *okay* noticeboards and chatrooms.)

The man has problems, but no-one seems to have a problem with that. His problems make him more, more something. Edgy, perhaps – a quality yearned for by sixteen-year-olds.

Edges cut.

I've known for quite some time that Crab was in serious trouble. But it never really hit me until he started up with the piss-routine. And then, about halfway through this tour, I overheard him, drunk on the plane, being interviewed by a journalist from Melbourne Australia. The words Crab said were these:

'Whenever I get out of rehab, I like to . . .'

Didn't matter what he liked to.

Whenever.

If I could have gone home right then, I would have done – I would have strapped on a parachute and bailed; I would have quit the band again, crawled back to Esther, howled in her arms, and then tried to figure out the right thing to do. The right thing for Crab.

Probably I shouldn't be saying this. I should be saying I would have intervened straight away. But what could I do? What could I do? Cancel the tour? Get him checked into rehab? Come on. Rehab, clearly, was now part of the problem – part of the rhythm and routine of his addiction. Another clean-up, another relapse. Tssk-BOOM.

Whenever.

On the afternoon of his tenth birthday, the boy who would later become Crab rode over to show me his new bike – golden leaves stuck between the spokes, because he had cycled straight through several piles of them.

His face gets brighter, the further away it is. His ten-year-old's face.

That bike made him happier than any other material object.

When it goes, Hope leaves a very clear outline, like a cartoon character running through a puff of smoke, like a God-shaped hole in the universe.

Two weeks later, his father took that bike and threw it off a river-bridge. He did this coldly, and without anger. It was a lesson.

Being an alcoholic, you could say that Crab was dying from the day he first took a drink.

Over the last couple of years, it has gotten much worse.

People say, after he leaves a room, *My God – he looks like Death.* But he's looked that way for so long I've started to think, *No, actually, Death looks like him.*

We all *drink*, the band, but for some people it's just a different substance – more necessary, more beautiful. It is *Good Morning, Vietnam* and *Goodnight Vienna*. It is *Happy House* and *Sad Café*.

Guitar is Crab's day job, a way of financing his vocation: C_2H_2OH.

So, I waited until the end of the tour, and then the end-of-tour party – and then I went back to Vancouver with Crab, and I stayed with him.

The first night, in a bar, he thought I just didn't want to go home.

'See your kids, come on. You haven't seen them in weeks. Go be Daddy.'

But I had already okayed it with Esther. She knew why I wasn't where I wanted to be.

'No,' I said. 'I thought I'd have a few more.'

I had a few more. Then we were invited to a party. Crab tried to lose me there, but I kept him in sight. We took a taxi to a casino. He tried to appal me by losing a vast amount of money – most of his takings from the tour – on the roulette table. I said nothing. Next came dawn, and coffee in a diner.

'Are you ready to go home yet?' he asked.

'No.'

So he led me off on further adventures. Around noon, we stopped at a fleapit motel for some sleep.

'I like this place,' he said. 'I may stay here for a while.'

The whole Bukowski thing.

He snuck out some time that afternoon.

I caught up with him back at the bar.

'Oh, hi,' he said. And the chase began again.

That night was little different to the night before, only a woman was involved. Around 4 a.m., she became maudlin and tearful. We ended up back at yesterday's motel, friends once more.

I turned in, slept and woke.

From the room, I called Esther.

'How's it going?'

'I can't keep up.'

'Talk to him.'

He had checked out, and disappeared for the rest of the day. I thought I'd lost him but he turned up back at his regular bar that evening. The woman wasn't with him. He was drunk. Yet, when he spoke, it was with absolute clarity.

'Look, I know what you're trying to do. I appreciate it. I love you for it. You will fail.'

I have never been that good at lying. Never have I wished more for the skill.

'I don't know what you mean.'

It wasn't the words themselves; it was the rhythm with which I said them. And a good drummer always knows when he's out of time.

Crab smiled, falling back into the woozy. But he knew exactly what he wanted to say: 'Give up. Go home.'

'No,' I said. 'I'm with you.'

There was a football game up on a screen at the end of the bar. One of the teams scored. Crab did not allow himself to be distracted.

'It's not a place to be,' he said. 'You're a good man.'

'I'm not.'

'Compared to other men, you are.'

'This isn't about me.'

He looked at me, focussed again.

'Of course it's about you. Come on.'

The barman brought us another couple of beers. I believe Crab ordered them telepathically.

'Come on!' he said, getting loud for the first time.

I'd misunderstood.

He led me across to an empty booth.

When we sat down, I found we were out of sight of televisions.

'What's this about?' he said.

I hesitated.

'No, tell me, what's this about?'

It all came out. My worries. The interview on the plane. The *whenever*.

'It's quite understandable,' said Crab. 'I make you feel bad. You want to be able to help, but there's nothing you can do.'

Lit from below, from a small lamp on our table, I couldn't help but see that Crab had started to look quite like a pig. His face was pink, bloated. The nose was bigger than it had been. I could kind of see up his nostrils.

He continued to talk. 'But you also feel other things. One of them is guilt. It's not guilt about me. It's guilt about yourself. Because I'm doing what you feel, in your heart, you should be doing. Not for you. You're not a person like me. You don't have my reasons. You don't have those reasons at all.'

I knew what he meant.

'We made a contract with the fans. They expect us to be like me. And Syph. No-one's interested in a Buddhist. Everyone thinks a Buddhist's a waste of time and everything. No offence. I respect you. I think you have it just about right. It's a better life. But you're too fucking clean, man. And nothing's going to come of that, is it? You've always been kind of clean-cut. It's a good look, when there are other people around you to rough it up. Make it attractive. But you've removed yourself from the fray.'

At *fray*, a bubble of spittle landed on the lamp's lightbulb and went fz.

'It's not what's wanted. The fans are important. I understand that in a way you don't. They have requirements. I'm not making up for you – those aren't my reasons. But . . .'

He needed a run-up to what he was about to say.

'There's Syph and there's me, and then there's you and there's Mono. And he has Major and fishing, and you have Esther and Sarah and Grace and the lord Buddha.'

Imaginary figurines were arranged in front of me on the tabletop. Mine, though it didn't exist, was the most grotesque.

I said, 'And you, you have drinking.'

'And I have drinking,' he said. 'I quite agree. Absolutely, old chap. That's what I have.' (Comedy Englishman was beside me.) 'Corking, what? And Syph has whatever the current drug *du jour* is. But we also have something else. Call it freedom. It's a shorthand but we're living the dream, baby. And if we don't, you can't. We're the guarantee of quality. One hundred per cent the real deal.'

This time I caught the finger-lift that brought us another

round of beers. What I couldn't figure was how that gesture had also added whiskeys to our order. Trebles.

'The people want to see you're living the life. If that's not happening, then they think you're living the lie. I know you look down on what I do. But I am devoted. We need to survive, as an entity. The band is my life. I love it.'

'I do, too.'

It sounded feeble.

'Look at me,' Crab said.

I did my best.

'Say it again,' he said.

'I love the band.'

It sounded more feeble.

'Is it *everything*?'

'No, of course —'

'You don't *love* the band. You *have* the band. You take it or you leave it. You love your family. I have no family. I love the band. Let's not try to compete because I'm going to win.'

To prove this, he drank off his whiskey.

To at least stay in the conversation, I drank mine off, too.

There was no coughing. My eyes hardly watered. But I felt my soul sag like the back of an old mule. I was carrying unaccustomed burdens.

'I'm not trying to compete. I'm trying to —'

'Rescue me.'

'I didn't say that.'

'No. You didn't *say* that. But that's what I *heard*. You're not comfortable here. This is a public place. I like to live where I can be seen. There's always someone can pick you up, if you need it. They'll rob you, as well. But people are astonishingly kind, when you're needful. I don't want to be on any other level. I'm not after enlightenment. You understand?'

I had got so used to him monologuing that, for a moment, I had no answer. I kicked the soul-mule. It moved, slowly.

'There's a difference between that and killing yourself.'

'Most people are killing themselves, or hadn't you noticed?

212

If you haven't got that far, I can't help you. I'm sure the Buddha –'

'Yes, he knew,' I said. 'That's what he's all about.'

'And you love me. And you don't want to see me die. Well, thank you. I'm flattered. And I am more moved than I can possibly allow myself to show you.'

For the first time, he wobbled along the winding wall-top of a sentence. To recover, he went simple:

'I like my life. I don't want your life, or any other man's life.'

'You're in denial,' I said, and immediately regretted it. He was making me feel priggish.

'I'll let that pass,' he said. 'I'm in denial of nothing. What am I in denial of? I'm in a bar and I'm drinking. I know what it's doing to me. Shall I describe it? I've had it talked at me enough times. My liver. I'm not Superman. There is damage. There is pain. I am being true to my freedom.'

This last statement seemed conclusive.

I began to speak, but Crab spoke for me, and against me.

'It is not enslavement. Please don't say it's that. I am gliding. I am gliding slowly down. This is not a crash. If it was a crash, I wouldn't be here.'

More drinks arrived.

'Will you listen to me?' I said.

'Of course,' said Crab. 'But there is nothing you can say that will change a damn thing. I am the person you see before you.'

He waved across the bar to someone he knew.

It was this gesture which defeated me. He was right. This wasn't my place. I was disgustingly superior, in attitude. I couldn't ditch that.

The Buddha took clothes from a dead man, when he gave up being a prince. But he washed them before he wore them. He washed them until they were clean.

I stood up.

'Well, at least you tried,' said Crab.

I sat down again.

'You are breaking my heart,' I said.

Crab let that hang, until it answered itself.

I stood up again.

'You will have nothing to blame yourself for,' said Crab. 'You did everything you could. Tell Esther hi.'

I came out from behind the table and took his right hand. It was covered in small cuts and gouges from hitting the strings so hard.

'That was a good tour,' I said. 'You were excellent.'

'Thank you,' said Crab. 'You weren't bad yourself.'

With that, I left.

A taxi took me home.

The driver recognized me, and told me about his son's band. They were good, he said. I should check them out. I asked what they were called. Then asked again, because I'd already forgotten. After that, I let him talk.

At home, Esther took me upstairs. The girls had been asleep for several hours. Esther chaperoned me into their room. Crab had been right. This here was my band, now.

'Tell me,' said Esther, when we relocated to bed.

'He's wise,' I said. 'He's beyond me.'

'How come?'

I went back over our conversation. How everything I wanted to say to him, he said first.

'He made me feel uncool,' I said.

'That was his tactic.'

'It worked.'

'But that doesn't change anything. He's still what he is. You tried to give him an opportunity.'

'No, I just slotted in line, along with all the other people who try to tell him what to do. I repeated the pattern. I made it worse. I wanted his bike. Oh God, I feel –'

I made it to the bathroom.

I mostly missed the toilet.

'I'll get a bucket,' shouted Esther.

Together, we cleaned it up.

Then Esther made me drink as much water as I could. Then we went to bed.

I woke up in a clean house.

I did not hate it.

MYSELF

I don't believe in myself any more.

Not in a gung-ho, dream-the-impossible-dream-and-fight-the-unwinnable-fight kind of way.

Not even in an I-will-survive way.

I don't believe in myself in the same way I don't believe in fairies at the bottom of the garden.

The difference is, I *never* used to believe in the fairies, but I seem to remember thinking that I had a worthwhile self and that that self, if it so chose, could do things to things that would affect things and perhaps even improve things.

Right now I don't even make it to ghost.

I wish I did – then I could haunt someone worth haunting: Esther.

I could buy odour of lavender from the ghost-stores, and drop it for her to smell in the passageways of our house.

She would know it was me, because I've told her that's how I'll communicate with her from beyond the grave.

I think, today, I am beyond the grave; beyond in the sense of the grave no longer being really relevant to me – if I tried to get into my own long home, I would just fall through: through the dirt, through the rock, the mantle and core, right through to the other side of the world and off into space.

This isn't what I should be feeling, husband of one, father of two: I remember the opposite – when every sensation, even the teensiest, was so intense it was like getting tattooed.

Look, needles on a tall tree, glittering in the frost: the greatest fucking most amazing thing I've ever seen!

Drugs did this, sometimes – for other people, never for me. Never truly.

Good cocaine, I admit, was Snow White, and on it I occasionally felt like a Handsome Prince, but all the other drugs turned me into one of the Seven Dwarfs: dope, pre-dictably, made me Dopey, ecstasy made me Happy (but in a really depressing way), heroin made me Sleepy, alcohol made me Doc (diagnosing everyone else's problems, governing the world), caffeine made me Grumpy, crystal meth made me Bashful (because I was so hyper-aware it should be having the opposite effect, hubba-hubba) and bad cocaine made me Sneezy.

I won't say *and then I discovered meditation* and I won't add *and it did everything for me that I'd ever wanted drugs to do.* I won't patronize you with a recommendation to try it or disgust you with a hippie testimonial.

You're on your own path, as they say. You can walk on gilded splinters all you like. You can choose to spend your alive-time doing what you wanna do. For example, you could go up to Lexington 125 and wait for your man. Or you could taste the whip. Or you could get on a clipper ship and sail. Your desires are your desires, whatever they may be. You can sometimes get what you want if not exactly what you need.

I don't have a story about drugs. Leastways, not one I want to tell.

Looking back, I can see that I was gradually on the way to where I am now. But I've been cuntishly slow in getting here.

The years have helped. Thank you, 2003.

Becoming middle-aged is like waking up, I mean regaining consciousness, halfway through writing a rock opera – forget dignity, forget cool. Instead, there's the distant prospect of much money and the comfort that's meant to bring. There's some laughs to be had, mostly at your own expense. There's a whole lot more drama backstage than ever crosses the footlights. And there's the inescapable awareness that you've become a person you would never ever have wanted to be.

I should know.

This I'm going to tell you about took place after six days of a two-week-long retreat – one of the ones where no-one speaks to anyone.

I won't even tell you where on earth it was because *it doesn't matter*. The time of day I'll give for free, early evening.

At the moment we join me, I am kneeling on the floor of my deliciously bare cell (one bed, one chair, walls bare apart from a photograph of the face of a statue of the Buddha) – I've been trying and failing to meditate, thinking too much of my distant family, when in walks someone I really don't want to see: me, aged twenty.

'Hey, maaaan,' baby-Clap says, 'reached enlightenment yet?'

Was this really me?

I am surprised at how good-looking I once was (shiny hair, clear-ish skin, good teeth); less surprised to meet myself this way – it is a showdown that's been in the offing for several years.

Still and all, I am not ready for it.

'Take a seat,' I say. 'Take *the* seat.'

Clap Jr chooses not to. He goes and inspects the Buddha-photograph with his head aggressively tipped to the left and then to the right. I have a body memory of doing this, the cocky confidence it was meant to express; the awkwardness it was meant to cover over.

The Buddha is Buddha Maitreya, the Buddha of the future.

I give up on the meditation but stay where I am, close to the floor.

When he doesn't speak, I know Clap wants me to be the one to start it. 'Are you here for any particular reason?'

'What?' he says. 'Ghost of Christmas Past? Kind of.'

'You have life-lessons to teach me?'

'Not exactly. It's about the music, the band.'

This last sentence makes my stomach and guts feel like leaving my body and going for a walk in the monastery grounds – maybe take in the Zen garden.

'What exactly about the band?'

'Stop it – just stop it. *Now*. Find lock and clawl under, Glasshopper.'

'What do you think I've been trying to do for most of the past decade? They won't let me.'

'Who's *they*? Because you're always blaming them —'

'The band,' I say. 'The management, the employees.'

'Boo-fucking-hoo. I haven't even put a record out and you're letting them release this musical turd with your name on the cover.'

He means the last album, of which I am truly ashamed. We should never have tried to update to a contemporary sound, involving hip-hop — not even after my number-one sample.

'I said no to that at the time.'

'But you didn't nix it.'

'I couldn't,' I say.

'Why not?'

'Tax. The girls needed new things.'

'Then sell a house.'

'I like my houses. Each one has a different function.'

'You used to exist in one room.'

'*Exist*, not live. You should know that.'

'True. But my dreams of life are a lot more noble than your nightmare of a reality.'

His lines sound more rehearsed than mine. Perhaps he's had more time to prepare.

'I'm not aware I ever thought much about *nobility* when I was your age —'

'Of course, because you've forgotten everything you ever knew that was worth knowing. It's all about nobility — it's about nothing else. We wanted to say something worth saying, not just fill the space. Make way for youth.'

'I do. Every day. My daughters.'

'Quit the band. And don't go back. Not like last time. Let them make fools of themselves by themselves.'

'How would you handle it different, if you were me now and not you then?'

The sun is going down outside, splashing a stretched circle of gold up the wall.

'I'd be a private citizen. I would go to Savile Row, London, and get them to make me some bespoke suits – not wear that semi-rock star crap you do. Ditch the bracelet –'

'They're beads. They're important to me.'

'They make you look old.'

'They're not about looks.'

'Bull*shit*. Learn to do something else, and do it well.'

I feel calmer than I should do – six days of solid meditation and garden-inspecting have achieved something.

'Why are you so eager to silence me? Isn't what I have to say as valid as –'

'No, it's not. It's not as valid as anyone. I want to silence you because you're embarrassing yourself – fucking up your own reputation. At one point, you were pretty good. And now people are just laughing at you. You're no longer valid. Fetch the mop-pushing porter from your local high school – *he's* got a story. You just have more anecdotes of weaknesses indulged and privilege taken for granted.'

'I don't disguise them as anything else.'

'Get real. Meet some *real* people – people who aren't successful – people who are going down, rapidly.'

'Believe me, I've met enough of those.'

I tried very hard not to think of Crab.

'You have *no idea*, man. You're so up yourself.'

'I know that.'

'What are you doing about it?'

'Well, for a start, I'm talking to you – correction, I'm listening to you and taking you seriously.'

'And?'

'I'm considering quitting, as you suggest. I don't think I'll be ordering the suits, though.'

'Just a suggestion, man. Have some dignity.'

Clap Jr has now moved across to the chair and sat down. From the side pocket of his jacket, he produces a packet of tobacco – and begins to roll himself a joint. I don't try to stop him.

'How did I lose my dignity?'

'The first time you did something without putting your whole soul into it, that's when.'

'Not when? How?'

'By deciding to rip off the fans – short-changing them.'

'Did I?'

'As good as. You've admitted as much yourself.'

'And how are you going to avoid this?'

Long pause. 'I'm not. I'm you. That's why I'm so fucking pissed at you.'

'I'm sorry.'

'You should be.'

'And you will be.'

'I am already.'

He lights up. The smell brings back further memories. I feel a powerful anti-nostalgia.

'So everything you do right now contains your whole soul? You must be exhausted.'

'And exhaustion leads to weakness – which is how it happens, the sell-out.'

'Can I tell you a story?'

'No. I've had enough of your excuses.'

'I am less angry than you. Stories may be one of the reasons why.'

'Very clever. No.'

'But I'm also less bitter. Even though I have a lot more to be bitter about – twenty years more. You're bitter in anticipation of things that won't even happen.'

'They might have done. I didn't avoid them out of virtue.'

'Listen – I made a decision – or perhaps it was all just an accident. Around your age, I invested my entire life in pop culture –'

'– in the music. No-one talks about "pop culture".'

'– in a sound that attracted me as much as anything ever had or would, apart from –'

'– pale and interesting young women.'

'Correct. But that investment, while paying dividends, also was subject to taxation.'

'You're talking like an accountant.'

'I've spent a lot of time in their company.'

'You shouldn't have.'

'Some of them are decent people –'

'And the majority deserve –'

'No worse than I do. Anyway, I am paying that tax now. It is larger and larger in proportion to my income, which itself is shrinking fast. Those first older generations that reacted to rock'n'roll, the spectacled back-from-the-war bunch, the Herr Musik Professors and the Church of the Holy Gook Ministers – they got some things right when they condemned this primitive and lustful new artform. They didn't *understand* it, because they never fell in love with the sound like we did, but they knew that it was part of a general decline in Western culture –'

'Oh –'

'You see, I call myself a musician, but I'm not. I'm not anything like as good as I should be – as I could have been, if I'd practised, if I'd had a discipline to practise. And I might still be improving, rather than getting worse and worse, as I am.'

'Now you're just making me sad.' He says it sarcastically, but I can tell that he means it.

'Fathers and mothers have reasons for saying the things they do – about settling down and getting a proper job, marrying and putting a little away for your retirement. They've counted a few more costs than you have.'

He begins to sing: 'Sometimes you cannot count the miles till you can count the cost.' Our lyrics.

'You're not wrong.'

'But you are.'

'And I'm you.'

'I know. I know you're me. That's what's so hard.'

We sit for a long while without talking. The light has gone

from the wall and from the window, too. 'We find ourselves and lose ourselves in the dark, in the dark.' More of our lyrics.

'I will quit,' I say. 'Maybe it will take a little time, but not longer than a year.'

He starts on another rollie.

'Maybe you shouldn't. Maybe I'm being too hard on myself. I'm not perfectly noble. Like you said, why am I so keen to shut you up? What am I afraid of?'

'You're just trying to protect me. And I thank you for it.'

I feel him considering his memory of what this room looks like, although I can't see him moving his eyes or head.

'Do you really like it here?'

'I love it.'

'That's good. It's good to find a place like that.'

'You will.'

'I'm sorry I got angry at you. I just feel frustrated. I want to get into what you're already beyond. I hate it that you're beyond it.'

'It's been a long time since one song took over my life – told me how to dress and live and how to *be* inside. But it still happens, sometimes, if only for the length of the song. I can be driving along a road, and, until it finishes playing, I'll be a completely different person. I'll drive in a different way. Often, it's a worse person I've become – more aggressive, more angry. Songs make me younger. Some of them make me you again.'

I become aware that he has gone without leaving, but I continue talking, to myself.

'When people write to us, as fans, I know that's what they're saying, or trying to say – that we change them in a way they want to be changed. They want to say thank you. But we didn't get anyone saying thank you about the last album. So, that's why I'll quit. Not because of you.'

I raise my voice.

'So you needn't feel guilty, maaan!'

224

I lower my voice.

'Not any more than you usually do.'

I don't speak again for the next eight days.

Q & A

A Swedish music magazine sent us a questionnaire. Our tour publicist, Karla, waited until we were stranded in the departure lounge of Reykjavík airport before presenting it to us.

With nothing else to do, the band sat down at four tables in the bar and applied itself to answering.

I don't know exactly how many of these things I've tried to be cool, clever, amusing or profound in, since we began. Let's say, one every three days, on average – which totals around twenty-five hundred.

The fog that was keeping us on the ground thickened, and, after another hour, we were told a decision had been made: we were returning to the hotel.

On an impulse, I asked to look at the answers the other guys had given. This was a mistake. I started to cry, although I made sure no-one noticed – I put my head in my hands.

'Can you photocopy these?' I asked, handing them back to the publicist as I got off the minibus. I had on my dark glasses.

'Sure,' she said, puzzled.

They were delivered to my room later that night. I sat up with them, a *Coke*, a vegetarian burger and fries, and Elvis Presley's Sun Sessions on my iPod.

I noticed that Karla had censored some of our answers, and filled in spaces we'd left blank.

Name?	**Syph**
Born?	**Yes! I was! Isn't it great?**
Star sign?	**Leo. What else? Roar!**
Place of birth?	**Saturn.**
First crush?	**My mom, of course! Then the midwife.**
First record bought?	~~**Hey, I always stole them!**~~ *Sex Pistols, Pretty Vacant*
First job?	**Explosives expert.**
Favourite colour?	**Paint it black!**
Favourite animal?	**Any party animal. Yow!**
Favourite book?	~~**Hitler. A study in Tyranny**~~ *Hammer of the Gods by Stephen Davis*
What do you usually do when you are bored?	~~**Heroin**~~ *Go to a club*
If you could go anywhere in the world, where would you go?	**The Playboy Mansion Hi, Hef!**
Would you rather have the ability to fly or be invisible?	**To fly. It would be so cool for concerts. Whoosh!**
Do you collect anything?	**Digits, baby! What are yours?**
Most frightening experience?	**Nearly dying in LA.**
Funniest experience?	**Nearly dying in LA.**
Desert island single and album?	**AC/DC, For those about to Rock! Led Zeppelin IV**
Hero/heroine?	~~**Myself**~~ *Jim Morrison*
Have you ever seen a ghost?	**No.** ~~**But I have made one**~~
Do you have final words of wisdom?	**Stay cool, children!**

Name?	**Crab**
Born?	**[Blank]** *1965*
Star sign?	**Scorpio**
Place of birth?	**Don't remember**
First crush?	**My English teacher, Miss Ullshawn**
First record bought?	**The Ramones, Rockaway Beach**
First job?	**Always proudly unemployable**
Favourite colour?	**Don't remember. What's that yellowish one?**
Favourite animal?	**Skunk**
Favourite book?	~~**The wine list**~~ *The Catcher in the Rye.*
What do you usually do when you are bored?	~~**Start a fight**~~ *Call up a friend.*
If you could go anywhere in the world, where would you go?	~~**Cognac**~~, **France**
Would you rather have the ability to fly or be invisible?	**Fly, fly, fly away**
Do you collect anything?	**Parking tickets**
Most frightening experience?	**[Blank]** *Losing my voice*
Funniest experience?	**Waking up this morning**
Desert island single and album?	**The Ramones, Rockaway Beach/Rocket to Russia**
Hero/heroine?	**Jesus Christ**
Have you ever seen a ghost?	**Yes. Seriously. I don't want to talk about it.**
Do you have final words of wisdom?	**Study hard**

Name?	**Mono**
Born?	**1965**
Star sign?	**Pisces**
Place of birth?	**Vancouver**
First crush?	**Paul McCartney**
First record bought?	**Pink Floyd, Wish You Were Here**
First Job?	**Assistant drum majorette**
Favourite colour?	**Blue**
Favourite animal?	**Rainbow trout**
Favourite book?	**Izaak Walton, The Compleat Angler**
What do you usually do when you are bored?	**Talk to my wife**
If you could go anywhere in the world, where would you go?	**The Great Barrier Reef**
Would you rather have the ability to fly or be invisible?	**Be invisible**
Do you collect anything?	**Nature books. Matchboxes**
Most frightening experience?	**Never been scared**
Funniest experience?	**My future wife not being interested in Syph**
Desert island single and album?	**Paul McCartney, Maybe I'm Amazed I don't like albums any more**
Hero/heroine?	~~**My wife**~~ *Jaco Pastorius*
Have you ever seen a ghost?	**No. I don't believe in ghosts**
Do you have final words of wisdom?	**Keep calm**

Name?	**Clap**
Born?	**June 29th 1966**
Star sign?	**Cancer**
Place of birth?	**Vancouver Canada**
First crush?	**Mrs Sylvie Ullshawn, English teacher.**
First record bought?	**Snow White and the Seven Dwarfs soundtrack**
First job?	**Paper route. Lasted two weeks.**
Favourite colour?	**Tortoiseshell.**
Favourite animal?	**Cicada.**
Favourite book?	**e.e.cummings, Selected Poems**
What do you usually do when you are bored?	**Drum.**
If you could go anywhere in the world, where would you go?	**Home. Bed.**
Would you rather have the ability to fly or be invisible?	**But I can fly, and I've always been invisible. You'll have to try harder than that.**
Do you collect anything?	**Sad stories.**
Most frightening experience?	**Syph's overdose.**
Funniest experience?	**That's private.**
Desert island single and album?	**Fleetwood Mac, 'Tusk' Joni Mitchell, 'Blue'**
Hero/heroine?	**The Buddha, obviously**
Have you ever seen a ghost?	**Yes. Recently.**
Do you have final words of wisdom?	**Yes. See over.**

Okay, here goes – my good advices, my road apples:

Always shave in the direction the hair is growing.

Look before you leap, but look *over your shoulder* – because that place you're leaping from, you'll never see it again.

Instinct will serve you better than any committee, even a committee of your best friends convened to decide what is in your best interests.

Be careful what you ask for, it'll get you. In fact, if you want it badly enough, it'll track your weary footsteps through the snow and ravage you until you're nothing but a pile of red mush.

Heartfelt experience concentrated to a diamond-like essence cannot be expressed as anything other than cliché. Sorry. This is a fact.

As Bob Dylan once said, 'Keep a clean head and always carry a lightbulb.' I don't know what it means, either.

Most people, as you'll learn, are essentially good; most people, you'll discover, are innately evil; most people, you'll find, are morally ambiguous. Kids, too.

I don't know what the sound of one hand clapping is, but I know it makes a lousy rhythm track.

If a tree falls in the forest, and no-one hears, no lawyers need be involved; with the creation of any other recordable sound, that is not the case.

Life is very short; life is very long; life is as long as a piece of string.

Beware those who moralize their incapacity.

Don't – whatever you were thinking just then: *don't.*

Be true to *who you really are*, unless *who you really are* turns out to be Adolf Hitler or Ted Bundy, in which case repress yourself as much as you possibly can.

Find your inner beauty and offer it the once-in-a-lifetime opportunity of plastic surgery.

If you're scared of clowns, don't run away to join the circus.

All will be revealed, but only if you tuck $20 in her garter.

It happens fast or it doesn't happen at all.

Don't mourn your own life.

There are no short cuts. Let me repeat that: There are no short cuts.

As soon as I was finished, almost as if it had been preordained, I coughed up a small black spot of blood.

There had been a few flecks before, but nothing to worry about. This was more like a haemorrhage.

It was midnight. Still evening for Esther, however. So I called her. She told me to see a doctor, immediately.

After I'd put the phone down (the girls are *fine*, I am *fine*, see a doctor *now*), I spoke to reception.

By quarter past, the doctor had arrived.

By ten the next morning, I had a diagnosis of lung cancer.

By three o'clock, I was on a flight home.

It happens fast or it doesn't happen at all.

*

On the airplane, I thought about death. I often think about death when I'm on airplanes – in fact, I rarely think about anything else. But this was different. This time it was as if Death were in the passenger seat beside me. It was as if Death were flying the plane – quietly steering us towards a mountainside in Greenland. It was as if the plane itself were Death.

I tried to calm down, be casual.

So, I might be leaving the party early. Well, that's always been my way, hasn't it? Because of which, I've missed out on some pretty wild stuff (after hours), because of which I've ended up with fewer regrets (Sunday morning coming down).

I didn't even regret having been the kind of guy to leave parties early.

I got out my notebook and wrote down my wishes for my funeral:

No music. No eulogies. No sadness. In fact, no funeral.
Cremate me somewhere crappy – where they ask cash or cheque when you walk in and then give you fifteen minutes for the service.

My will was in good shape: Esther got the lot, including my ashes –

– these she could dispose of as she wished, which would probably be somewhere shady in our garden. I knew the spot she'd choose, and wouldn't have been able to dissuade her even if I'd wanted.

It meant she'd never be able to sell the house but, my money being what it was, she shouldn't ever have to.

Over the next week, I found myself interviewing myself. Questions. Always more questions.

Are you angry?

Yes, I am angry.

Do I feel it's unfair?

My whole life has been unfair – entirely in my favour.

This counts as a minor belated adjustment. What I had, all of it, I did not deserve.

Am I going to fight this thing?

Yes.

Do I have a message for the fans?

No.

Haven't you learnt anything you wish to pass on?

Yes. And I wrote it all down. Looking back, I think that was a foolish thing to do. If I'd kept all my wisdom secret, I might have been granted a little longer.

Has your faith given you strength?

It's shown me how pointless is the quest for strength.

God, that came out pompous.

How did the band take it?

Those guys – they never believe anything I say, thought it was a put-on, that I was shitting them.

I don't feel all that great. Can we end here?

One final question: How would you like to be remembered?

On my bedside table is a bowl of flowers – their roots are in earth, not water. I've asked, and they're called marguerites. They have a dial of propeller-shaped petals, twelve or thirteen, arranged around a disc of egg-yolk yellow. They are a very simple flower, like one of my girls would draw and be dissatisfied with. Their leaves have a difficult-to-describe shape: dragon's feet. Coloured a very delicate silvery green, they are far more complicated and morally ambiguous (if you want to have it like that, and right now I do) than the flower-parts. Lure those bees in with a happy face but then what those buzzers are keeping alive is actually a bit monstrous. I haven't seen a bee in a while. I haven't been in a summer meadow. I didn't last summer (on tour). I would like to and it's likely I won't unless I insist – unless I make it through to next spring, or fly to somewhere where it's a different season. But then it wouldn't be a real meadow, just a rich man's fake.

I am forty-two years old.

BENEFIT

Genital warts.

The joke between me and Esther is that this was the first gift I ever gave her.

Since then, I have been desperately trying to make up for it – really *desperately*.

I have given her three houses, a half-dozen cars, a piece of silver jewellery from every city I've been, a forest of flowers.

The first thing I remember Esther giving me was an old fob-watch her great-grandfather had kept thirty years in his waistcoat pocket. It didn't work, hadn't since the 1940s, but I found someone to fix it.

I don't know why she entrusted me, wart-bringer, with something so important to her and her family; this was only a month after we'd met – perhaps because she saw that responsibility was what I needed. (In that, she wasn't wrong.) And I have managed, so far, not to lose or destroy the watch. Mainly by having it screwed to the music-room wall, framed behind tungsten and bulletproof glass.

I have given Esther every getable object mentioned in her favourite-ever song, Dylan's 'Sad-Eyed Lady of the Lowlands': one copy of the *Missionary Times*, a silver cross, some silk, some glass, some Arabian drums, some metallic sheets, a deck of cards (I removed the Jack of Hearts and the Ace of Spades), some clothes bought from a basement store, a specially commissioned Victorian-style silhouette of Esther in profile, a matchbook that plays a tune when you open it, a recording of gypsy religious music, a list of Australian convicts (not easy to source), a rug made only between the hours of midnight and 6 a.m., her mother's drugs (antihistamines, I should point out – that took some explaining), a signed first edition of Steinbeck's *Cannery Row*, a picture of someone's husband cut out of a magazine *belonging* to one of her friend's husbands, a medallion bought from the Vatican and personally blessed by the Pope – is that holy enough for you? etc.

She, of course, topped all this by giving me the girls – although she hates it when I speak of their birth as a gift.

'We made them together. You gave them to me, just as much as I gave them to you.'

Didn't look that way in the delivery suite, I'll say.

And now, to put an end to all gift-competition, she – along with about eighty thousand other people – has given me a second death; the first one, so it seems, has been dodged.

Yippee! Whoopee! Whoop-de-doo!

Let's be silly.

I feel that now, let's be really silly, having faced down **THE FEAR** – as Stephen King would no doubt put it.

THE FEAR!

Tinkle-tinkle goes the music box.
I am going to die.
La-la-la go the spooky children.
Black fear.

I am as good as dead.
Slam goes the metal door. Clank-clank go the chains.
Solid fear.
There is no hope.

Not fear like mist or water – fear like a slab of marble that you have to try and walk through. And you know it's impossible but suddenly you find yourself inside it – black marble – and you're obliged to keep moving, and you don't know how: if you think about it, you're paralysed; if you don't think about it, you can't move. You begin to be afraid of thought itself, so you try to stop thinking – which takes a lot of thought.

THE FEAR!

After my prognosis came in, Esther hit the internet so hard it flinched. She spent all night in medical chatrooms, three at a time. She gathered enough information to write several PhDs. She emailed clinics across the world – and, when they didn't email back, she called them.

Eventually, she found the hint of a possibility of a treatment.

It was experimental. It involved lasers. It was expensive, even for us.

To make the treatment worthwhile, at least nine other people had to undergo it as well. And we would have to pay for them. A new hospital didn't have to be built from scratch, but the cost wasn't far off.

And then, even though only band-members can call a band meeting, Esther called a band meeting.

The other guys showed. Usual booth.

'No shit,' said Syph.

'At least there's hope,' said Crab.

'Of course we will,' said Mono.

And, with that, the benefit concert was put into play.

All bands re-form eventually: The Velvet Underground, The Sex Pistols, The Who, The Beatles (sort of).

Their reasons are, usually, not complicated. Usually, they are the reverse of complicated.

Dylan's '78 tour was known as the Alimony Tour; our second-last jaunt was privately known as the Paternity.

I am not the only member of *okay* to have become a father. But I am the only one to be personally raising his children.

Crab went out to get the I-divorce-you-I-divorce-you-I-divorce-you pack of cigarettes. He sees his son, maybe once a year. Not Christmas.

At the last count, Syph had nine legally certified offspring, sprinkled far and wide across the world – five girls and four boys. Most were conceived before DNA-profiling became widely known and used. Not all – Syph, as you know by now, takes a long time to learn his lessons. There are three more suits pending.

Mono won't and, fittingly, Major can't.

The Paternity Tour had been a cynical, and remunerative, exercise.

This re-formation was different: my life depended on it.

True friends, I've realized, are the people who will come and visit you in hospital *more than once*.

If I'd known this a while ago, I'd have included it among my good advices.

Yoyo (hi Yoyo!) came more than once – as did ex-roadies Monkey Boy and Shed, Clarissa Publicist and Maggie Marketeer.

Mono and Major were at my bedside around the clock. I know that, because we often spent the wee small hours playing backgammon. (For some reason, I became obsessed with the game – as if it, too, could help save me.) The two of them moved in with Esther and the girls. They were a great help at home, cooking and babysitting.

'But we're not *babies*,' I can hear Sarah and Grace say, together.

Ever since the Golden Music Teacher incident, Crab has had a phobia of hospitals. We spoke every day on the phone, however. Behind him, I could hear the sounds of bars – they made me feel bad, but he made me feel good. He told me I was tough, and, coming from him, I took that as one of the highest compliments I've ever received.

The real surprise was Syph. He used to hang out all the time, partly because he was going through a medical fetish phase, and wanted to meet nurses.

He met nurses.

But he also sat and talked to me in a way that was so intimate and compassionate that – well, I won't say it made being ill worthwhile, just to see; that would be untrue: I wouldn't for a moment wish myself back in that white condition. It was one of the unexpected gains, let me leave it at that. Syph is a true friend. He even wrote me a song. ('Isn'tism'.)

240

Being ill, like becoming a parent, makes you realize just how normal you are. To the outside world, you can be Mr Big Stuff, but your lungs could care less – and, neither, for the most part, could the medical professionals.

I had one guy, a consultant, who, after telling me that my prognosis was much worse than it had been two weeks previous, wanted to discuss the wrist technique of flams, drags and paradiddles. (Technical drummer stuff, don't worry.) Apart from him, though, everyone treated me like a totally run-of-the-mill rich-and-dying person.

I'm under no illusions that a poor version of me, given the same cancer, would have faced a completely different world of shit and pain.

As a famous person, I'd been called upon, in my pre-illness life, to visit the sick'n'dying – also the perfectly healthy but vastly disabled.

Confession: I never felt comfortable.

There's excruciating footage of John Lennon, on-stage during The Beatles 1964 American tour, doing what these days would be called 'spazzing out'. He sticks his tongue down behind his bottom lip, smiles with his cheeks, crosses his eyes and puts his head at an angle. Then he contorts his arms and legs until they look sufficiently palsied. And then, to make it even funnier, he does a little sideways spazz-dance towards Paul and George.

This happens so frequently that, even on *The Beatles Anthology*, it can't pass unmentioned. (It looks, at points, like Lennon couldn't face a camera without first making a spazz-face.) One of John's talking-head chums helpfully explains that, although the popular image of Beatlemania is of four moptops singing *oooh!* to stadiums crammed full of screaming teenage girls, in actual fact, the first three or four rows at each concert were usually taken up by the severely mentally and physically handicapped. When they played, this was what The Beatles saw – a glistening sea of wheelchairs. Lennon, the head-friend says, was just trying to cope.

I, too, finding myself confronted by ill people all day every day, spazzed out. Not physically, mentally.

THE FEAR!

'I can't cope,' I said.
Actually, I screamed it.
Esther was called.
'You can cope. You have to cope.'
For a week, I stayed in my private room.
Sedated is the word.
Then I went out again into the communal spaces.
Here, I met Mike.

He was fifteen-years-old, wheelchair-bound and thought my band sucked. Mike liked only the heaviest grindcore. (Cannibal Corpse was, he said, 'shitty pop'. His favourite group was Anal Cunt.) Apart from that, we had a lot in common. For instance, we both played backgammon, and we both had only six months to live.

'Your band are pussies. You don't rock. You're easy listening, man. Hey, six and six. I'm doubling up.'

On top of serious-as-fuck cancer, Mike also had really bad acne and braces. I couldn't see the point of inflicting braces on him, seeing how his teeth would never be sorted. His parents, although divorced, were united in wishing to see him die with an orthodontically satisfactory smile.

You might be expecting me to say that Mike made me realize how lucky I'd been, in my life. Even if I were to die, I would at least know that I had achieved something.

And he did make me feel that. But not in an obvious way.

'You suck. And you're playing too slow.'

We talked about him and what he wanted to do – what he would have done, if he hadn't been in hospital, in a wheelchair.

Mike was without ambition.

He didn't make me feel as if I'd lived his dream. He made

me feel as if I'd lived way beyond anything he was capable of dreaming. In a way, his modesty was Zen.

Yes, he loved grindcore, but he was happy to leave the playing of it to other, more disqualified souls.

In 1996, Anal Cunt released an album called *40 More Reasons to Hate Us*.

'What about travel?'

'I can see pictures. Why would I want to be there? I don't like it to be too hot or cold.'

Checking first to see there were no nurses around to overhear, and report me: 'What about losing your virginity?'

'Oh, come on. I did that years ago.'

'Years?'

'When I was twelve. She was fourteen. She was so ugly no-one else would do it to her.'

'What was her name?'

'Jane McManus. It was in the basement of our building. There's an old couch there that everyone uses. It's gross.'

'That's a very romantic story, Mike.'

'She sucked my cock, too. So I've done that, as well.'

'I'm glad.'

'Were you going to offer to get me laid? You can still do that, if it makes you happy.'

'No,' I said, though I had considered the possibility.

We resumed our conversation a few days later.

'What about growing up? You want to grow up, don't you?'

Mike didn't answer. At first, I thought I'd really upset him.

'I'm sorry,' I said.

'I do want to live longer,' said Mike. 'But I don't want to become, like, old. I don't want to be like you.'

'What am I like?'

'You're kind of finished.'

'Is it that obvious?'

'There's stuff for you to do, but you're not as into it as you were into stuff before.'

'They call that middle age.'

'I don't want that.'

Again and again, he beat me at backgammon. He wasn't just lucky, he was way better than I was. But, when he lost, he didn't even seem to notice.

A third time, I tried finding out his ambition.

'Food?'

'My parents bring me McDonald's when they come.'

'Drugs?'

'I've had enough of those.'

'Money?'

'What for?'

Mike's six months, so it turned out, had been more optimistic than mine. After two of them, he went into renal failure and caught pneumonia.

Towards the end, I contacted Seth Putnam from Anal Cunt through a friend of a friend of Syph's. He flew in with the band and played a short set for Mike. At his request, they finished with a cover of Motörhead's 'Killed by Death'.

'Thank you,' said Mike, the next day. 'They were quite good.'

He died the following week.

Soon afterwards, the benefit concert went ahead.

Eighty thousand people in GM stadium.

I joined the band on tambourine for a gentle acoustic version of 'Sea-Song $^{\#}2$'. It was all I could manage.

I've never heard an audience like it.

ƒUCK ƬHE ƒEAR!

All I had to do was stand there.

Hanks.

The money came in.

Yippee!

I got treated and went into remission.

Whoopee!

Five out of the other nine people are still alive.

I invited all of them, and all their families and true friends, to a costume party at our house. It was clear we had very little in common, except gratitude. But we had the greatest time. Esther came as the Virgin Mary. I went as a skeleton.

Whoop-de-doo!

ROADKILL

Roadkill.

For Canadians, it's a fact of life.

And, of course, death.

Pet Heaven only knows how many bugs, birds and beasts I've massacred in my twenty-two years of qualified driving.

Since becoming a Buddhist, however, I mind about it more.

My Religious Studies teacher, a committed Christian, once told an anti-Buddhist story in class – in a blatant attempt to try and put us off this rival religion. He said that a friend of his knew a Buddhist monk, and this monk had just bought a car. The friend asked the monk how he was going to square his belief in reincarnation with, essentially, roadkill. Wasn't it terrible karma even to hit all those bugs? The monk had a simple solution: get someone else to drive. Then it would be *their* karma that was impacted.

Even aged twelve, I didn't believe the teacher. For a start, I didn't believe he had any friends at all – let alone one who knew someone as cool as a Buddhist monk. Misguidedly, I imagined the monk-friend as a cross between Obi-Wan Kenobi and David Carradine in *Kung Fu*.

To be perfectly honest, I still haven't worked out what I think about this. It's not orthodox, whatever that may mean. I can't really believe that some guy who leads a really shitty life, and comes back in the form of a slug or a rat, isn't going to want to get out of that body as soon as possible.

I would.

Some reincarnations are better than others. But then, I suppose, some – like my current one – give you a bigger chance of majorly fucking up.

Pretty often, I look back over what I've done, over the totality of what I'm guilty of, and I can almost feel myself metamorphosing into a cockroach. On bad days, an amoeba.

It's not for me to judge, luckily.

And I know what I should believe – that every existence is of infinite individual value, that the smallest single cell creature is beyond glorious.

So, therefore, avoid doing harm to others, including life-forms you would hate to be.

Like, I'm sure there's a lot of warmth and camaraderie among rats. You get to spend time hanging out with your extended family. But I have enough trouble remembering birthdays as it is. And if I had any residual consciousness of how much Esther hated me and my kind . . .

And what about viruses? If Sarah or Grace go down with throat infections, I'm not going to worry that I'm prolonging the samsara of strep. They get dosed.

There is a hierarchy.

Yes, Buddha-nature is in everything.

Yes, I can just about imagine sparing a mosquito that I catch chowing down on my forearm.

But should I give up my car completely and walk every-where just because a couple of dozen bug-reincarnations are going to move on up to a higher level for each mile I travel?

To the voices who say, *Yes, if that's what you believe,* I say, *Gimme a break, I'm still working all this shit out.*

To the voice inside which says, *You don't know exactly what's wrong with your spiritual life, but you know it's pretty much in the vicinity of everything,* I say, *Shut up for one fucking second, won't you?*

So, I am driving down an empty moonlit road, between trees, returning home from a friend's – call him Fred. He lives in Southern Alberta. I have a ritual of flying there and driving back. I like the empty time.

There's music in the hire car: Nick Drake's *Pink Moon,* appropriate to the night and the way I am feeling.

Fred is almost divorced. He has reached that stage where he looks back and thinks of all the good times.

The rear-view mirror is an empty black. I always feel this

is wrong, and there should be at least a smear of the car headlights in it.

I am driving and not thinking.

It has been a sunny summer's day, and for much of it I have worn a hat – a grey fedora to go with the suit I've recently returned to wearing, along with a white collarless shirt. I did, after all, go up to Savile Row to buy it.

Dignity uniform.

As I drive, the hat sits in the passenger seat. But I can feel the ghost of it all around the circumference of my head. I have to keep checking that it's there and not there.

From my left, two suddenly incandescent rabbits rush the road, diagonally. They are moving too fast for me to avoid them. The lead rabbit, smaller of the two, makes it to the opposite verge. But rabbit the second doesn't freeze, as cliché would demand. Rabbit two goes between my front wheels and keeps on running, until it meets my rear right wheel.

I can't say I really feel a bump. There is a sound, more of a thud than a crunch. I become aware of a death, behind me.

Roadkill.

Like I said, a fact of life.

But because I'm increasingly bothered, I pull over, stop the car and walk the twenty yards back.

I am carrying my glove-compartment flashlight, but the rabbit is clear in the moonlight.

I feel as if I can see every detail of it more perfectly than by daylight. Each hair on its still body seems to be illuminated from within.

The rabbit is dead – I don't need to touch it to know that. However, there is no blood. The wheel didn't squash it in any way.

Sad to say, it's a beautiful sight, the paleness and stillness of it. If it were alive, I'd never get this close.

I kneel down, aware that I have to listen out for other cars – even though (despite the tinnitus) I'd hear them a mile off, at least.

I don't touch the rabbit. I don't want the guilt of its warmth. And pretty soon, I've gone from *I don't touch the rabbit* to *I can't touch the rabbit.*

It isn't disgust that stops me. The emotion is something much more like terror. This, here, is the fact of death. However many times we encounter it, it's always the first time, because we are only born into the present moment an instant or two before.

But I know I should at least carry the rabbit over to the ditch. Some critter or other will probably have it before the night's out. If I leave it where it is, a truck will flatten and splatter it – destroying its perfect intactness.

I leave it.

I walk away, following the flower-shape my flashlight makes on the ground: chrysanthemum.

There is no good explanation. Maybe I just want to do a worse thing than kill it, out of self-disgust.

Esther is asleep when I get home, and the next morning I tell her about the divorce, not the rabbit.

I certainly haven't forgotten.

When I don't tell her, I'm deliberately *not* telling her, just as I'd keep an affair secret, although I've never cheated on her, not since the Japanese girl.

A day passes, then another, and the rabbit becomes the affair I've never had but was secretly having.

It would be humiliating to tell Esther now. She thinks vegetarians are essentially rampant egoists who hate society and use food as a means of revenge. I'm not sentimental.

Two weeks later, Major calls me and tells me straight out, Crab is dead.

I ask how:

'You won't believe it,' she says. 'A lightning strike got him. He was asleep in Stanley Park under a tree, and it just got him.'

'How did you hear?'

I am jealous – I want to know why I haven't been called first.

'Someone from the Vancouver police department called an officer here. It hasn't been announced anywhere. He drove right over to tell us. He's still here. Can you contact Syph?'

How much don't I want to?

'Okay,' I say. 'Thanks for calling.'

Then I ask, 'How's Mono taking it?' but Major has already hung up.

I don't know how *I* am taking it. For so long, I have expected to hear that Crab was dead. He has been hospitalized increasingly frequently, during the last couple of years. (Not as much as me, though.)

'Esther,' I shout, and she knows from my voice that death is involved.

She has been having lunch in the kitchen with the girls.

One of them starts whining; Grace, left with macaroni cheese and no access to ketchup.

Esther hugs me hard, then has to go back to them.

I think about calling Syph, then decide I need to see at least one member of the band face-to-face that day.

All through the drive, I think of how long I'd known Crab and how long it had been since I'd really known him.

Traffic is backed up, after a truck rollover, and the journey takes an extra hour.

'I know,' says Syph, opening the door. 'I heard.'

We talk as we enter the circular room. He has redecorated, again. It is 1930s modernist, very restrained.

'Did someone call?'

'I was online. Yoyo messaged me. Condolences.'

'How do you feel?' I ask. The question is again for myself.

'I feel, *the bastard, how could he do this to us?* I feel, *here is an excuse for drugs.* I feel, *I will never have a better friend.* I feel, *shouldn't I be feeling more?*'

251

It is a long time since I've heard Syph this eloquent. His words are almost like his song lyrics.

We sit in leather and metal chairs.

'What about you?' he asks.

'The same,' I say. 'It's quite a cool way to die.'

This is what I would have said, aged seventeen or twenty-five. I should have something different to say, now.

'He always thought he was going to be electrocuted on stage, like Keith Richards in 1965.'

'Remember that rainstorm over Glastonbury?'

'I heard him chanting the Lord's Prayer all through that gig,' says Syph.

'Really? I never knew.'

Syph makes some coffee and the calls start to come in. We let the management write a response for us. There is a brief conference call with Mono.

'We have to talk about the band,' says Syph.

'What band?' asks Mono.

Syph doesn't press him.

I can remember the thunderstorm the night before. Half-woken by it, I had worried that the girls would start freaking out. The next time I had any kind of conscious thought, the skies were silent. How could I have known anything significant had happened?

We buried him.

His father, tough old fucker, was still alive to see the day. I had never known him sober before. His mother I won't describe, out of respect.

There was resignation and pointless anger and black humour and something missing. The service was very traditional. It surprised me to learn that Crab had often gone to this big old Catholic church. When the priest spoke, briefly, it was clear he'd known the man.

Crab had made a new will only two weeks before. Half of everything went to his mother, the other half went to establish a music school. Classical music, not our stuff. Acoustic instruments only – that was what the will stipulated. This fact moved me.

Little else did.

Mono stayed a week after the funeral but refused to talk about the future.

The management suggested a memorial concert.

Syph liked the idea.

Secretly, I did, too.

Over the next month, Crab's death became like the ghost-hat. I wore it all the time, consciously.

I tried crying and it just didn't work. Tears came, but they felt forced.

I made further efforts at grief.

I went to the charred tree in the park and stood there for an hour.

I played all our old albums. I watched the tour video. I read the distraught emails and letters from fans.

And then the hat was gone.

One night, about three months later, I am driving back from Fred's, from my now-divorced friend's house. There is no moon. The night is different than before. That was summer. Now it is December and snow everywhere. It is a little stupid to be driving back in a blizzard. But I have chains on the wheels, and the 4×4 I've hired is a mean old bastard.

When I reach the point in the road where I hit the rabbit, my foot comes off the gas.

I cruise to a halt, unable to see for strong crying.

The front right wheel hits the soft shoulder.

I get out and stumble back up the road.

I am a wailing thing, not myself at all.

The words coming out are a song more than a sentence.

'I should have moved you. I should have moved you even if I didn't bury you. I'm sorry. I'm sorry, rabbit. I shouldn't just have left you there, all dead. I didn't mean to kill you.

I hate those fucking trucks. Did they mess you up? I hope you're okay. Why didn't I bury you? I wasn't being disrespectful. And you were such a beautiful rabbit.'

DOG #2

'Rpt ad lib to fade'
    (No specific song. Most of our songs end this way.)

'A three-legged dog is still a dog' – that's what Syph said, with sorrow, in one of his post-Crab interviews, quoting Michael Stipe, without acknowledgement, ha ha.

And so, when we went back on the road, earlier this year, we called it 'The Three-Legged-Dog Tour'.

But the sound was too empty, too exposing. No middle. We found that we needed another leg, and we ended up with another couple: ex-roadies Monkey Boy and Shed were recalled to active service.

It was a much better solution than employing some session musician.

okay went slightly folky, which chimed with the times.

Still, we missed Crab like hell. All of us.

Syph had stood to his right for over twenty years, was regularly jabbed by his elbow, cut across the face by his swinging-round headstock; when he looks to his left these days, Crab is missing – even off-stage, he's not where he should be.

His life, the end of it, was more complicated than we initially thought.

In what turned out to be the final year, Crab met a woman – the one he introduced me to, that night I tried to keep up. Things must have moved fast, afterwards. Perhaps he was in control of them, and himself. I like to think so. It went something like this: Courvoisier courtship, Moët et Chandon marriage, Jack D divorce.

But he hadn't signed the papers, because he'd lost the papers, because he was drunk, because he was an alcoholic, because he hated everything so much, because nothing would make it go away, so she is claiming all the money.

Until we use our mint-tea lawyer.

Then the money will go to his mother and the music school. This may take time.

As for my own children, I'm sometimes asked whether becoming a parent wasn't a huge shock, after the cosseted life that people assume I'd led.

In fact, being the drummer in a mid-level indie rock band was the best preparation for parenthood: the general sense of bewilderment and disorientation, the hours of boredom, the moments of all-redeeming joy, the ubiquity of bodily fluids, the subservience to endearingly unreasonable ego-monsters, the love of exhaustion and the exhaustion of love.

I like touring, but I prefer being at home.

I've never really enjoyed pleasure.

I realized this recently. It's too re-re-re-repetitive. The moral of debauchery is always the same: *It's not worth it, in the end.* And I think I'm intelligent enough to have picked that up from other people, ones around me.

Restraint (mine) leads to curlicues of moral ambiguity. I think that's why I've spent my life – ignoring certain well-documented periods – just saying no. There were binges, like after Esther left me, but they were anomalous: I was being weak, and to do so took a certain strength of character.

Where does Syph get the energy?

I still love the music.

I love the music so much I've made myself deaf.

When I go in to check on the girls, I can't hear their breathing from the door – I can't hear it bending over them – I probably couldn't even hear it with my head an inch above their chests.

No, to tell they're still alive, I have to touch them (sometimes because of this they wake up) – in the quiet of their room, I can hear a piledriver being used by a banshee while an air-raid siren warns of a whistling bomb which never lands: tinnitus.

In this, among drummers, I am far from alone.

But the convention is, we don't talk about it. It's un-rock'n'roll and ungrateful.

When you're fifteen, the stage is the only place you want to be. At forty-four, consider it as a working environment. Some nights, you might as well be shovelling iron ore into a blast furnace.

Drumming is manual labour.

Boo-fucking-hoo.

In *The Last Waltz*, Robbie Robertson – bullshitter *extraordinaire* – called The Road 'a goddamn impossible way of life'.

That may well be. But you certainly meet some interesting people out there.

I don't have a story from the Three-Legged-Dog Tour. We now have enough money to protect us, by and large, from amusing events.

And so, I thought I might bring you up-to-date on a few of the interesting people we've met along the way, interesting and otherwise.

Because of publishing these ramblings as a book, I had to check out with most of them (those who could be traced) that they didn't mind me including them. Names have been changed to protect the innocent, and the guilty, and the morally indeterminate but shy.

Of course, this is going to be sad, in parts. But, here goes.

Cast in order of appearance.

WHERE ARE THEY NOW?

MINOR CHARACTERS

I've never managed to track down *Inge the Beautiful Dog-Rescuer of Rotterdam/Amsterdam*. (Probably for the best.) And I might as well dispose, here, of all but one of the other untraceables:

Ginger who was Crab's On-Off Girlfriend, Celia the Matchgirl who was around for Syph's Overdose, Lydia Who Fell in Love with Me and Whom I Cruelly/Kindly Left, The Girl in Room 333, Shirley from Lubbock Who Introduced Mono to Jesus, The Buddhist Monk Who Gave Me the Beads, Lula-Maybelline from the Tourbus, Honey Ditto, and *The Butterfly Swimmer Who Kicked My Ass and Saved My Life.* It's just, you meet so many and remember so few. I remember you all. Be in touch, if only to let me know you're still around.

Lindsay the Librarian sent me an invitation to her wedding, c/o the record company. I got it two days late. It turns out she moved to Nottingham, England, and met a Recruitment Consultant called Colin. They now have a daughter, Bryony. Lindsay published her first book of poetry, with a small Scottish press. It's called *Our Hosts.*

Miss Watts the Head Librarian is still working. At eighty-five.

For *Yoyo from the Fanclub,* see the entry on Syph, below.

Syph's Mom has remarried, twice. There's no-one out there good enough for her.

After school, *Katie Proudhon (aka Catty Proudhorn)* had a brief modelling career. Then she took an MBA, and is currently very dull.

It's impossible to separate *Shed* and *Monkey Boy,* so I'll do them together. After the Three-Legged-Dog Tour, they went and recorded their ninth album. Thanks to you, the buying public, it was a hit, like always.

Kerrie Who was Crab's Ex is doing a fine job bringing up Crab's son. We have seats near them at Canucks games.

Our Management from the Time of Syph's Overdose are still in LA, and welcome to it.

The Divine Miss Sylvie Ullshawn Who was Crab's and My English Teacher, and Our First Crush took early retirement, and moved to New Zealand, where she gardens and paints. She has never married.

Scary Asian PA from Our First Big European Tour Who Mono Fell in Love With has become one of the world's leading designers of S/M figurines. It is a growing market. She specializes in latex-clad nurses.

My Mother's Friend Betty, Who was Around When My Father Died, herself died of breast cancer a couple of years ago. I will always be grateful to her memory. She made a bad time slightly more bearable.

My Mother is fine, thank you for asking.

Skullfukk, the Deathmetal Band in Whom I Took Solace split, sadly. But their monster of a drummer went on to become a mainstay of Maggotdikk.

Dorothy in South Africa Who Introduced Me to Her Aunt, and Set Up a Drumming Party for Me is HIV-positive but getting antiretrovirals. She was raped, which is how she became infected. She stopped to give the guy a ride. He pulled a knife. I warned you this was going to be sad.

Barbra, the Model Trying to Figure It All Out made lots of money and retired aged twenty-five. She does take photographs, but not professionally. From what I hear, she will soon be coming out of retirement.

Friend One, Friend Two and Friend Three from the Black Forest email me occasionally. They've all completed their educations. Two of them have children. Slowly, they are becoming less Goth.

Crab Senior outlived his son, but only by two weeks.

Tony and Jordan, Our Ex-Management are once again our management. More, I cannot say. And *Cindy, Their Former Assistant* is now managing other bands, and doing very well thank you.

Clarissa the Publicist remains a stalwart friend and supporter of the band. She has a good man – Jeremy-of-the-firm-handshake – who is big in sports equipment, and two lovely daughters, who are small in flowery dungarees.

Maggie the Marketeer wants to know what's so horribly wrong with her. (That's what she asked me to put.)

Irina the Russian Superfan turns out to have been working for the Russian secret service all along. After bringing off a major-league mafia bust, she had to go into hiding. I do not know her whereabouts. She is not in Canada.

Joyce Cloud, Esther's Mother cannot be praised highly enough. I think I have been forgiven.

The Commode-Fox, Esther's Stepfather has taught me a thing or two. And not just about antiques.

The Kid Who Followed is the one I left out of the list of people we couldn't track down. Of course we couldn't track him down.

The Japanese Girl I Almost Married, and Her Fishing Village Family are doing fine. The financial settlement helped them no end.

They now have three boats. And she married the boy she should have married all along. They have a button-cute son.

Leonard Cohen aka Jikan, the Silent One is back up Mount Baldy. In fact, I think he never fully left – I was misinformed about that.

The Record Company Executive with the Inspirational Desk-Calendar is still, I am sorry to have to report, a knob.

Mint-Tea Lawyer is still TCB.

Craigie the Surfer and *Jenny* and *Boo* came to stay last Easter. Boo got on very well with Sarah and Grace, despite the age gap. After we met in Barbados, Craigie managed to become an exhibition surfer, but hated the commercialization of his art. However, he'd earned enough to set himself up as a board designer and manufacturer. After building the business up to the third biggest in Hawaii, he sold it off. Currently, he is fronting a surf-forecasting website and learning high-end yoga.

Jenny has written two very successful novels, *The Wide Wide Blue* and *Spillikins*.

Boo likes horses better than waves.

As for *the Rapper Who Sampled 'Holding'*, I can't tell you how rich and successful he is.

Big Boy, Sent to Meet Me by the Rapper Who Sampled 'Holding' was still there in the videos, last time I checked. Still nodding in slo-mo, looking both venal and smug.

Jean Wallace and Aaron Benjamin, Parents of Otis are fine – though fine, I have to say, on a fairly modest scale. These things never go away. I mostly hear about them through their daughter, *Caroline Wallace-Benjamin*, who came to work for *okay* as a sound-technician. She will go far, if she turns the kick-drum up just a little more.

We exchange Christmas cards with *Chester, Otis's uncle.* He runs a successful business servicing golf-carts.

Karla, Our Tour Publicist in Iceland drowned whilst swimming off the coast of Croatia. She was only twenty-six.

Fred, Call Him Fred, My Friend in Alberta is just about over his divorce. I have never told him about the rabbit, so he's going to learn something about me if he reads this book. (So is everyone.)

MAJOR CHARACTERS

Major. Rocks. Majorly.

Mono (along with Major) has become a committed environmental campaigner. It happened like this: during the winter months, when he couldn't do much fishing, he started to become obsessed with levels of chemical emission from nearby factories. He is now campaigning for tighter restrictions on industry, not just in Canada but right across the world. He has Bono on speed-dial.

Get this: *Syph* hasn't taken a drink since the day after Crab's funeral. And I'm pretty sure he's kicked his other addictions, too. For a few months, after coming out of rehab, he went to live with Mono and Major. They tell me he did a lot of fishing, and crying. Then he turned up on our doorstep, in tears. He told me – he told my right shoulder – that he'd always loved and admired me. And this was before I'd even invited him in. Once over the threshold, he became even more distraught – telling me that, really, he'd always wanted to *be* me. 'You're so solid – and I'm hardly there at all. I feel like I've been absent for the past fifteen, twenty years. Right from our first success. Look at what you have. Your beautiful wife and your family. You have a support network.' After he'd calmed down, I gave him a couple of these anecdotes to read – just to show him how solid I really wasn't. (If you're interested, they were 14, 22 and 25.) 'These are great,' he said, when he returned them, late that evening. 'You should publish them.' I told him they were entirely private. He dropped the subject immediately, then brought it up again a few days later. Meantime, he had been quizzing me about Buddhism. He'd seen me go off to meditate, and had asked if, next time, I could teach him. We did some basic mindful breathing together. After that, he went completely wild with it, sitting for hours on my *zafu*. He wanted me to become his guru. I told him to stop shitting around. 'Please,' he said. 'I need your wisdom.' I gave him a couple of books to read – other people's wisdom. He'd finished them by the following morning. 'More,' he said. When he'd exhausted my small library, he started ordering all the other books by the same writers. It only took him a fortnight to manage the full lotus; those slinky hips of his. Also, he'd asked to read the rest of my stories. 'They're all great,' he said, when he was done. 'You really should think about putting them out there. I think they'd help a lot of people understand what it's like.' He could only mean *What it's like to be a drummer.* Before this, though, he acknowledged my justifiable resentments against him. 'I'm so sorry,' he said. 'I can't tell you how sorry I am. I was in a lot of pain. I had a lot of anger.' In number 16, he came across the mention of Mount Baldy. He left us for California a few days later, having cajoled his way in there. 'Please,' I said, 'whatever you do, don't mention my name to Leonard.' 'I promise,' he said. The next we heard, a month later, he had been joined there by Yoyo (hi Yoyo!). And then they got married. And then, two months later, they got divorced. But they're still together. And Syph still meditates, sometimes. He's back in Vancouver, though. I see him around. He keeps dropping by. He wants to do a new album. 'Mono's in,' he says. 'All we need is you.'

Sarah and *Grace* have made me promise not to say anything embarrassing about them. But what else are dads for? They are the most oodlesome girls in the world.

Esther is love. Esther is pregnant.

And *Me?* I play the drums in a band called *okay*. And that's cool.

OKAY DISCOGRAPHY, INCOMPLETE

OKAY

Sea-Song #1
Work
Gustav Klimt
Withdraw
Walls
Sea-Song #2

Sea-Song #3
Into Space
Click
With Strings
Queen Victoria
Sea-Song #4

ARRIVE

Anæmic
Blissfully
Call
Thousand
Jane-Jane
Beachcombed
O

Arrive
Moon
Waltz
August
Haven't
Motherhood
Zero

THE SOCIETY FOR MUTUAL AUTOPSY

Different Types of Sugar
Isn't, Wasn't, Won't
Prohibition
Nikki's Gone to America
The Unhip
Vancouver Drug-Hoover
SS

Cutey π
Gnostic Jewellery
Easel-Weasel
Art-junk-shop
Groteskimo & His Penguin
    Gimp
Nature vs Nurture
Rat Mansion

4TH

Cleaning up
Spangle-jangle
I love love love you

Giggling
Save it
Wolves (The Most Honest Words)

LIVE ALBUM (DOUBLE)

Isn't, Wasn't, Won't
Idiot Boy
Giggling
Anæmic
Jane-Jane

Sea-Song $\#_1$
Sea-Song $\#_2$
Sea-Song $\#_3$
Sea-Song $\#_4$

The Unhip
Haven't
Queen Victoria
Click

Waltz
Beachcombed
Wolves (The Most Honest Words)
Rocks Off

SONGS AND SNOGS

Retro-futurism
Jealous
My Dead Shoes
She Spat Me
Bitte Schön
With You (Out of Doors)

Gunk
Unnamed
Bitterness
Exit Strategies

UNDERLINGS:
B-SIDES & EARLY RARITIES

Celibacy

You are the girl

Cicada

Underlings

Saw you last

Castor & Pollux

Chicken Rhythm #2

August Strindberg

Vancouver Drug-Hoover

2 a.m. song

Hippie Summer

Bookends

Helicopters

Take me away (from you)

Hush-hate-hum

Wipeout

TREE

So holy

Woods

Green again

Rust

Cassette

Tree

Back to where

Holding

Battery

Envelopes

Long-shot

Mist

9TH/DARK DARK DARK

6-6-Sixties

Lord and Master

Heaviosity

Spunk-burger

Hello, Hell

The Subterraneans

Hole of Nobody Knows

When I wasn't me

Shadow-walker

Incandescent Twilight

Blinder than Thou

Masterpiece of Pain

Agony Threnody

The Scream (We all scream)

Killingly

Luciferous

Ride the Metal Steed

Zero Sum Game

Decimate

Planet-killer

Total Blackout

SS Nature

SONGS OF DEFEAT A.K.A. COUNTRY ALBUM

Sleeping on the sofa

The Drinker's Song

Long Cold Lines

The Heels of Her Shoes

Where I'm Calling From

The Song

Thanks a Million

What Daisy Knew

6

Saved by the Bell

ISN'TISM

O Love	LA (OD)
Lindsay	Unsaid
(I used to be your) Poster Boy	Confessional
Caravaggio	Better than Not
The Left-behind	Isn'tism

OKAY: MTV UNPLUGGED

Sea-Song $^{\#}1$	Click
Waltz	When I wasn't me
The Left-behind	Woods
Long Cold Lines	Holocaust
She's Lost Control	So Long Ago, Nancy
Kooks	Wolves (The Most Honest Words)
	Sea-Song $^{\#}2$

SOLO ALBUMS / SIDE PROJECTS

MOUNTAIN MEN
BY MONKEY BOY AND SHED

Basement Testament

Hung Up on Glory

Grunky Girls

So English It Hurts

Spare

Back of my Truck

The Cold Fire

Moshpit Romance

In Sunderland

Wilfulness

Mountain Men

Honey Child

The Revolution

Hymnal

HOOK, LINE & SINKER
BY SYPH

Coup de Fou

I can't even talk to you

Perfume

Drum Majorette

Beatbox Romeo

Croix de Guerre

My friend, the winner

No hard feelings

Bastard

What I Wanted & What I Got

Pull Out the Roots

The Yearning

Nothing, No-one, None

Spendthrift/Spindrift